THE BARFLY BOYS

Also by John D. Wells

The Plague Year

THE BARFLY BOYS

A NOVEL BY
JOHN D. WELLS

iUniverse, Inc.
New York Lincoln Shanghai

THE BARFLY BOYS

iUniverse, Inc.

For information address:
iUniverse, Inc.
2021 Pine Lake Road, Suite 100
Lincoln, NE 68512
www.iuniverse.com

ISBN: 0-595-27492-7

Printed in the United States of America

Contents

▼

SPRING

SUMMER

THE UNIVERSITY OF MICHIGAN ANN ARBOR, MICHIGAN WINTER, 1991

CHARLOTTESVILLE,
VIRGINIA
WINTER, 1990

Here There and Everywhere

The bedroom was cloaked in murky darkness, making it difficult for the young lovers to distinguish each other's features. She could barely see the outline of his face. A lone blue candle on the nightstand flickered nervously while casting shimmering shadows on the walls. Behind him, she saw ghostly splinters of light shooting off in all directions, creating a dizzy black and white animation of drunken stick figures dancing down the street. They were lying naked together on the rumpled bed, silent in the afterglow of making love. The woman's cheeks were flushed like two tiny pink rose buds as she turned her body over on her side. She moved closer to him, wrapping her arms around him. Responding in kind, he inched his way toward her, easing gently into her arms. Her lover consumed her thoughts. She felt he looked more beautiful than handsome, as the luminosity from the candle softened his features, forming an angelic, choir boy physical symmetry. She looked at him more closely, marveling at the flashes of tiny golden stars twinkling in the microscopic universe of his eggshell blue eyes. She ran her fingers down his back. His skin was soft to the touch. He was thin, but his angular body felt taunt and muscular. His lips were almost too feminine, heart-shaped and perfectly formed, like the rest of his face. Suddenly, from outside the apartment, a lumbering snowplow with chains rattled the frozen street below, rudely breaking the quiet, intimate rhythm of the moment. He lifted his head in the direction of the window, pausing until the clattering became fainter and fainter into the night.

Soft, melodic sounds, scarcely audible, whispered from the radio beside the bed. She stroked his long, curly light brown hair, twirling the ends with her fingers. She thought, at this moment, he looked more like a boy than a man with his drop-dead flawless looks, his robust complexion, high cheekbones, finely chiseled jaw, and lonesome, sad eyes. She could feel him watching her; she could sense the quietude of lovemaking in his heart, the warm intimacy of his not-yet-cooled body. His hands moved from behind her back and traveled slowly to her breasts. He clutched them both, then gently kissed her, resting his head on her shoulder. A tingling sensation shot through her body, like a current of erotic electricity from a libidinous generator. He released a low, sensuous murmur of pleasure as he sank between her breasts. She moved her head from side to side, creating movements of shadows on the wall. Leaning slightly away from him, she strained to hear the song coming out of the radio. It sounded familiar. She reached over and turned up the volume, immediately recognizing one of the *Beatles* heartfelt ballads.

> *To lead a better life, I need my love to be here*
> *Here, making each day of the year,*
> *Changing my life with a wave of her hand.*
> *Nobody can deny that there's something there...*

"They're playing our song," she said.
He raised his head, glanced toward the radio, then back to her.
"Good timing. How did they do that?"
"It must be cosmic."
He rolled over on top of her, bracing his weight with his arms, careful not to crush her.
"Do you think we're a little old for a favorite song?"
"I hope we never get too old for a favorite song."
He leaned down and kissed her again. "Maybe we should get a new one...something by *Iron Maiden*, or *AC/DC*."
"Very funny. You're a hopeless romantic."
"It's better than being just hopeless."
"I love you, Chris."
"I love you too."
Chris rolled over and the couple assumed their former position. They stared at the ceiling once more, watching the shadows from the candle, listening to the song.

But to love her is to meet her everywhere,
Knowing that my love is to share,
Each one believing that love never dies,
Watching her eyes and hoping I'm always there.
To be there and everywhere
Here there and everywhere...

"I wish things could be like this forever," she said.

"We can make it happen. We'll always be together."

" I hope so..."

"Do you have any doubts?" he asked.

"No...it's just that I don't know what I'm going to do."

"What do you mean?"

She lifted her head and stared into his eyes.

"Well, I have to do something besides make love to you all day, don't I?"

"Hey, that's plenty of life for anybody. You just stay in this room all the time and I'll bring you some food once in a while."

"Thanks for the offer."

Once again, they heard the deliberate rumbling noise of the snowplow making another round outside the apartment.

"You know, I don't know what I'm going to do either," he said.

"You mean if the band doesn't make it?"

"What if we do make it?"

"Lots of money...sold out stadiums..."

"That means time on the road..."

She wondered what was going through his mind. Was he looking forward to going on the road with the band? Did he want to take her along? She was afraid to ask, afraid of what he might say.

"You mean you might be gone for some time?"

"I guess..."

He turned away from her and clasped his hands behind his neck. The shadows were still playing tricks on the walls; this time creating a psychedelic movement of flowing images, like black cumulus clouds racing across the sky. There was so much unspoken about their relationship.

"Well, that won't be so bad," she said.

"No, but sometimes these road trips take a long time—months even."

"I don't want us to be apart..."

"Don't worry. Everything's going to be okay. We don't even have a steady gig yet, let alone a road trip."

She turned away from him and fumbled in the dark for her nightgown. She found it at the foot of the bed. Slipping into it, she got up from the bed and wandered over to the dresser. She glanced in his direction, then back to the dresser. Standing in front of the mirror, she picked up a hairbrush, and smoothed out some tangles from her long, straight blonde hair. She took her hand and swept the hair away from her face, then tossed the brush back on the dresser.

"Chris, I don't think I can handle you going on the road with those guys."

"What do you mean?"

"You know all those stories…drugs…sex…"

"I love you, Sarah."

"But you're going to leave me."

Chris rose slowly from the bed and came over to the dresser. They were both standing in front of the mirror. He took her in his arms.

"Who said anything about leaving? I might go away for a couple weeks, but I'm not going anywhere."

"What about us? Where are we going?"

He dropped his arms and gazed vacantly out the window. A car, turning into the parking lot, flashed his headlights past the window, sending a sudden burst of light into the room.

"How about Jake's?"

In the darkness, he could see the outline of her body sagging, as if someone had just squeezed all the air out of her. He knew it was the wrong thing to say. The words, as if sealed in a helium balloon, drifted up to the ceiling, and hung there, motionless. In the silence, he thought he heard her sigh.

She picked up the brush again, looked at him, then back to the mirror. She was going to comb her hair again, but decided against it. She tossed the brush back on the dresser.

"Sure, Chris. Let's go to Jake's."

LOVE AMONG THE RUINS

For the past hour, the light powdered snow was falling more steadily, and it was beginning to stick to the roads, so Sam Winston decided to spend the night in Charlottesville. He pulled off the interstate in his 1988 Bronco and began searching for a place to stay. Plodding along cautiously on one of the side roads leading into the city, he finally spotted a brightly painted orange and blue sign in front of the Wahoo motel. He turned into the motel, registered, and walked over to a nearby bar to drink a couple beers before retiring for the evening. As he opened the door, Winston was momentarily blinded, unable to see anything in the dimly lit room. It seemed darker than the night. Gradually, to his immediate left, he was able to discern a rectangular, ageless, mahogany bar that looked as if it was confiscated from the prop room of a Hollywood western. A blackened, boot-heeled brass rail rimmed the bottom of the bar, heightening the wild west atmosphere. A straight row of popular brand liquor bottles lined the back of the mirrored bar and an assortment of various shaped glasses and pitchers were bunched together beside the beer taps. Winston spotted the long, wooden-handled labels of Old Milwaukee, Budweiser, and Coor's Light. To the left, on the inside of the bar, a cracked and yellowed sign reading "Expresso Yourself" hung crookedly over an antique, rusted out coffee pot. Taped to the mirror, a "Miss Pauli Girl" calendar incorrectly disclosed today as Wednesday and the red and blue Bud Light clock above the calendar was twenty minutes fast.

The items placed haphazardly on the bar reminded him of a Montana hunting lodge: silver tin ashtrays, match boxes in a plastic cup, cheap cardboard salt and pepper shakers, pale blue napkins, Slim Jims, beef jerky, a jar of pickled eggs, a rack of small sized potato chips, and a bowl of complimentary peanuts. An eld-erly, craggy-faced bartender was perched on a stool behind the bar, reading a newspaper. Winston wondered how he could possibly read in such poorly lighted conditions. Several older men, uniformly dressed in plaid flannel shirts and bib overalls, were sitting impassively at the bar, silently sipping their draft beers. Bleary-eyed and sullen, they rotated their heads toward the new patron in perfect unison, like puppets manipulated on the same stage. Pausing for a second, they swirled their heads back to their original positions.

Winston grabbed a stool at the far end of the bar near the bartender. Directly behind the bar he noticed a large picture Hank Williams clutching his guitar, dressed in a tan Cowboy suit with the black musical notes running down his sleeves and pant legs. A few run-down delicatessen booths lined the perimeter of the large expansive room and a set of four rickety card tables and chairs were bunched together in the middle to form the restaurant part of the bar. Two coin-operated billiard tables were positioned on the right side of the restaurant where Winston saw about six or seven rough-looking biker types hanging out, drinking beer, and shooting pool. The walls were covered with dull brown panel-ing and the low hospital-green ceiling supported three wooden fans revolving lazily above the patrons. Thick, sturdy, four-by-four beams separated each section of the interior. Three young ladies were sitting together at one of the booths nearby engaged in furtive looks and earnest conversation. Winston thought the place evoked a faint odor of varnish and gasoline.

Heavy metal music blared from a music video coming out of a large TV screen suspended to the left of the pool tables. Winston glanced at the video and saw a shot of a gang of longhaired motorcyclists with guitars screaming on top of a mountain. Winston thought the choice of music was odd because he knew this was a university town and he expected to hear something like *The Cure* or *10,000 Maniacs*, but there were not any college kids in here as far as he could see. The customers, except for the patriarchal regulars at the bar, were mostly in their early twenties. They looked shabby and tattered in their bleached-out levis worn out around the knees, and in spite of the cold weather, wearing T-shirts with names of rock groups like *Aerosmith* and *Guns and Roses*. Winston felt a sense of weary despondency about the place. No one seemed to be talking, dancing, joking around, or anything. He concluded that perhaps the rock music was dulling their senses.

"Great picture of ole Hank," Winston noted to the bartender.

Like a languorous lion, rudely disturbed from his daily nap, the bartender managed to raise his head slightly enough to acknowledge the new costumer.

"Best ever," he replied, returning to the world at large.

"I'll take a Budweiser."

The bartender dropped his paper and garnered enough energy to rise from his throne-like stool and secure a beer from the stainless steel bowels of the bar.

"That'll be two dollars."

Winston handed him two one-dollar bills.

"Are you from around here?" the bartender asked unexpectedly.

"No, I'm from Arlington. Just passing through."

The bartender reached over and shook Winston's hand.

"Well, welcome to Jake's. I'm Jake."

"Sam Winston. Glad to meet you."

Jake returned to his reading and Winston sat at the bar in silence. Within minutes, one of the three women whom he had seen talking at one of the booths, wearing zebra-stripped spandex pants and a T-shirt embossed with the name *Winger* walked up to him.

"Hey, stranger. Why don't you play some songs?"

"What do you want to hear?"

"Oh…anything," the girl said, sliding on to the stool next to Winston.

Winston walked over to the jukebox and played a couple of songs by Eric Clapton. He returned to the bar and sat down next to the girl.

"Will you buy me a beer?" she asked.

"Sure. What's your name?"

"Alicia. What's yours?"

"Sam."

Winston turned and looked closer at her face. She was attractive, but Winston concluded that she was definitely not the homespun cheerleader type—maybe an ex-cheerleader with ten years and a hundred bottles of bourbon whiskey down the road. As she spoke, her long brown hair continually fell in her face and she constantly brushed it back in a flirtatious manner. She had thin lips, a pointed nose, and high cheekbones, so that she looked both young and rough at the same time. Her eyes were like dark liquid pools of chocolate brown, murky and dense. She slowly surveyed Winston from head to toe. He could feel her checking him out, but he was not sure about her intentions. Maybe, he thought, she just wanted a drink.

"Can I ask you a question Sam?"

"Sure."

"Do you hate people?"

"No, I don't hate people. Do you?"

"Wrong answer. New in town?"

"As a matter of fact, I'm just passing through. I work in Arlington. What's the right answer?"

"In this bar, there's only one answer. If someone asks you if you hate people, you say, 'No, but I seem to feel a lot better when they're not around.'"

"I don't get it."

"Guess you're not a barfly."

The girl abruptly walked over to the other side of the bar and talked to one of the pool players wearing a *Rolling Stones* T-shirt with a big red tongue splashed across the front. He had a tattoo on each knuckle of his left hand that spelled out the word o-z-z-y. While he was waiting, he heard the sound of *Stairway to Heaven* filling the air, prompting a couple to dance near the pool tables. Winston watched them gently swaying to the music, cuddling up to one another. He thought it was strange to see a lone couple moving so tenderly together in such an unromantic atmosphere. As he watched them gaze into each other's eyes, they appeared genuinely in love. It reminded him of the title of a book or play called "Love Among the Ruins." The couple continued to dance in between two faded, green felted pool tables while surrounded by a "hot shot" basketball game, rusty old state license plates, a "Space Cadet" video game, gaudy beer and whiskey signs, and other signs proclaiming "No Whining" and "Buy or Bye-Bye!" A programmed, mechanical phantom voice bellowed from a hidden speaker, "*Quit talking and start chalking.*"

Alicia finished her conversation, returned to the bar, and sat down next to Winston.

"Sorry about that," she said. "I had to talk to that creep over there."

"That's okay."

Alicia noticed that Winston was staring at the couple. She leaned over and whispered to him.

"That's Todd and Leslie. Do you think she's pretty?"

"Yes. I think she's very pretty. Don't you?"

"Sure…if you like that type."

Winston glanced over again in their direction. The girl was tall and slender with long, straight jet black hair cascading down her back, almost reaching her waist. She possessed a blemish-free, crystalline complexion, sculpted high cheekbones, and astonishing almond-shaped eyes. She had an aristocratic look about her, carrying herself with dignity and grace. Although she was dressed in simple torn and frayed blue jeans and a bulky red knit sweater, she projected an air of elegance and quiet sophistication. Her boyfriend was also tall, ruggedly handsome with shoulder length hair, wearing a small gold earring. He also possessed the same disheveled, ragged blue-jeaned appearance as the rest of the men in the place. Alicia also kept looking over in their direction.

"Are they friends of yours?" Winston asked

"Well, yeah…kinda. We grew up around here. We all went to the same high school."

"Do you go to the University?"

"UVA? No way! That school's full of snobs. That guy Chris over there goes to a community college, but that's about it. A couple of these guys have a band called *Mean Streets* and they think they're gonna be the next *Led Zeppelin*. They used to practice all the time, but not lately. See that guy in the green T-shirt?"

"Yes."

Winston looked over and saw a short, wiry customer dressed in a pair of black jeans littered with brightly colored patches, wearing an Iggy Pop T-shirt.

"Well, that's Dutch. He thinks he's a guitar player, but I bet you he hasn't picked it up in months. He also claims to be some sort of tortured poet, but all he does is ride his stupid motorcycle and vegetate in his room. No…nobody does anything here."

"Well, you all must do something."

"That's what you think. These losers all refuse to get real jobs."

"Listen, I've got to be going. I've got a long day tomorrow."

"Want some company tonight?"

Winston was surprised by her offer. It was so direct and obvious.

"Sure."

"Get a bottle, okay?"

"Okay."

Winston ordered a bottle of Jack Daniel's from Jake, and then they got up to leave. As they were going out the door, Dutch abruptly stood up, wildly waving his arms around while holding a shot glass.

"TO ALL MY FRRR…IENDS!!! TO ALL MY FRRR…IENDS!!!"

To Winston's amazement, the whole bar spontaneously exploded into a frenzy of everyone toasting drinks to one another.

"What's that all about?"

"Oh, that's the barfly cheer—don't worry about it. It's just children playing a game."

In the midst of the celebration, Winston and Alicia left for the motel room.

Billy Saxon saw Alicia Powers leaving with the stranger and her behavior further reinforced his hatred of the girl. He thought she was a sleazebag, two-bit whore, and he wanted to tell the stranger he better wear a condom or his dick would fall off. He looked and saw Todd and Leslie dancing in the middle of two pool tables, as Larry, the pinhead was attempting to sink the 8-ball. The couple moved out of the pinhead's way, so he could make the shot, but he blew it anyway. Billy looked once again at Todd and Leslie and envied their attachment to one another and their ability to be romantic and affectionate. Billy had no conception of romance and the only time he danced is when he slammed into a bunch of guys in the mosh pit.

Billy scanned the bar and noticed the usual crowd of hangers-on, looking permanently screwed to their bar stools. The bar stools had long since yielded to the angle of their sedentary asses. Billy felt every old cranky barfly should have a gold nameplate attached to his favorite stool. Billy did not like very many people, but he did like the veterans at the bar.

Chris Hamilton, Billy's fellow band member, emerged from the crowd of pool shooters.

"Hey, who are you not going to be tomorrow?"

"An airplane pilot."

"Why?"

"Because, said Billy, "I have a friend who works as a mechanic for American Airlines and all he does is smoke dope on the job."

"Good reason."

"So, who you not going to be today?" asked Billy.

"Bricklayer. I mean, all those red bricks look alike. How would you like to stare at the same size rectangular bricks every day of your life?"

"Not me."

"I gonna split," said Chris. "We gonna practice tomorrow?"

"I don't know. Dutch's amp is probably broken."

Billy was about to leave, but someone played a *Ratt* song he liked, so he decided to stay a few more minutes. Todd left Leslie and came over to talk to Billy.

"What's up?" asked Todd.

"I'm not being an airplane mechanic because all the mechanics get stoned on the job."

"I wouldn't trust the pilots either. You holding?"

"No," said Billy, "But I should have some next week. What are you going to do with the money you won on Remote Control?"

"I don't know. Got any ideas?"

"I'd buy a 49 Merc. Just like James Dean."

"Maybe I should get four horses."

"Four horses?" asked Billy.

"For the apocalypse…"

"Huh?"

"Never mind," said Todd.

Todd went back to the pool tables to rejoin Leslie. Billy was about to leave when he heard a scream from across the bar.

"HEY, CRATER FACE!!!"

It was Joey Culbertson, a local hanger-on, who was not part of the regular scene at Jake's. Billy considered him a certified loser who worked for a trucking company hauling vegetables.

"Who are you not being tonight?"

Billy wondered why Joey Culbertson would ask him about the barfly game. *Was he making fun of me for some reason?* Billy decided to give him a straight answer, but sensed a trap.

"A fireman. All you do all day is sit around on your ass, bored to death, playing cards with old farts who get a hard-on seeing houses burn down."

"You could never be a fireman," Joey asserted. "It takes guts to fight fires and you're too chickenshit to put your life on the line."

The patrons were stunned. No one had threatened Billy in a long time. They quietly waited for his next move. Billy calmly walked up to Joey and stared him down.

"Let's step outside."

"Sure, tough guy, but don't get too close. You smell like tobacco spit."

Obeying the ironclad Jake rule that no one fights in the bar, the two men marched out with a rowdy gang of stragglers and spectators following behind.

On the way out Billy was beside himself wondering why this local nobody would want to pick a fight with him. Then he remembered that he took this guy's girlfriend home with him. She came into Jake's alone one night, and after they drank heavily for hours, he took her to his apartment. Unfortunately for Billy, she took one look at his grungy apartment and demanded a ride home. Now a stupid fight was about to erupt for no reason.

The alley was very dark. As the two men circled each other, girding for battle, Billy could barely discern Joey's shadowy figure moving stealthily around him. Suddenly, Joey hurled himself forward, catching Billy with a solid left hook. Billy stumbled backwards, completely caught off-guard by the ferocity of the blow.

Jesus, has this guy been lifting weights? Stunned, but still conscious and standing, Billy quickly became more serious. Maybe he had underestimated this punk, but now he was ready to finish him off. Billy rushed toward Joey and tackled him, sending his body crashing into the hard pavement of the alley. Joey landed on his back with a gigantic thud. Billy, seizing the advantage, pummeled him with a flurry of hammer-like blows to his head. Joey screamed and covered his face with his hands, completely defenseless and bleeding profusely. Then, without warning, Billy was tackled from behind by two of Joey's friends. One of the guys pinned Billy to the ground, as the other one smashed him in the face while kicking him in the ribs with his heavy boots. Joey struggled to his feet, staggering badly, wiping the blood away from his face with his shirt. He stood over Billy, laughing hysterically.

"You stupid fuckin' townie."

Joey landed a boot heel to Billy's face, loosening several teeth, then continued his assault, landing a volley of punches to Billy's head and chest. Billy was having trouble breathing, choking on the bits of teeth and blood stuck in this throat. Gagging and twisting his head violently from side to side, Billy struggled to get some air in his deflated lungs, as he dodged the next barrage of blows to his head and ribs. Rolling into a fetal position, he tried to spit out the debris in his mouth, but one of his assailants kicked him in the groin, taking his breath away. Lying helpless, Billy decided to give in to the torture and closed his eyes, hoping that the next series of punches and kicks would not leave him crippled for life.

But the expected attack did not happen. Out of nowhere, Todd, Chris, and Dutch appeared from the crowd of onlookers. Todd and Chris grabbed one of the men and sent him flying into a trashcan. Dutch, wielding a baseball bat, slammed it mightily into the face of the other torturer. Instantly, blood gushed from his face like a lawn sprinkler as he ran frantically into the bar, crying for an ambulance. Billy, freed from his captors, took off for Joey who was running for his life down the alley. Billy tackled him from behind and landed several fists to his head, breaking his nose in the process. Joey tried in vain to protect himself, but Billy was pounding his entire body with the ferocity of a heavyweight champ. Joey was about to slip into unconsciousness, but Billy eased up enough for him to regain his senses. *I want this son-of-a-bitch awake.* Billy went over to a dumpster and picked up a scoop of rancid garbage.

"Hey, Joey," Billy taunted. "You want some dinner?"

Billy shoved the pile of filth down his throat and held it in his mouth so he couldn't breath or spit it out.

"SWALLOW IT!!!"

Joey swallowed the rotten garbage, then choked and vomited.

Billy raised his fists in triumph, and before delivering his final knock-out punch, leaned over and whispered to Joey:

"Now who smells like tobacco spit?"

The barfly boys raised their arms, slammed high fives together, and taunted Joey who was crawling on his stomach down the alley.

"Let's get some beers," said Billy. "This alley stinks."

The overamped guitars blazed a Hendrix-like blare into the night. Raving trash metal chords consumed the tiny, atmosphere of Zipper's Café as a gang of gyrating metalheads jumped up and down on the worn-out blistered floor. The lead guitarist, playing with fierce abandon, ripped a full-blown, hardcore assault on the stoned-out senses of the bare-chested boys in the pit. Todd and Chris were on the sidelines grooving to the music as he laid down a helter-skelter barrage of pummeling riffs, as the rest of the band sizzled and cracked with volcanic distortion. Chris swore he heard a thousand guitars clashing to the ragged, pulsating beat.

Above the din, Todd yelled something in Chris' ear, but Chris could not understand what he was saying. *Did he say, Let's get high?"*

Poised for a climatic finish, the tattoo-riddled singer belted out a blood-curdling scream in the midst of a fuzz-wah riff from his sweaty, bony-faced lead guitarist. And in one final frenzy, a scorching solo rocked the place with a nasty, searing sound as the torrid performer spat and snarled, hurling expletives into the wild hormonal snake pit before him.

Gradually, with impeccable timing, the heavy, throbbing beat slowly wound down as the screeching guitar evolved into a slow, dark and rumbling sound. The singer moved around the stage like a caged black panther, spinning his torso like a drunken ballet dancer, until he was writhing on the floor…

"Make me feel it, baby…Make me feel soooo…good…"

Chris thought he looked like a crazed Jim Morrison reincarnated from Paris, curled in a fetal position, wailing the blues, like a drunken soulful preacher of the damned.

The house lights diminished and the crowd swayed lightly back and forth, rocking gently to the toned-down rhythm of the band. Unexpectedly, a priest emerged from back stage and approached the singer. He leaned over the body, crossed himself, and tenderly placed a blanket over the stricken corpse. The priest removed a cross from his neck and placed it upon the dead man's chest.

There was a brief moment of silence from the stunned crowd before total pandemonium broke out.

"MORE!!! MORE!!! MORE!!!"

A hundred matches glimmered in the night, but there was no sound or movement. Suddenly, the lights returned, but the stage was empty. As the club erupted with a burst of applause, Todd yelled again:

"LET'S GET OUT OF HERE!!! I CAN'T HEAR A THING!!!"

The two barfly boys struggled through a mass of smoky humanity, escaping into the frozen street. The sleet had turned into a light snowfall. Chris turned toward Todd.

"What were you saying in there?"

"I was just wondering who Dutch was not being today."

"He said he was thinking of not being a carpenter. He had this crazy dream the other night. There were giant tweezers circling him in the desert and they started swooping down like vultures, plucking tiny splinters from all parts of his body. Then he said he was eaten alive when the tweezers turned into birds of prey and performed a crazy dance of death."

"That guy's nuts."

"Where'd Billy get to?" asked Chris.

"I guess he split."

"Wanna go to Jakes?"

"No thanks. I'm going out with Leslie."

"How about tomorrow night?"

"I'll be there later on. Believe it or not, Leslie and I are going to a Chevy Chase movie."

"I thought you didn't like movies?"

"I don't. But Leslie gets tired of drinking every night at Jake's. She thinks we're taking this barfly thing too far."

"We gonna practice later on?"

"Dutch is having trouble with his amp."

Dutch is always having trouble with his amp."

"Yeah, I know."

"That band was awesome, wasn't it?"

"Yeah, best local band around—except us."

"Do you think we could ever be that good?"

"Sure. I really do, but we gotta practice. It's been about three weeks. We're gonna get rusty."

"Dutch's amp is broken."

O-Z-Z-Y

Billy split from Zipper's early because his guts were on fire and his nerves edgy from the powerful crank that he snorted in the men's room. He thought he forgot to tell Todd and Chris he left, but he was too stoned to remember exactly what happened. He woke up the next morning with a massive headache, and after downing four Tylenol, he decided to go to the CD store at the downtown mall. It was bitterly cold outside and, as usual, his beat up old pick-up truck refused to start. He began to walk into town. As he ambled gingerly down the icy streets of the historic section of Charlottesville, he gazed at the throngs of people strolling along University Boulevard. He couldn't help but feel like an outsider—an alien from another planet, distant and immune from the people surrounding him. Billy told everyone who would listen that there were two major types of natives in the town: University of Virginia spoiled brats who never worked a day in their life and homegrown redneck locals raised on starchy foods and cigarettes. Passing by the Blue Bird café, he noticed a homeless tramp, his face reddened and stained like an old bottle of Mad Dog 20/20, slouching on a corner in a drunken daze, begging the students for some spare change. None of the students paid any attention to the old bum. Billy heard cynical phrases like, "Get a job" and "Get a life." He dropped a dollar in his hat.

My God, I am surrounded by a mutant army of pleated Duck Heads, covering the earth in orange and blue, so they could end the world by boring it to death. There's no doubt about it. I am a condemned prisoner, suffocating on this arid pomposity, blinded by a bombardment of orange and blue bullshit from every conceivable direction. I am living in the in the heart of the pretentious Izod capitol of the world, or maybe it's the arrogant Laura Ashley black hole of the universe. Either way, I'm fucked. Omygod, what have we here? I see all around me a loathsome assemblage of oozy slimoids traipsing merrily down the bumpy cobblestone sidewalks. Here they are—the whole repugnant spectacle of humanity multiplying before my very eyes: a rowdy group of butt-wasted beer sloshers, knocking over a couple of clean-cut Bible students; three muscle-headed sports guys driving by in their Range Rover shouting obscenities at two sorority sisters dancing together and waving pompoms; a couple of non-descript computers nerds programming their life away; one future lawyer of America talking on the phone, planning his country club existence, two greedy-looking guys in suits, hustling their souls on the money market. Jesus, so much blue-blood Virginia in-breeding has spawned a whole new generation of young, geeky razorcuts carrying on a tradition as outmoded as the bathroom at Monticello. As far as I'm concerned, the only thing worth preserving in this overblown historical junkyard is the dormitory room of Edgar Allen Poe.

To his surprise, Billy ran into a young Jamaican with dreadlocks sprouting out of his head like tentacles from a large insect. He was wearing an oversized Bogart trench coat and mirrored sunglasses, although the day was gray and blustery. The ground was frozen rock-hard and a thin layer of snow had blanketed the town from the storm the night before.

"What's happenin'?" said Billy to the man.

The Jamaican flashed him a mischievous grin, hoisted a "thumbs up," and sauntered down the street like he knew the riddle of life and death. Billy figured he must be a fellow musician.

He arrived at Back Alley Disc. He was going to make a quick purchase of an old *AC/DC* album, but they did not have it. He wandered around and surveyed the types of music that was currently selling: *Madonna, Vanilla Ice, and New Kids on the Block.* Billy concluded that it was hopeless.

He could not make up his mind whether to buy the new *Ozzy Osbourne or Aerosmith*, and then he remembered that *Aerosmith* recorded a rap song, so that put them out of the picture. He also considered *Poisson*, but Chris told him they were a girls group. He finally decided on *Judas Priest.*

Walking out of the store, Billy spotted Alicia on the other side of the street. He tried to duck into a phone booth, but Alicia saw him.

"Billy!!! I've been looking for you all day!!!"

Jesus, what a dull, uneventful life she must lead, if that's what she's been doing all day.

Alicia approached Billy wearing the same black and white spandex leggings that she wore two nights ago and a brown furry overcoat that looked somewhat like a grizzly bear rug.

It's Smokey the Bear dressed up for a Bon Jovi video.

Alicia's coat was open, revealing a T-shirt beneath it. Billy could only read, "mn Yank" through the opening of her coat.

"What's that T-shirt?"

"Damn Yankees."

"Oh."

"Are you holding?"

"No."

"Do you know where I can get some?"

"Chris might have a quarter ounce. You can see him at Jake's tonight."

"Awesome."

"It's just average dope from his uncle, the lawyer."

"Who are you not being today?"

"Look, I gotta split. I'll see you at Jake's, okay?"

"Sure."

Billy could not tolerate Alicia. He figured he was about the only guy in town who had not slept with her. She reminded him of a leper who strayed from the colony, wandering around scaring the hell out of everybody. He called her "Black Death in Spandex."

Billy hatred of Alicia was exacerbated by the fact that she had conceived a child out of wedlock and given the child away for adoption. To Billy's way of thinking, that was unforgivable. Billy thought Alicia was extremely selfish and thoughtless because she cared more about doing drugs and having a good time than bearing the responsibility for raising a child. He was especially hard on women who did not accept the responsibility of motherhood.

His thoughts about Alicia shifted to getting another tattoo. He liked the o-z-z-y on his knuckles and thought that perhaps the *Guns and Roses* scull and crossbones would look good on his left bicep.

DAYDREAM

Alicia was sitting at the bar in Jake's wondering why God put some people on earth, especially Billy Saxon. Every time she thought about him, it reminded her of the bottom of a garbage pail. Why, she thought, are so many young girls forced to face the ugliness of this world. Todd Zimmerman was so different than most men she knew. She had a terrible crush on Todd and was very jealous of Leslie. At the moment, the couple was deep in conversation at a nearby table. She did not understand what Todd saw in Leslie because she felt that Leslie could not possibly please men the way she did. Alicia prided herself on her ability to please men. In fact, most of her thoughts centered on sex with different men. But she was especially interested in Todd.

One of her vivid memories was when she was thirteen and had just discovered the pleasures of sex. At this young age, she was routinely having sex with about two or three guys a week. One time she was with a local guy in a car and after they had sex she started to feel sick to her stomach. She cried profusely all over his seat covers. The guy looked at her contemptuously and asked her if she wanted to go home to mommy. Alicia told him to stick it up his ass. In retrospect, Alicia realized that she did want to go home to her mother, but that was exceedingly difficult. Alicia's mother was not around very much because she was single, irresponsible, and also dated many men in town. Alicia remembered being in the fourth grade and Sammy Edwards asked her if he could come over to her house to get some from her mother.

"Some what?" asked Alicia.

Sammy Edwards just laughed his head off.

The two Valiums that Alicia took earlier were beginning to kick in as she once again looked over her shoulder at Todd Zimmerman sitting with his girl friend. The Valium made her woozy, putting her in a dream-like state laced with sexual tension and desire. Her thoughts drifted to one of her reoccurring fantasies. She is sitting on a psychiatrist's couch...*tell me about your dream...the one about the sea...Do you remember? Yes...the sea...I remember...I am a little girl...You're a little girl? Yes...no...I don't know how old I am...maybe too young to have these thoughts...But I have them anyway...Is that okay? Is there something wrong with me? Go on...I am spending endless hours by myself playing on the beach. I am strangely curious about this awesome blue-green body of water that beckons to me from beyond the golden sands and tidal pools. I feel somehow that this dark giant marks the boundary between my little world of shovels and sand castles and whatever mysteries lay beyond. I remember like it was yesterday.... What? What do you remember? I learned how to swim. I went into the sea. I was overcome by the strength of the ocean, but I was equally aware of its gentleness. As I grew stronger, and ventured beyond the breakers, I found the rocking motion of the mighty beast to be like a mother gently rocking her baby. The sea had become the driving force in my imagination. I began to be obsessed with fantasies about sex and the sea.*

I would imagine in the quiet hours of the night that the sea was calling to me. The moonlight glistens over its sleek body and shines into my bedroom, waking me gently and patiently. I put on my bathrobe, crawl out my open window and walk to the beach. I am constantly aware that the voice of the sea is growing louder as I approach it. As I reach the beach, I must pause to marvel at the giant unyielding beast. Is it tonight that I am to meet the very source of my lifelong infatuation?

A sudden sea breeze lifts my bathrobe over my shoulders, carrying it to the dunes behind me. I am naked, yet unafraid. I walk softly down to the shoreline and put my feet in the water. Its warmth, contrasted to the cold sands of the beach, comforts me. The waves crash against my thighs and breasts, awakening me to the excitement that is to come...

I am drawn out past the waves by a strong current, drawn out where I can barely see the few lights that are left on overnight at my beach house. My smooth ride brings me to deep water, much deeper than I have ever been before. The depth, however, does not frighten me. This is where I want to be.

Without warning, a pair of strong hands reaches around my body, drawing me underneath the water. I try to struggle free, but in vain. Whatever is holding me is too strong, so strong that I am immobile. Where am I going? Gradually, my fears turn to excitement. I feel at ease with the creature. He is strong, yet gentle. He lets me loose and I surface. I am not where I went under water, but in a cave. I crawl up onto a large smooth rock, overcome by curiosity.

Abruptly, he surfaces. He has the appearance, not of a man, but of a God. His deep sea-green eyes illuminate the once barren cave, revealing its true identity as a garden of love. As he emerges from the water, I am astounded by the size and beauty of this Man-God. He must be seven and a half feet tall with golden hair and a deep dark tan. His physique is perfect. His shoulders are broad. His manhood is large, but it does not frighten me. As he walks toward me, it grows with anticipation. Could it be that this superman is attracted to this shy, innocent young woman?

He lifts me from the rock and delicately places me on a soft bed of clover. I desire him—I am wet with anticipation. He caresses my neck, sending me into a world of disbelief. How could someone so strong be so soft? His lips work down my neck and between my breasts. He kisses both of them, not missing a spot, making me eager for more. He moves down my stomach and into my thighs, kissing them inside and out. His tongue and lips finally reach their goal. I am writhing with passion and desire. I need him. Although I am speechless in my world of ecstasy, he seems to sense this. He places the head of his throbbing muscle against the entrance of my womanhood. I pull him gently inside of me. Feeling only joy—no pain—I pull him deeper and deeper, until finally he is all the way inside me. With the ferocity of breaking waves he crashes in and out of me, sending me into paroxysms of joy. He fills me with warm love juices and I keep coming more and more...

Still erect, he slows his tempo down to a tender, rocking motion. We make love this way for hours, having orgasm after beautiful orgasm. I have been drained of all my energy and filled with love. With his powerful, sensitive fingers massaging my back, I fall into a deep sleep...

"ALICIA! WHAT THE HELL ARE YOU DOING!!!"

"...Huh...what...?"

"I SAID, WHAT THE HELL ARE YOU DOING? STARING AT THE BUGS ON THE CEILING?"

"No...I was just...daydreaming..."

It was Billy wanting to know if Alicia would lend him twenty dollars to buy some crank.

"I'm broke," said Alicia. "Who's got crank?"

"Nobody you know."

Billy left Alicia sitting at the bar. Alicia turned and saw him leave.

"God, I hate that guy," she said to no one in particular.

You're James Taylor

Billy knew it was hopeless asking Alicia for twenty bucks, but he could not resist bothering her. He went over to the other end of the bar to see Todd who was momentarily by himself. .

Alicia's a fuckin' scumbag," he said.

"Why?"

"I don't know. She's just a whore. She reminds me of a frog croaking in the low rent district of a toxic waste dump."

"She that bad?"

"Look at those stoned-out eyes, for God's sake. She's a fuckin' horror show all by herself."

Todd looked over in Alicia's direction, but did not say anything.

"Okay, forget that bitch. When are we going to practice?"

"Dutch's amp is still busted."

"So what? We can practice anyway."

"I don't know…

Billy left Todd and went over and stood by the "Hot Shot" basketball game.

"Hey Chris. When are we gonna practice?"

"Dutch's amp is down."

"Who cares? He can play acoustically, or we can go without a rhythm guitar player for awhile."

Chris ignored Billy, focusing his attention on the video screen.

"Check this out."

A young woman was feeling herself in various places on her body with nothing on except a bra and panties. She stood up on a bed, started dancing and waving a scarf around her head.

"I've seen that one. When do we practice?"

"Dutch's amp…"

"You know what?"

"What?"

"The last song you wrote for us sucked."

"What do you mean sucked?"

"I'm not going to sing wimpy shit about a rain forest."

"Christ, Billy. That song was about preserving the environment."

"Fuck the whales."

"You're an asshole. Do you want to sing about motorcycles and girls all your life?"

"It's better than singing about a bunch of trees and marine life. Nobody gives a shit about this whole earth crap. We're a rock 'n roll band, for chrissakes. You think Elvis ever sang a song about a whale?"

"You're hopeless."

"Yeah? And you're James Taylor!"

Chris gave Billy a disgusted look and returned to shooting pool. Billy followed him to the pool table.

"Hey word man," said Billy apologetically. "Maybe Elvis should have sung a song about a whale. Maybe he would have been more contemporary, instead of a fat has-been in Vegas."

"Do you think *Slash and Burn* really sucked?" asked Chris.

"No. It's a good song. I'm just pissed cause we ain't practicing."

"You're right. Hell, let's get together Wednesday night. I'll get Todd and Dutch."

"Now you're talking!"

"Who's talking? James Taylor?"

"Boy, that was a low blow, huh?"

"About the lowest."

"Hey, speaking of Todd," said Billy. "He called me the other night and asked me what Lo Level Jo and the Antichrist were doing on MTV."

"That's kind of strange, even for Todd."

"What was I supposed to say? I mean, I think Lo Level Jo sucks too, but MTV can play anything it wants to, right?"

"Is that all he said?"

"Yeah, then he hung up."

"What's with the Antichrist?"

"Don't know. Maybe he's freakin' out."

"Did you know Leslie is trying to line us up a gig at Trax?" asked Chris.

"No."

"She said she might be able to persuade the manager to let us open for *Megadeth*."

"When?"

"I don't know. Maybe in a couple weeks."

"We're not ready for the garage—much less *Megadeth.*"

"Maybe we need a manager," said Chris.

"It might get us off our butts. Get a hold of Todd and Dutch, okay? I gonna split."

Later, Billy returned to his apartment. It was a room in a garage next to a funeral parlor. He turned on the television and clicked the remote control until he landed on an MTV special called "Heavy Metal Rockers With Their Mothers." Billy found it too ludicrous to think about, but he did ponder for a second what would happen if Jesus chose this moment to make his Second Coming. He pictured Jesus descending from the clouds, landing right in the middle of the show when the *Ramones'* mother was saying what a great bunch of guys her sons had become. Billy liked the *Ramones,* but vowed never to have his mother on television with him, no matter how famous he became.

Billy heard a movement outside his window and looked to see two sturdy guys in heavy-duty overalls carrying a body in a large sack. The telephone rang. Billy went over and picked it up. It was his landlord Mr. Winkleman informing him that he was raising his rent fifty dollars.

"RAISE THE RENT??? YOU GOTTA BE KIDDING! I'M PAYING TWO HUNDRED DOLLARS FOR A ROOM IN A GARAGE NEXT TO A FUNERAL HOME!!!"

"Calm down," said Mr. Winkleman.

"Look, normal people look out their windows and see trees and streets and shit. What do I see? Dead bodies wrapped in body bags, carried on stretchers, or slung over some goon's back."

"The utility bills are getting too high."

"That's not my problem. I'm the one who feels like a guest in the Addams family household. And by the way, it's always cold in here, so don't give me that utility bill bullshit."

"The rent is two hundred and fifty dollars starting on the first of the month—and you play your music too loud."

"Oh really? Who am I going to disturb?"

"You have no respect for the dead."

"And if you had any respect for the living, you wouldn't raise my rent!"

Billy slammed the phone down, knowing that he was fighting a losing battle with the landlord. He felt the little guys in this world had no hope over greedy landlords, or anybody else for that matter. He figured he would have to find another place to live, or start working more overtime at the plant. He called his boss at the frozen food factory.

"Hey, Mr. Perez. This is Billy Saxon."

"What can I do for you?"

"I need to work some more hours."

"You mean overtime?"

"Yeah, whatever."

"Well, I might need someone for the graveyard shift."

"I'll take it."

"Good. Be here tonight at 11 o'clock."

Billy hung up the phone.

My God, I'll be repairing frozen food machines at four o'clock in the morning when everyone in their right mind is sleeping. What a life. I go from living in a graveyard to working on one.

ABYSS

...Getting chilly...

Reluctantly, I got up from my easy chair, lumbered over to the fireplace, and tossed a log into the fire...

...Glad Leslie gets MTV and the Book of Revelation. She just finished her shower...can tell because a few seconds ago I heard her hair dryer come on...don't know why, but the droning noise really gets on my nerves...reminds me of my life right now...ZZ TOP flashed on the screen...about time they played something decent...video is "Legs" and they sure picked a gorgeous girl for the part. Her legs are really incredible...thought about Leslie...she is naked in the bathroom...thought about paying her a visit, but decided against it...don't feel like going to the trouble right now. Besides, she might be the ancient harlot, but I can't be sure. Sometimes I see her garbed in purple and scarlet and adorned with gold and pearls. I think the earthly dirges have lamented the loss of voluptuousness, and thus, the end of music. Video is over and Adam Curry is talking about the next MTV theme of the week. He said, totally serious, that they are going to conduct a Madonnathon—the thought of which really repulsed me...just thinking about watching 100 Madonna videos in a row makes me want to put a gun to my head...I know I have to accept the hard life, to deal with outright stupor, to lift the coffin lid, and suffocate.

...I keep hearing the voice of the great multitude and the sound of many waters and mighty thunder peals. Isn't it time for the end of Satan's evil age?...felt a headache coming on, so I went into the kitchen to get a beer. Fortunately, by the time I got back, Billy Idol had replaced Billy Joel, and a young hardbody is crawling across the floor like a cat in heat, stalking some preppy-nerd... Girl is hot although she's only

about fourteen years old, but she doesn't have the mark on her forehead or hands like the rest of the martyrs who will not be there for the resurrection. I think she should be cast into the lake of fire with the rest of the harlots, whores, and thieves.

Leslie emerged from the bedroom and walked down the hall toward the living room. She bent over the back of Todd's chair, leaned toward him, and gave him a big kiss on the lips.

"You look great."

"Thanks. Was it worth the wait?"

"It sure was. Do you want to watch the Madonnathon?"

"Very funny."

Leslie came from behind the chair and collapsed in Todd's lap. Todd put his arms around her for support.

"Todd, I want you to know that I am here for you if you need me."

"What do you mean?"

"Those drugs are affecting your personality. You're drifting off more and more..."

"I'm okay."

"Will you promise me you'll lay off those awful pills—and whatever else you're doing."

"Okay, I promise. I think you're right. They do strange things to my head."

Leslie got up from the chair and went back into the bedroom to make a phone call. Todd glared at the television.

...Still a chill in the air...

...Singer comes on MTV who is actually more ugly than Billy Idol. I recognize the group as Midnight Oil. They are singing a song about being "king of the mountain" and the lead singer is bald-headed, wearing a T-shirt with a slice of a lemon pie splashed across the front. He's performing on a platform in New York City...had a discussion with Billy the other night and he said he thought Steve Tyler was uglier than Mick Jagger. I said that was a toss-up, but hell, look at this guy...I don't think Tom Petty looks so good either. Thank God, Adam Curry just finished the "Top 10 Countdown" which is the worse part of MTV, except the rap shit...who cares if Billy Joel doesn't know why he goes to extremes?...wonder what Billy Joel's idea of extreme is...maybe wearing a black leather jacket...

...Lit a joint, popped a couple percodans...found myself drifting listlessly into the kitchen to grab a Budweiser from the refrigerator...only have two beers left...returned to the living room. Nothing happening...went back to the bedroom, and looked in on Leslie, who is talking to someone on the telephone. Perhaps she is talking to the great

multitude...wandered around the apartment...everything is vacant...saw one of Leslie's Cosmopolitan magazines on the coffee table. Notice the feature article is called "Where The Men Are."...Flipped through the magazine and found the article...large, two page spread of a map of the United States, isolating the "hot spots" for men. Places like Aspen. Los Angeles. Seattle. What kinds of guys live in Seattle?...I remembered that Jimi Hendrix was from Seattle, so maybe it's okay...

...Discarded the magazine...floated back to my easy chair...percodans are beginning to soak up my brain...collapsed in a state of rubbery consciousness. Sometime later...sprinkled a bit of angel dust on a joint, lit it, and wandered off into Jerusalem. MTV and the apocalypse are calling me again. My eyes are heavy-lidded, drunk and drowsy...What? Perchance to dream and fill this dull vacancy of the mind?...Reached into my pants pocket and produced three darvons...gulped them down with a swallow of Bud. Maybe that will put me out completely...I felt as if my eyes were being pushed down, like they were large pillows stuffed into small pillowcases. Is this all about transmutation? This is the blood that makes the outlaw. I have been of an inferior race forever. I understand a new epoch is at hand, full of sordid terror. What low and vile nature is about to commence? Modernity is the peasant's grasp of the world untouched by miracles. I have to bury my imagination and my memories...must escape my filthy childhood education and upbringing. Does this farce have no end? Who is that? Some Australian VJ named Andrew Daddo is playing The Time's "Jerk Out."...Don't know who told American audiences that the Australian accent was cool. They all sound like a bunch of wimps. Look at Downtown Julie Brown...now there's a piece of work! Club MTV. That's what I'd like to do to her. Club Downtown Julie Brown—right over the head!

MTV is getting stranger every day...hard to describe, but the videos are getting more symbolic and violent. I'm sure there are lots of messages coming out of MTV that I should be paying attention to...like a couple of minutes ago, I saw, once again, "The Antichrist is coming" flashing on the screen...When are we going to see the judgment of the harlot? There are certainly enough of them on MTV. I see two olive trees and two lampshades next to Downtown Julie Brown, which is very confusing, if you ask me. I am still anticipating a demonic beast to appear from the bottomless pit to make war against the witnesses and kill them. But all I see is a trembling world, waiting for an earthquake, and the kingdom of our Lord. It's an ancient agreement, right? With evil and personal intention. I must refrain from lonesome soliloquies on pride and ambition, and avoid glimpses of the divine essence, erotic flowers, and drowsy melodies from an ancient family. Another video appears. This time it is a woman clothed with the sun, with the moon under her feet, and on her head a crown of twelve stars singing, "Any day now, I shall be released." We all need a place prepared by God and

. Michael with his angels. The morality of wickedness must be controlled. Leslie comes into the room, looks at me strangely and says something I can't make out very clearly. I think she said something about going to Jake's. I'm getting tired of this black guy slinging a lariat around in a country and western bar, so I decided to call Chris.

"Hey, man, what's going on?"

"Nothing much," said Chris. "What are you doing?"

"Just watching MTV. Do you know the Antichrist is coming?"

"Huh?"

"Never mind. What's Wayne Newton doing in a Billy Idol video?"

"Who's Wayne Newton?" asked Chris.

"Nobody. Who are you not being today?"

"A truck driver."

"Why not?"

"Because," said Chris, "There are too many gears on them semis. Like sixteen, or something like that."

"That would be tiresome. Shifting gears all the time."

"Who are you not being?" asked Chris.

"An IRS agent,"

"Why?"

Because I was watching Family Feud the other day and they asked one hundred people what occupation was the least liked in the United States and they said IRS agent. So the IRS is out. I mean, who wants to be one of the least liked persons in the country?"

"We're trying to be rock musicians and they aren't exactly loved by the American people."

"But it's money for nuthin' and the chicks for free."

"Sure."

"Talk to you later."

…Slouched even lower in the chair…began to lapse into another dimension…pales and trembles slumping into the unfathomable abyss…the strange shadow of evil lurking behind my easy chair…. A frightful half-smile appears, then disappears down the boulevard of broken dreams…There's a ballet being fought in the tenement slums, crusty old bums, and weathered old crones…I must say I have certain deficiencies…why else would the waters of my dead loves leave me bleached along the silent aching shore? TV screen blurred and metabolized into celluloid breakdown, as images of color blending and green melting liquefaction go blobbing along with oozy slime,

molting into blood-boiled plasma...Leslie and Jake are calling me to love and dance among the green felt tables and garish neon signs...

LOVE AT FIRST DRINK

Sarah arrived at Chris' apartment on a sunny Monday afternoon carrying a copy of a new *R.E.M.* bootleg. She sat down on his cluttered sofa, somehow finding a spot between two disheveled mounds of books. Her left heel inadvertently rested on the latest draft of Chris' new song.

"How was the band?" she asked.

"Awesome. You shoulda come. Some guy dressed like a priest and gave the lead singer his last rites. Really weird."

"I had to study Chaucer."

"How are classes going?"

"My senior project is harder than I thought."

"Don't worry. Your father could always buy you another college if you flunked out of this one."

"What's bugging you?"

" I'm just joking around, that's all."

Chris reached over and grabbed the bootleg and put it on the stereo. Soon the plaintive sounds of *Murmur* were wafting from the speakers.

"Sounds pretty good for an amateur copy," said Chris, pushing a stack of books on the floor and sliding on the sofa next to Sarah.

Sarah did not respond. They sat together quietly for a few minutes. It was Sarah who broke the silence.

"Do you want to go a poetry reading at the Prism?"

"It's kinda cold outside, don't you think?"

"So, you don't want to go?"

"I'm not crazy about poetry readings."

"But you *are* a poet," she protested.

"I'm not anything, especially a poet. Besides, all I've been doing for a year is writing lyrics for *Mean Streets*. I wouldn't exactly call that T.S. Eliot."

"I don't understand. Everybody has to be something."

Chris wanted to tell her that he *was* something. Something holy and barbarian, like a crazed Zen motorcycle madman careening through the dark American night; something noble and chivalrous, like a young, valiant Sir Lancelot slaying a dragon for his beautiful damsel in distress; something powerful and foreboding, like a giant Polynesian tidal wave swelling twenty feet into the air before crashing onto a beach.

"Chris…?"

"Oh…well…not really. Not everybody has to be something."

Sarah audibly sighed. She went over to the other side of the room and turned down the stereo. She came back to the sofa and sat down. She looked Chris firmly in the eyes.

"Only children live in a world where they don't grow up."

"I don't think Todd has been practicing his drums."

Sarah rolled her eyes toward the ceiling. "Well, Todd has his share of problems. Maybe he should straighten out a bit."

"What do you mean?"

"I think he has been doing too many drugs, don't you?"

"Yeah. He has been acting more strange. He seems to be having trouble concentrating."

"Leslie tells me all he does is sit around watching MTV."

"Well, it's better than working. I'd hate to think he might have to get a regular job."

"What's wrong with that?"

Chris reached over and made an awkward attempt to hug Sarah, but she twisted out of his grasp.

"What's the matter?" asked Chris.

"I can't figure you out. You're smart, talented and you come from a good family. You know I like all the people at Jake's and your interest in music, but I just don't see why you don't get into anything else."

"Like what?"

"Well, like some of my friends or a poetry reading."

"Look, let's go out. We can talk about it later,"

"Out? You know that means. We'll just go to Jake's and drink beer."

Chris went over to the stereo and turned the music back up. Sarah reached for a magazine on the coffee table. It was *Newsweek* with a picture of President Bush on the cover. Chris came back to the couch and sat next to Sarah.

"What are you going to do this weekend?" asked Chris.

"I'm going to Hampden Sydney with Susan and Patty."

"More fraternity parties?"

"It's mid-winter's."

"So?"

"It's fun."

"I guess spending weekends with five hundred guys would be fun. Maybe I'll check out the girls' schools."

"You know I'm not interested in any of those guys. They're just friends."

"Sarah, don't be so naïve. Every one of those guys would sleep with you on a moment's notice."

"No, they wouldn't."

"Yeah, sure. Why don't you try it?"

"Try what?"

"In the middle of one of your beer blasts, ask one of your so-called friends to sleep with you."

"Don't be ridiculous."

"You don't know men very well."

"You put too much emphasis on sex—"

"—And you don't put enough on it."

Chris got up and went back over to the stereo. He inserted the new *Travelin' Willbury's* CD and cranked it up real loud. On the other side of the room Sarah shouted something that sounded like, "The Pope is even less."

"WHAT???"

Instead of answering Chris, she gave him a disgusted look, and went into the bedroom, shutting the door behind her. She plopped on the bed and picked up a copy of Joseph Campbell's *Hero With a Thousand Faces*. She heard Chris turn the television on in the other room. She wondered if Chris really did have potential, or was just another townie that would never amount to anything. She did not think he would reach his potential by limiting his life to Todd, Dutch, and Billy and she was sure he could be a terrific poet, or hold a decent job if he put his mind to it. For her, the whole barfly routine had gotten completely out of hand. She could not understand why every one of those guys had seen the film count-less of times, knowing virtually every line Mickey Rourke utters in the movie. She could not understand their logic. She wondered what was the point of picking out an occupation that you didn't want to be? Wouldn't it make more sense to try and figure out what you *want*ed to be?

She heard a knock on the door.

"Yes."

"Can I come in?"

"It's your apartment, remember?"

"You know what I mean."

"Sure. What are you doing?"

"Watching TV. Nothing's on."

"Does this have something to do with the other night?"

"What about the other night?"

"We were getting along great. You remember. Then you said something about me leaving...about going on the road...I told you I wasn't going anywhere."

"You don't know where you're going. That's the problem."

"Do you want to go to Jake's? We're gonna watch the movie at Dutch's later on."

"Chris, I've seen that film too many times. Aren't you sick of seeing it?"

"Not really. What are you going to do?"

"I'm going back to my place. I've got an early class tomorrow."

"Okay, I'll call you tomorrow."

"Good night."

Sarah went back to reading her book, but her thoughts again drifted to Chris and his infatuation with a movie that practically no one ever saw. It seemed like such a terrible waste of time. She could not understand the attraction of hanging out in a bar pretending to be a degenerate character in a movie. She questioned her own motivations for being attracted to Chris in the first place. Sarah had plenty of chances to go out with regular college guys, but she felt they were ordinary and predictable. She liked the way Chris and his friends communicated as they sat in their favorite booth, slouched over draft beers, peering into each other's eyes, repeating lines from *Barfly*. They reminded her of some lost bohemian poets, rambling chains of rythming images over dimly lit coffee house tables. But at other times, she admitted to herself that they were just a bunch of working class guys going through a ritual that protected them from admitting to themselves that they were going nowhere. They acted like pauper philosophers and undiscovered artists who could not be troubled with the mundane aspects of life. Their booth at Jakes' served as the special, private place that no one else could penetrate.

The phone rang, interrupting Sarah's thoughts.

"Hello."

"Hello, Sarah. This is Leslie. What are you doing?"

"Just reading. Nothing much."

"Are you going to Dutch's?"

"No, not tonight. It's late, and besides, to tell you the truth, I'm sick of that film. Are you going?"

"Yes, just for a while. Why don't you come?"

"No, thanks. I'm sure I'll get another chance to see it. I'm tired."

"Okay. Well, see you later. By the way, can we do lunch next week?"

"Sure."

"How about the Ivy Inn on Wednesday around twelve noon? My treat."

"Sounds great."

"See you then. Bye!"

Sarah stopped reading her book. She reached for the entertainment section of the university newspaper to see what films were playing. As she was scanning the paper, she noticed that the film *Barfly* was playing at the Vinegar Hill theatre. She could not believe it. The movie seemed to be following her around. Beneath the announcement, she read the review of the film:

> *Barfly is a descent into the lower depths of poet Charles Bukowski's deadbeat East Hollywood streets. It is the story of a lively and bedraggled alcoholic couple played by Mickey Rourke and Faye Dunnaway. In the beginning, we encounter the character of Henry (Mickey Rourke) being beaten to a bloody pulp in a back alley by a bartender. Henry is a battle-scarred survivor of the streets; a wreck of a man who lives to drink and write poetry. He stumbles into a bar and meets Wanda (Faye Dunnaway) who is also alcoholic, but terribly self-destructive. It is love at first drink. Under the seedy surface of the film emerges a cunning comedy and touching love story.*
>
> *Wanda is being supported by a sugar daddy until Henry tells him to get lost. Henry loves Wanda so much that he is even willing to get a job, but as a voluntary dropout of the rat race, Henry has no discernable market skills. He tells Jim, the bartender that it overwhelms him thinking about all the occupations that he doesn't want to be—like an airplane pilot, a priest, a cab driver.*
>
> *In the meantime, Henry is pursued by Tully, a rich upper crust patron of the arts who loves Henry's writing and begins to fall for him. It's hard to believe that Tully would fall for a barfly/poet with scabby knuckles, dirty fingernails, and a filthy T-shirt, but she is drawn to Henry's search for truth by living amongst society's rejects.*
>
> *In this weirdly romantic tale, Wanda leaves Henry for the night and sleeps with a bartender because he "had a bottle of whiskey." Henry stays overnight at*

Tully's, but quickly returns to the streets the next day because he can't live in a "cage with golden bars."

   Henry returns to the street scene with Wanda. Tully comes back for one more try. She enters the bar and Wanda immediately perceives Henry had been with her. They have a classic catfight and Tully is chased from the bar. The movie ends with everyone piling out of the bar to watch Henry fight the bartender once more.

   Barfly is deeply moving in ways that go beyond laughter. It is a touching story of two lost souls among the ruins of the East Hollywood streets.

Sarah clearly understood from the review why Chris and his friends found the film so appealing. They also think they are romantic dropouts from society. But she had no intention of playing the part of Wanda and she did not see anything remotely romantic about drinking yourself to death. Sarah was growing tired, but she did not feel like spending the night at Chris' apartment. She wanted to be back in her own place.

She got up from the bed, gathered her things together, and quietly slipped out of the apartment.

THE BANALITY OF WESTERN CIVILIZATION

"Modern poetry," the professor intoned dramatically, "is usually a completely formless mishmash of puerile yearnings about nothing of any substance."

One of the students in the class, whose name was Bernard, raised his hand energetically, like he was ordering a hot dog in Yankee Stadium.

"But professor, Bernard said, "Isn't Sylvia Plath a modern poet? Surely, you can't say she's without substance."

The professor paused for a second, carefully measuring the full weight of the comment.

"Bernard," he said, "Have you ever *read* Sylvia Plath?"

"Yes, sir."

"Well, then you should know Ms. Plath couldn't write a decent poem if a gun were held to her head."

Chris Hamilton was sitting in class taking in this exchange with more than a small degree of cynicism and distain for academic pomposity. Personally, he thought that the "gun to the head" phrase was a weak comparison. He should have said she couldn't write a decent poem if she put her head in an oven—which is what she really did in real life. Chris had a soft spot in his heart for poets who committed suicide and resented the professor's arrogant put-down of the famous poetess.

The class ended, and Chris was glad they were spared further musings on the banality of modern civilization. He vowed not to be a professor in this life. He felt they all possessed an exaggerated sense of self-importance and besides, he figured, he couldn't possibly motivate these students. Last semester a girl in his class wrote down that she was taking "Oral and Terp." Later, she came up to him and asked him when the "terp" part of the course would begin. "What do you mean by "terp?" he asked. Chris looked at her schedule card and realized that she had signed up for "Oral Interpretation." Of course, she had heard everyone speaking about taking "Oral Interp."

Chris left campus and went shopping for new guitar strings at the Downtown Mall. As he passed Miller's Café, he ran into Alicia.

"Hey Chris, Wassup?"

"Nothing. Just got through classes."

"You holding?"

"No. I was supposed to get some from my uncle, but he hasn't come through yet."

"No big deal. You going to Jake's tonight?"

"Yeah, I guess so."

"Do you want tickets for the *Faith No More* concert?"

"No thanks. I'm broke."

"See you later."

From the mall, Chris decided to see Sarah because he knew things were not right between them and he felt he was avoiding her, or maybe she was ignoring him. It had been two days since he had left to see the movie without her. Chris called her at her parents' house and asked her if she wanted to do a late lunch. Sarah would occasionally spend a weekend at her parents' palatial estate in Scottsville. He drove over to the Carson residence and along the way, Chris had time to think about his relationship with Sarah. He knew he loved her and he was sure that she loved him. But it was more complicated than that. He wondered how they could spend beautiful, intimate nights together, making love, and giving of themselves completely, and still be having so many problems. He loved everything about her; the way she smelled like blooming lilacs during sex; the way she smiled seductively when he told her how sexy she looked; her eclectic, cultivated taste in music, books, and movies; her sardonic sense of humor, and especially the way she loved him unconditionally. Of course, he figured, perhaps he was fooling himself. Maybe she did not love him unconditionally; maybe she wanted more out of life, more than just being Chris Hamilton's girlfriend. If he was confused about how she felt, he was even more confused about he felt himself. He reasoned that he must not love her unconditionally, or else he would not put the band as a top priority. He made it very clear that the band came first, and that was probably the biggest hurdle in the relationship. He felt he was being split down the middle; half of him wanting to live the rock 'n roll lifestyle and the other half wanting to spend the rest of his life loving a beautiful person. He knew, deep down, he could do both, but right now, he could not reconcile the two opposing forces in his life. He also knew there was another big issue that was hindering their progress. In simple terms, he was the guy from the poor side of the tracks and Sarah was the girl in the mansion on the hill. The situation made for some great song lyrics and soap opera plots, but in real life it was not so easy. Sarah made the mistake of telling her father about the barfly scene and he was absolutely incredulous. "You mean he just hangs out at a bar with a bunch of do-nothings? What does he put down as his occupation on his tax return—barfly?"

Sarah realized her mistake, quickly covering by adding, "…but he's going to community college, plays bass guitar in a band, and writes some great lyrics!"

It was too late. Things had not been the same since that conversation. To Sarah's father, Chris was just another local loser.

Chris drove down route 20 toward the Carson's house, passing through rolling countryside where there were few actual houses to be seen, but plenty of private roads branching off from the highway with signs proclaiming farms and estates in the area. He observed names like "Meadowbrook Farms," Mountain View Estate," and "Windom Hill Farms" as he cruised down the curvaceous country road. Approaching "Carson Farms," Chris turned left on a narrow, paved, Leland cypress-lined driveway, which led up to the Carson residence. He passed through an elaborately designed wrought iron gate, and eased the Chevette into the asphalt parking area of an expansive, eighteenth century white colonial house with a grand, wraparound porch and marble steps, flanked by two round, dominating black stone columns. There were pristine pathways jutting out from the house in all directions, leading to a lush garden, a swimming pool with a waterfall, and various outlying guesthouses. The front of the house was immaculately landscaped with green scrubs, English boxwoods, assorted colorful flowers including geraniums, roses, and rhododendrons. The estate was also blessed with a clear blue pond with sculptural stonewalls, stocked with ducks, fish and frogs. From the pool, massive granite steps were set into a grassy hillside descending to a boardwalk, where guests could stroll amid the tall, rustling grasses. A turn to the right revealed a stone path leading to a bench in the shade of an ash tree. Bright flowers glowed against the backdrop of the richly colored foliage.

Chris got out of the car, walked up the steps and rang the bell. Momentarily, her mother answered.

"Hi, Mrs. Carson. Is Sarah here?"

"Oh, hello, Chris. Come on in. She's expecting you. She'll be down in a minute."

Mrs. Carson was an attractive middle-aged woman who was always impeccably dressed in designer dresses and wore fine, tasteful jewelry. Her hair was clipped short, hanging loosely about her youthful, rounded face. She led Chris into the foyer that was twice as large as Chris' living room. She left Chris alone as usual, so he did his regular routine. He carefully sat down in a chair he thought might be from eighteenth century France. He knew the chair was very fragile, so he sat perfectly still, cautious not to break anything. He glanced over and asked, "What's goin' on?" to one of the several shiny brass cranes standing on one leg in a blue-watered fountain.

Sarah finally made her appearance; descending a flight of stairs that were so grand Chris always thought he could grow a beard by the time she got to the bottom.

"Well, hello," said Sarah.

"Hi. Do you want to get a sandwich at the deli?"

"Sure. Let me get my coat."

Sarah retrieved her coat from the closet, and then yelled to her mother upstairs.

"Mother! I'm leaving now."

"Fine, dear. Don't forget, dinner at eight."

"I won't."

Chris walked out to the car and he opened the door for Sarah. As he was getting in the car, it occurred to him that there probably were not a lot of Chevettes in the neighborhood.

It was called the New York Deli, but located on Main Street right next to the university. As they stood in line, Chris looked around at all the college types in the place.

"Please, honey, do me a favor."

"What's that?"

"Don't ever go out with a guy who wears a sweater around his waist, okay?"

"Don't worry."

They both ordered a "Thomas Jefferson" and waited a few moments at the counter for their sandwiches before taking a seat in one of the booths in the back.

"I wonder what Thomas Jefferson would think of a sandwich being named after him," mused Sarah.

"He probably wouldn't care. He was a ham anyway."

"You have a sick mind."

A song by the *Cowboy Junkies* began playing.

"Do you like the *Cowboy Junkies*?" asked Sarah.

"They're okay, but do they ever play an up-tempo song?"

"Do you expect a band with a name like *Cowboy Junkies* to play upbeat music?"

"Well, the *Dead Kennedys* play fast songs and their name certainly isn't upbeat."

"My father hates the Kennedys."

After a few moments of silence, Sarah's mood turned more serious.

"Chris, where do you think our relationship is going?"

Chris stuck a tomato with a toothpick and played with the lettuce in his sandwich.

" I don't know…I just don't know where I'm going right now, so it's difficult to make plans…"

"I'm not asking for a something carved in granite. I just want to know how you feel about me and if we have a future together. Sometimes I feel like I'm wasting my time."

"No, you shouldn't say that!" exclaimed Chris. "We're going to make it together. I just need some time to figure out what I'm going to do."

"But Chris," Sarah quickly noted, "You spend all your time with those guys pretending not to grow up. How much longer do you think I can put up with that silly nonsense?"

Chris lifted the lettuce out of his sandwich, tearing away pieces and dropping them on his plate.

"Well," began Chris, "I need a few more years to figure all this out and I don't think that's too much time to wait."

"For what?"

"What?"

"To wait for what? What am I waiting for?"

"…You know…something serious."

Chris wanted to end the discussion. He was tired. His eyes felt droopy and he was getting a headache. Sarah stared vacantly into her sandwich. Chris wondered what she was feeling. Did she want to cry or hit him over the head with a large metal object?

"I'm sorry," Chris said, "I'm being a jerk."

"You finally said something that makes sense."

"I love you, Sarah. You know that."

"You should say that more often. You used to say it a lot."

"I know. Do you know why I don't say it as much as I used to?"

"No."

"I'm afraid you will desert me. Deep down inside I think you will dump me."

"Why?"

"It's hard for me to explain. I don't think you are really dedicated to me. You spend too much time with your friends and studying. I guess I'm jealous of your time. Remember last semester when you started going to all those fraternity parties?"

"Yes."

"Well, I think you changed when school started. You didn't see me as often. You went to too many fraternity parties."

"They're just friends. What's wrong with that?"

"Nothing. But tell me what you can get from them that you can't get with my friends and me? In the beginning, we did all kinds of things together. Now, we're lucky to spend two or three nights a week together."

"I don't think you understand."

"Why the fraternity parties?"

"They're fun."

"And going to the movies with me isn't?"

"Of course."

"Well...?"

"I guess I never thought about it. I suppose it's the attention."

"Why? Are you insecure or something?"

"No, I don't think so..."

"I can't compete with fraternity parties."

"They're just fun, that's all."

"Hey, no problem. You can have all the fun you want. Just don't hassle me with this 'where is our relationship going' bullshit. You gonna lot of nerve bringing up the word commitment when you can't wean yourself from phony, stupid fraternity guys hitting on you."

"I'm sorry."

"About what?"

"I'm sorry I brought the whole thing up. You're right. Maybe I'm not ready for a full-time relationship. I like my friends too much."

"Well, you got them. You can go to a thousand fraternity parties. Don't worry about me."

"Chris…"

He stood up, reached in his pocket and tossed a twenty-dollar bill on the table.

"See ya," he said, as he turned toward the door.

Sarah looked away toward the offerings of sandwiches on the wall and noticed one of the names for a sandwich was "Wahoo."

Tequila Pig

Sarah's friends sometimes accused her of being a "neat freak" because her apartment was always kept so tidy. Sarah was bemused by the comments because she did not think she was as meticulous as everyone thought. She liked to think of herself as someone whose life was organized, but not in an obsessive way. She thought housework was good therapy, and a welcome break from the rigors of academic life. Usually on Saturday mornings, she would wake up, put on a pot of coffee, slip some folk music into the stereo, and clean the house. She thought John Prine was the best person to listen to while cleaning. Her apartment was an older duplex with rust colored shingles located near the campus with the entrance through the kitchen. The kitchen was a clean, tan wallpapered room with white mini-blinds covering the lone window. The room was simple and efficient. The most colorful feature was the refrigerator, which was littered with a mass of miniature-scrambled words that could be arranged to spell out phrases. Yesterday, she was fooling around with the words and left "traveling some day soon" prominently on display. A row of houseplants were bunched together on the inside windowsill.

Sarah may not have thought of herself as a "neat freak," but she did consider herself a "plant freak." Her apartment was a virtual flower shop housing all sorts of plants from every conceivable variety. The white windowsill in the kitchen contained a spider plant, a philodendron, forest cacti, and a piper plant. A braided hemp hanger hung from the ceiling maintaining a blazing yellow narcissus plant. The kitchen was adjacent to a comfortable living room with light brown wall-to-wall carpeting, a walnut entertainment center with a television and stereo, a black futon, and a cream-colored popeson chair. A thin, black halogen lamp with gold trim was stationed in the corner by the futon. Numerous prints and pictures were mounted on the walls. There was a Diane Arbus print of an obese transvestite lying on her bed, surrounded by party balloons; A black and white picture of reggae singer Bob Marley was placed over the popeson chair. A slick billiard player with a brown felt fedora was shown making a shot while a voluptuous raven-haired beauty eyed him seductively from the back of the pool hall. There was another photo beside the halogen lamp of a slouching, brooding James Dean walking down a rainy side street in New York City. The entertainment center contained a host of photos sealed in stained glass frames: her parents, young and in love, smiling broadly on a river bank from a ranch in Texas; her three small God children waving their arms frenetically at Disney world; her grand parents, who were deceased, hugging each other by a fireplace; Chester, the family golden retriever looking goofy with a piece of wood gripped in his mouth; a faded, worn picture of her father as a little boy proudly wearing his brand new Roy Rogers cowboy outfit; and several photos of her and Chris enjoying fun times at parties, cookouts, and baseball games. There was also one picture of the two of them and Jake hanging out at the bar.

The living room also contained an assortment of houseplants. Sarah liked to add plants to her surroundings because she felt plants could enliven what she considered the dull features of her apartment. The apartment had a non-functioning fireplace and she felt an empty hearth was unattractive, so she festooned the mantelpiece with shade-loving foliage plants and temporary flowers like kalanchoe, pink jasmine, and aphelandra. She hated the ordinary appearance of radiators so she improved the look by installing a shelf on each one and adding a pebble tray with plants like succulents and cacti, ones that liked high humidity. In her bedroom she made a display window featuring an arrangement of flowers and greenery. She placed shelves of plastic fixed across the window opening at convenient heights, and pots arranged along each shelf. In her large, well-lit bathroom, she cultivated colorful exotics like anthurium, calathea, caladium, and maranta. She chose wickerwork for potholders, a choice she thought ideal because of the Victorian feel of the house. At this moment she was watering the plants when Chris knocked on the door.

"Oh, hi. Come on in."

"Hey, how's it going? You not answering your phone?"

"I just don't feel like talking to anyone right now."

"Including me?"

"Including you."

Chris walked across the room and sat down on the futon. "I came to apologize for being such a jerk."

Sarah continued watering her plants. "Don't worry about it."

"Look we can work this out."

Sarah avoided looking at Chris. She went to the sink and filled up her water pitcher. "Work what out?"

"You know…our problems."

"Name one."

Chris leaned forward on the futon, resting his elbows on his knees. "I guess the biggest one is that we don't have a plan…we don't know agree on what we're going to do in the future. What do you think?"

"I think you're right. The fact is, I'm tired. Maybe you can go on indefinitely, but I need something."

"I'm not sure I understand you."

Sarah turned her back on Chris. She finished watering a dipladenia and walked over to the fireplace. Turning toward him, she slammed the pitcher down on the mantle piece. "Damnit, you're fuckin' hopeless! And you *really* piss me off. You're making me act like a loser trying to draw something out of you. Well, fuck you! Normal adults do make plans. They don't act like children playing silly bar games. Face it, you're not ready for any kind of commitment besides the band, so why don't you just leave…"

"Hey, calm down! I'm sorry. Calm down, will ya?"

He rushed up to her, taking her in his arms.

"Sarah, I love you."

"Words, Chris…just words. When you love someone you organize your life to be around him or her. You just don't get it. It's beyond you…" Sarah moved away from Chris. She went over to the mantlepiece and picked up the pitcher of water. She walked back into the kitchen, turned on the tap water, and slowly refilled the container.

Chris sat back down on the couch. "I told you. I may go on the road for a little while, but I'll be back—"

"And then what?"

"We'll be together."

"For what?"

"For us…we'll be together."

Sarah walked over to the saintpaulia hanging in the dining room. A ray of sunlight splashed her face as she opened the blinds. "My God…three years of my life…"

Chris stood up and faced Sarah. "Are you talking about getting married? Well, let's face it, Sarah, we're too young for that...I mean, we have plenty of time to get serious."

Sarah watered the plant, then turned toward Chris. "That's not the trouble, Chris. Maybe I am too serious...Maybe, I'm just an insecure bitch. Maybe I want to blow your fuckin' head off." As she spoke, she swung the pitcher in Chris' direction, spilling a few drops of water on the floor.

"I'm just not ready for marriage."

Sarah set the pitcher on the counter and retrieved a paper towel from the kitchen. She bent down to wipe up the spilled water. "I never said anything about marriage—you did."

"Sarah, what's the matter with you? We were getting along fine until you started in on me about leaving you behind if we ever left town. Hell, we don't even have a gig anywhere. Who knows what's going to happen with Trax?"

"That's not the point. Whether you go or stay, doesn't make any difference. It's not a question of location, Chris. It's an affair of the heart and you don't have a clue." She took the paper towel and dumped it into a trashcan.

"I love you Sarah. What more do you want?"

Sarah did not respond. Instead, she went over to a plant in the dining room.

"You see this plant, Chris? It's pilea. It needs water. It needs attention, and it needs tender loving care. That way it can have healthy roots. Do you know what happens if I don't water this plant? It shrivels up and dies. The roots die, Chris. Are you getting my point?"

"Sure. I've neglected you. I'm sorry."

"It's more than that, Chris. Roots don't mean anything to you. Emotions...feelings...empathy...It's just beyond you. You can write a song about it, but ironically you can't feel it or express it. Just words, Chris. You're a writer of emotions who only thinks about emotions. You analyze, philosophize, dissect, try to make them rhyme...anything but a spontaneous display of emotion. You're smart, Chris, but it's like your mind deadens your ability to feel anything."

She slowly made her way over to the mantlepiece again. She looked at her night-blooming Cereus plant. Suddenly, it reminded her of the relationship.

"Chris, this is a night-blooming cereus plant. It flowers once a year if it has the right conditions. Once a year, it blooms. Maybe that's where we are right now."

"This is all news to me. Since when did I get this terrible tragic flaw?"

"I've been thinking about this for a long time. I think you think emotions are a weakness, an Achilles heal of some kind. You don't lose anything by expressing yourself, Chris. This is not a sports contest for survival where the wimpy guy loses the ball game."

"I'm not playing a game with you. You're wrong. I know I've had feelings...and I've shared them with you."

"When Chris? When did you share these feelings?"

"We make love, don't we? It's not just sex, you know that. I tell you I love you and we make love. That's not expressing myself?"

"Yes, you're right. I know you are expressing yourself and that's one of the reasons I fell in love with you. You do have an emotional side, but it seems to only happen when we're in bed together."

"So, I'm emotional cripple because I'm emotional in the bedroom, and you're Miss Perfect because you talk about them on the phone with
your girlfriends."

"Sex is fine, Chris, but the rest of the time you walk around like a zombie. You want me to love someone who only feels comfortable expressing his feelings while having sex?"

"That's not the only time."

"Yes, it is. You just don't realize it."

""I've got to go. We're rehearsing."

"Fine. See ya."

"We can talk some more, okay?"

"Sure. We can talk until the cows come home."

It was early Thursday evening. Billy and Dutch were sitting in their favorite booth, drinking beers. Chris was at Sarah's apartment and Todd was watching MTV at Leslie's place. There were a few regulars shooting pool, and the Irish soul sounds of *U-2* could be heard faintly from the speakers. It was a relatively quiet hour at Jake's.

"...and so this guy, an American named Fred, takes this pig into a Mexican bar down in Tijuana...a real dive with nasty looking banditos in it...and you know, like man, the pig is his best friend."

"The pig is drinking?" asked Billy.

"Oh, yeah, pigs drink," said Dutch.

"Get out of here,"

"Hey," said Dutch, "They can get drunk, just like us. This was the guy's best drinking buddy."

"...And this is a true story?"

"Would I lie?"

"Yes. You better not be setting me up for one of your stupid jokes."

"No way. It happened to Burt Louderman. He just got back from backpacking in South America."

"Alright, go on."

"So, the pig's getting drunk and drunker, and so's his owner, Fred. Then Fred decides to meet one of his buddies at the train station, and leaves his pig tied up to the bar, and tells the bartender he'll be back in an hour. Well, the train is late and Fred doesn't get back for three hours. He walks into the bar and there's no pig. In fact, the whole place is empty, except for this one drunk in the corner. He goes up to the drunk and asks where everybody is. 'Out back, out back,' he screams. So Fred goes out back and he runs into this Mexican dude who says, 'Do you want some pig?' And Fred says, 'No, I don't want *some* pig. I want my pig.' Then Fred goes over to the barbecue pit and sees his pet pig roasting over a fire, burnt to a crisp. They took his best friend and made a pig roast out of him."

"Do you expect me to believe that story? That guy was bullshitting you."

"No, he wasn't. And I'm going to write a song about the whole incident. Do you know what I'm going to call it?"

"No."

"…TO-KILL-A-PIG!!!"

"You asshole. You got me again."

"Oooooh, Pretty good, huh?"

"You're a regular Eddie Murphy. Congratulations."

Billy and Dutch took a sip of their beers. They both looked around, but nothing seemed to be going on.

"What's up with Todd?" asked Dutch.

"What do you mean?"

"I mean, he's acting kinda strange. He called up Chris and told him the Antichrist was on MTV. Don't you think that's a little weird?"

"Todd's been dipping into the angel dust, plus who knows what? He'll be okay."

"I hope so…" said Dutch, "I'd hate to think he was wigging out."

"Todd's lucky. He's got it made, but he keeps fuckin' up."

"No shit," said Dutch. "Leslie is gorgeous—and he doesn't have to work."

"I wish I had some righteous babe supporting me," said Billy. "I'd be in heaven."

"Instead, you're in Jake's with me."

"In other words, welcome to hell."

"Hell ain't so bad. At least we got *U-2* and some pool tables."

"Alright, let's shoot."

Dutch and Billy went over to the pool tables to check out the action. The regulars who were all good shots occupied most of the tables. Everyone at Jake's played eight ball. There was one table where two college guys were shooting. They looked virtually identical in their tan Docker pants and American Eagle plaid shirts.

"Let's challenge those dorks," said Dutch.

Billy walked over to them. "Wanna play partners?"

"Sure," said one of them. "After this game."

Billy and Dutch went back to their booth and waited for them to finish their game. After 10 minutes, the college guys motioned for them to come over and rack the balls. Billy grabbed the rack and set up the balls for the match. A young woman in her early twenties was sitting at one of the nearby tables, impassively watching the action. She was a petite, round-faced young woman with lively, bright blue eyes, and a clear, rosy complexion, wearing a blue floppy hat under her short-cropped light brown hair. She was simply dressed in blue jeans and a black T-shirt. She also was wearing a button on her T-shirt bearing the picture of a cocker spaniel.

One of the college guys came over to Dutch and shook his hand.

"Hi, I'm James."

"Hey, what's up? I'm Dutch. This is Billy."

Billy shook James's hand and the other college guy came over.

"I'm Arthur."

They all shook hands and James broke the balls, sinking a low ball. James ran two more balls, then Billy sank two high balls.

Billy came over to the table where the young girl was sitting.

"Okay, if I sit my beer here."

"Sure," said the girl.

Billy left his beer and proceeded back to the pool table to take his shot. He lined up and barely missed a difficult combination. The college guys were up three balls to two. When Billy came back to get his beer he noticed the girl with the button pinned on her chest.

"Okay, I give up. Why do you have a picture of a cocker spaniel on your shirt?"

"I'm a vegan—a vegetarian and an animal rights advocate."

"Are cocker spaniels endangered or something?"

The girl laughed. "No, I just love them. They're my favorite dogs."

Arthur, who had been eavesdropping on their conversation, seized an opening.

"I got the best dog."

"What kind do you have?" asked the girl.

"Pit bull. Mean as a sonofabitch."

"You have a mean dog?" asked the girl.

"You bet your ass," said Arthur. "Attack anybody who comes near him. Got loose one day and almost killed my sister. If I say, 'sic 'em,' he'll go for your throat."

"I wouldn't want to have a dog like that," said the girl.

"He's a great dog. He's the best dog a man can have. He's loyal, brave, and will do anything to protect me."

Dutch had been shooting and listening in on the conversation. He missed a shot and came over to the table and sat his beer down next to the girl.

"Hello."

"My name's Ginger, what's yours?"

"Dutch. Nice to meet you."

Billy left the table to take his shot, and Dutch stood next to Arthur waiting to shoot. The college guys were down to the eight ball and Billy and Dutch had two high balls to sink.

"So, you got a killer dog?" asked Dutch.

"Yup."

"I'm just curious," said Dutch. "Why would you want to have a dog like that?"

"Are you kidding? To protect me from the rednecks."

Dutch turned toward Arthur, sticking the pool cue in his face.

"You don't have a dog. You have a robot! That dog doesn't even have a mind! All that dog can do is what you programmed him to do. He can't even think without you giving commands like a storm trooper."

Arthur pushed Dutch savagely away and grabbed his pool stick.

"YOU ASSHOLE!!! YOU DON'T KNOW A FUCKIN' THING ABOUT DOGS!!!"

Dutch rushed up into Arthur's face.

"That's right. I don't know anything about dogs. I have two mutts who eat me out of house and home, chew up my carpet, bite my furniture, and dry hump everybody who comes into the house. But we live together because we like each other…and they come and go as they please! Nobody has to worry about being killed either."

Arthur's face boiled red with rage. He swung his pool stick at Dutch's head. Dutch reacted quickly, ducking to his left, as the stick whizzed violently over his head. Dutch came up swinging, hitting Arthur on the left shoulder, sending him reeling into the table, just missing the girl. The girl scrambled away from the table, as Dutch reared back, slamming Arthur again, right across the stomach. He fell awkwardly over the table, sending beers and ashtrays flying. Billy and James came charging over and they both grabbed Dutch.

"Hey! That's enough!" yelled James.

"Cool it!" screamed Billy.

Meanwhile, Jake came running over from behind the bar, motioning to Arthur and James.

"OKAY!!! OKAY!!! THAT'S IT!!! YOU GUYS, GET THE HELL OUT OF HERE!!!"

Arthur slowly got up from the floor, wiping spilled beer from his pants.

""What about those guys?" asked Arthur. "They started it."

"This is my place—and I decide who comes and goes—and you guys are going."

Jake led the two guys out the door. Dutch and Billy set the table back up, and Ginger emerged from the corner where she was hiding.

"Gosh, I'm sorry about that," she said.

"Hey, it's not your fault. They were the assholes," said Billy.

"Do you believe that guy?" asked Dutch. "He's got himself a killer dog and he's calling someone else a redneck! Unbelievable!"

Billy, Dutch, and the girl went back to the boy's favorite booth.

"I'm really sorry," said Ginger. "I feel like it's my fault."

"Heyyyyy…, don't worry," said Dutch. "You didn't start anything. How about a beer?"

"No, thanks. I don't drink."

"You don't drink?" asked Dutch.

"No, it's not good for you."

"Do you know this is as good as you're going to feel all day?"

"I feel fine."

"Okay, how about a Coke?"

"Great."

Dutch went over to the bar, obtained two beers and one Coke and returned to the booth. Billy was asking the Ginger about being a vegan.

"…So what can you eat?"

"Oh, anything that doesn't come from an animal. I don't eat meat, cheese, milk…lots of stuff…honey."

"Honey?" asked Billy.

"Bees."

"What about bees?" asked Billy.

"Bees are an animal."

"Huh? Bees are an animal?"

"They're alive."

"I thought bees were an insect," said Dutch.

"It doesn't matter," said Ginger. "We don't eat anything that comes from something that's alive. It causes too much pain for the animal."

Billy took a sip of his beer and looked at the girl. "You know plants cry when you kill them too. You just don't hear them."

"I think plants are different from animals. Animals have a face. I just couldn't eat something that has a face."

Todd and Leslie came into the bar, followed closely by Chris. They all joined them at the table. After introductions, Todd announced that a newcomer was going to play the barfly routine and take the test. Fifteen minutes later, a college kid with a crew cut, dressed in a button-down, blue oxford shirt, a pair of khakis and cordovan loafers came up to the booth.

"Hey, my name is Crawford. I'm ready."

Todd went over and grabbed a chair and placed it in front of the booth. He offered the chair to Crawford. Several locals began drifting toward the booth.

"Now tell me," Todd asked in an authoritarian manner, "What is the only thing that lasts?"

Crawford gazed at the ceiling. He pulled on his earlobe and shrugged his shoulders. A bead of sweat formed on his forehead. He pronounced the answer in a stuttering, halting voice that cracked and quivered with indecision…

"D…D…Desire…?"

No one said anything for a second, then Todd broke the news.

"Sorry, wrong answer. Get 'em next time."

Crawford shrugged his shoulders again and laughed. "Oh, well. Guess I'll have to do more homework. See ya."

Crawford went to the bar, and the locals left for more action on the pool table.

"Gee, I thought that was a pretty good answer," said Ginger.

"You do?" asked Billy.

"Sure, desire never goes away."

"Desire for what?" asked Billy.

"Oh, I guess the desire for love," said Ginger.

"I think you're right," said Leslie. "Desire never does go away."

"Well, that may be the case," said Todd, "but it's definitely the wrong answer."

"Okay," said Ginger, "What's the correct answer?"

"You really want to know?" asked Dutch.

"Sure."

Dutch peered directly into her eyes. "Are you ready?"

"Yes."

Dutch paused for dramatic affect.

"Hatred."

Ginger gave Dutch a quizzical look. Todd and Leslie left the table to go back to her apartment, followed closely by Chris who wandered over to the pool tables and challenged the next game. Dutch and Ginger were left alone at the table.

"Isn't that a pessimistic answer?" asked Ginger.

"It's a pessimistic movie," said Dutch.

The two young people sat in silence for a moment. Dutch was waiting for the girl to make up an excuse to leave. Instead, she surprised him by clasping her hands together, leaning over the table, and staring directly into his eyes.

"So, what do you do, Mr. Dutch?" She asked, lowering her voice in hushed, intimate tone.

The unexpected rush of sexuality emanating from the girl took Dutch back. It seemed to him that she suddenly changed from an innocent lost waif into a vibrant sexual animal. He was not used to girls flirting with him.

"You mean besides drink?" asked Dutch.

"Yeah, I guess," she said, flashing a wide smile while taking a sip of her Coke. "It's hard to just drink all the time, right?"

"Not for me."

"Do you have a job, or anything normal like that?"

Dutch gazed into his beer, absentmindedly swirling the mug, making beer waves. "I work here—bartending, cleaning up, bouncing, stuff like that. I have a room in the back. It's not much, but it's all I need. I'm also a guitar player in a band, but we're not very active right now. What about you? What do you do besides stay away from meat?"

"I go to school—UVA."

Dutch was aware that she was continually making eye contact. He felt mildly uncomfortable, but flattered at the same time. "You don't look like you're from UVA."

"You mean I don't look like a sorority girl?" asked Ginger, taking off her hat and shaking her curly hair loose, flipping her bangs back over her forehead.

"Yeah, I guess so."

Ginger took another sip, slowly stirring her drink with the straw. "I'm not from Virginia. I grew up in California. My parents were typical hippies. We lived on a farm upstate and I was raised on Tim Leary, Zen Buddhism and marijuana. They didn't even send me to a regular school. I was taught at home."

"What? How to smoke dope?"

"Yes, among other things."

"Kerouac was into Zen."

"Jack Kerouac? The beat writer?"

"Yeah, he volunteered to be a lookout in a fire tower for three months. All he did was pray and meditate all day."

"I thought he drank himself to death."

"He did—but that's kind of Zen-like, right?"

"Not the kind of Zen that I studied. But I guess if that's your choice…"

"Are you into poetry?"

"Yes, I love poetry."

"I write poetry all the time."

"What kind?" she asked.

"I don't know—the drunken kind, I guess. Just a minute…"

Dutch fumbled in his pants and shirt pockets, pulling out a ring of keys, a bottle opener, and some coins, as scraps of paper, like large balls of confetti, jettisoned out of his pockets from all directions. "I think I've got one here."

"What are those pieces of paper?" she asked.

"Well, they're all poems. I just don't have them organized."

"I'll say…"

"Wait! Here's one! I wrote this last night while listening to Tom Waits."

Dutch handed Ginger a wrinkled Kroger's supermarket receipt with a hand-written poem scrawled on the back. She read the poem out loud to Dutch:

> The lost butterflies, the flowerless grass
> Stirred by the whirlwinds of furious fire
> The velvet whiteness of a women's body
> ……………devoured long ago
> Where the sleep of the dead
> ……………intoxicate an acrid love
> As she lies vestal waiting,
> trembling in the empty ancient tombs…

"You've got a nice voice. You read very well," said Dutch.

"I like your poem. You've got others?"

"They're all over the place. My pockets are full of them—so is my room. Speaking of my room, would you like to go there and listen to some music? I've got more poems if you want to see them."

"Okay."

Dutch went up to the bar, paid the tab, and then returned to the table. He could not believe this was really happening. Dutch was notoriously shy around women and did not possess the self-assured confidence of many guys his own age. He had not been out on a date with a woman for three years and had lately given up on the idea of ever finding a girlfriend. But Ginger seemed to genuinely like him and his spirits were buoyed by her interest in him and his poetry. It was way too early to tell, but perhaps this girl was right for him. Even though he was feeling anxious, Ginger seemed to have a more calming affect on him than most girls he met.

Dutch lead her through a narrow hallway, passing the restrooms, a utility closet, and a stock room, before entering his room in the rear of Jake's. Ginger thought that Dutch was underestimating his lodgings by only calling it a room, but she quickly realized he was not being modest. As she entered, Dutch switched on the light of a small, brown-paneled room dominated by a dusty, black couch and wooden coffee table. To the right, she spotted a solitary window revealing a view of red bricks in a back alley. A portable space heater was positioned beside the coffee table. Several pictures from magazines were duct taped to the plain unadorned walls. She saw torn and faded black and white photos of James Dean, Jimi Hendrix, Allen Ginsberg, Lenny Bruce, and Walt Whitman. In the rear of the room near the bathroom door an electric guitar rested against a worn out 50 watt Marshall amp. She also spotted a Pioneer receiver and an ancient turntable with Advent speakers on a couple of orange crates below the window. Beside the stereo several old record albums leaned against the orange crates.

"Would you like to hear some music?" asked Dutch.

"Sure," said Ginger, sliding on the couch.

"What kind do you like?"

"Oh, anything. Blues, rock, country…You still have a turntable?"

"Yeah, I've had it for years. I just can't seem to enter the CD age. I thought vegan people listened to real loud punk music that nobody else buys."

"They do—most of them. But I'm not typical. I don't like to follow trends. I like albums. They have a much more intimate sound. CD's sound too cold and technical."

"They also cost fifteen dollars apiece." Dutch went over to the stereo unit and turned on the receiver and turntable. He lifted an album out of its cover and placed it on the turntable. Momentarily, the sound of Nick Drake came wafting out from the stereo:

Saw it written and I saw it say
Pink moon is on its way
None of you will stand so tall
Pink moon gonna get you all

"Who's that? It sounds real nice. Folk singer?"

"Yes, Nick Drake. I think he's from England and I think he died young. That's about all I know about him. He can write too."

"Pink moon?" she asked. "Is that a pill to get you high?"

"I never thought of it that way, but I guess you're right. Pink pill shaped like the moon. Makes sense."

Ginger glanced at the stereo and noticed an old black and white photo on the wall above the record player. She peered closer and recognized a man and woman on a motorcycle stalled on a muddy road beside a forest.

"Who is in that picture?" she asked. "Are they related to you?"

"That's my grandfather driving. One of his daughters is on the back."

"When was it taken?" she asked.

"Around 1920. The bike is a two cylinder 616 cc Wanderer."

"I don't know anything about motorcycles," she said.

"I didn't mean to be so technical. Basically, it was a very fast bike for the times. It reached a top speed of 90 miles an hour."

"He looks pretty rugged. Is he still alive?"

"No. He died rather young. The saying in our family is that he died from motorcycling."

"How's that?"

"He died of a kidney ailment. Everyone says that it was caused by bad springs on the bikes
and the condition of the roads. Luckily, the motorcycle virus never touched me or my father."

"The motorcycle virus?"

"Death by motorcycle. We call it the virus."

Ginger paused for a second, then her eyes drifted over to the guitar in the corner.

"Do you practice your guitar very often?"

"I used to, but not lately. That amp over there is broken and our band hasn't been practicing lately. We're pretty good, really, but we're in a rut right now."

"Do you write songs?"

"No, it's strange, but my mind only works with poetry. I can't seem to put the words in my head into music. My buddy Chris writes the songs for our group."

"What's your band's name?"

"*Mean Streets.*"

"How did you come up with that one?"

"It's the name of an old movie with Robert DeNiro. I think it's his first one. Say, how about a beer? I've got some Milwaukee's Best."

"No, thanks. I don't drink, remember?"

"Sorry. Let me see what else I have." Dutch went to the refrigerator, opened the door and looked at the contents. He saw a six-pack of Milwaukee's Best, a pack of hot dogs, a bottle of ketchup, and a day-old container of sweet and sour pork.

"Sorry, I don't really have anything to drink besides beer. I just have water…"

"That's fine. I like water."

"I never thought I would meet anyone who liked water better than beer." He ambled over to the sink, poured Ginger a glass of water, then returned to the couch and handed it to her.

"Thanks," she said.

Dutch sat down next to Ginger. There had not been a girl in his room for a long time and he was feeling a bit nervous, and apprehensive.

"I don't have any munchies, or anything. Maybe we could order a pizza."

"I don't eat pizza, remember?"

"Oh, right. It's the cheese, I guess."

"Right."

"Don't you think you're missing out on some good things in life, like beer and pizza?"

"No, I'm really happy not drinking and eating healthy foods."

"What can you eat?"

"Vegetables…fruits…nuts…"

"Gosh, you're gonna live to be a hundred."

"I have my weaknesses."

"Oh, like what?"

"I'm into unusual people. Sometimes, I really get burned because I fall for guys who are somewhat crazy. I have a weakness for people with weaknesses."

"Well, you certainly came to the right place. Nobody ever called me a fortress of strength, as far as I know."

Dutch paused a second, then walked over to the record player. He reached behind an orange crate and produced a bag of marijuana and some rolling papers. He came back and sat down on the couch.

"Do you have a weakness for marijuana too?" he asked.

"As a matter of fact, I do," she said.

Dutch rolled a joint, lit it, and took a deep drag, holding the marijuana in his lungs for a few seconds before sending a lazy blue plume of smoke toward the ceiling. He handed the joint to her. She puffed on the joint, held her breath, and then released a billowing lungful of smoke. They both eased back onto the couch, as Ginger handed the joint back to Dutch. Within a few minutes the joint was finished and the room was consumed with silence. Ginger glanced at the vast array of slips of paper scattered willy-nilly on the couch and littering the bare cement floor.

"Let me see some of your poems."

"Sure."

Billy rifled through a stack of loose strips of paper on the coffee table, then bent over and searched through more scraps of paper the floor. Unsatisfied, he went into the bathroom and looked beside the toilet. He returned to the coffee table and looked again. After rummaging through more slips of paper, he finally settled on one poem, scratched in pencil on the back of an opened envelop from a loan company.

"Here's one I like. I wrote this last week on a gigantic hangover." Dutch handed the poem to Ginger. She read the poem slowly in her mind, taking care to try and capture the rhythm and meaning of the poem.

Blood of Exile

She stuck out her tongue with an obsessive love
Forgetting that her fabled flesh was soaking, rotting
In the preternatural dawn, as her astral tears
..............fell from blue eyes
Gazing at her now, full of horrible appetites
The rays of moonlight struck her like a sword
A child under a red rustling tree with tender roots
..............filters the black poison

My lips moved and I made a sign of the cross
A diamond of affection glittered from her breast
And I saw that the dead have bad dreams too
...............fighting the burgundy tyrants

"It's very beautiful Dutch," said Ginger. "It's black beauty, but beauty none-theless."

"I wrote it while thinking about an old girl friend."

"It's really quite touching. I love the line, 'as her astral tears fell from blue eyes.'"

"Thanks. Too bad it's not worth much on the open market."

"Did you ever try and publish your poems?"

"No, I wouldn't know where to start."

"Well, you should try. I think you have real talent."

"Keep talking. If you don't watch it, I'm going to make you president of my fan club."

Ginger placed the poem on the coffee table, inching a bit closer to him. She was relaxed and confident while Dutch's body stiffened as he felt her knee touch his. Dutch liked the stoned-out, hazy feeling of marijuana in his head, but it often made him slightly paranoid. He was seldom at ease with women, even when he was straight. She took a sip of her water and looked again into his eyes. He felt it was the right time to make his move, to reach over and hold her hand, or give her a kiss. He sensed she would not resist. But his whole body seemed to betray him. He could sense his muscles constricting, his armpits sweating, and his mouth go dry.

She was aware of his anxiety, but she was not sure what to do. She felt attracted to him, sensed a painful self-consciousness on his part. They listened in silence to the record playing near the window.

And I was green, greener than the hill
Where flowers grew and the sun shone still
Now I'm darker than the deepest sea
Just hand me down, give me a place to be

Dutch rubbed his pants legs with both hands, attempting to dry his sweaty palms. The moment reminded him of walking across the cafeteria in sixth grade, painfully aware that his classmates were watching him, overwhelmed by self-doubt and insecurity. He turned and faced her, staring into her luminous, oval blue eyes. He thought she was the most adorable thing he had ever seen in his life. Tiny strands of blonde hair cascaded over her forehead, seductively hiding portions of her left eye. Her lips were luscious red, full and moist and her flawless complexion was highlighted by a tiny row of freckles dotting her nose. He felt himself melting into her, wanting to consume every part of her taut, well-proportioned body.

"He has a gentle voice, doesn't he?" she asked.

"Yes," he said. "It's a quiet sound—like you would hear in a coffeehouse somewhere."

She edged slightly closer to him, placing her hand on his thigh. He instantly tightened up, then caught himself and relaxed. He reached over and placed his arm around her, moving slowly toward her. He turned and looked at her again, then placed a gentle kiss on her lips. She closed her eyes and kissed him back. He leaned toward her until the weight of his body on hers created one slow, long descent into a prone position on the couch. He was on top of her now, but he was careful not to crush her. He put a pillow over her head and kissed her again on the lips, then followed the soft line of her cheek and slope of her neck. She wrapped her arms around him and pulled him closer to her.

"Wait, one second," he said.

Dutch slipped off the couch and went over to switch off the bare 60-watt light bulb that was lighting the room with a painful intensity. As the light went out, Dutch could barely see, but in a few seconds his eyes adjusted and he could see her outline on the couch, as a ray of light filtered from a lamppost near the window. He came back to her and whispered in her ear.

"You're the most beautiful girl I've ever seen."

"You must be a beautiful liar."

"I'm not kidding. You look like a goddess to me."

"I'm no goddess, believe me."

He slowly removed her jeans and T-shirt, then removed his clothes. They lay together for a while, caressing each other, murmuring gentle words in the dark. He made love to her like never before. Exhausted, they both fell asleep, as the yellow light from the lamppost cast a glistening shadow over their drained bodies.

A Devilish, Stoned-Out Look

Leslie Kramer was doing her best to get *Mean Streets* a working gig. During her break at the restaurant, she called her uncle and asked him if he would come and listen to the band. She hoped he would sign them to a record contract if he thought they were any good. Her uncle told her that his record company normally requires that groups send a demo for review, but as a favor he said he would send one of his employees to Charlottesville. He asked Leslie to make all the arrangements. Leslie also called the manager of Trax to see if he would consider letting the band warm up for *Megadeth*. The manager said he was still undecided. He asked what kind of music they played and Leslie told him she thought they were a great rock band.

"Do they play top 40?" he asked.

"No," she told him, "They play mostly their own material."

Leslie thought the manager was not very enthusiastic, but he did say he would think about it. Leslie hoped the band could get a break soon or she feared they would just give up on the whole idea of making it as a rock band. They were doing pretty well a couple years ago playing small local bars, but recently the band had reached a stalemate. She was especially worried about Todd who ceased playing the drums altogether and lately had been smoking way too much dope, popping pills, and drinking every night. At this moment, she was in her bedroom and he was in the living room watching MTV. She heard him laughing to himself. He had never done this before. She went into the living room to see what was going on.

"What was so funny in here?"

Todd gave Leslie a devilish, stoned-out look.

"He just said something funny."

"Who?"

"John."

"John who?"

"John Revelation."

Todd doubled up in a fetal position in his chair, lifting his legs high into the air, laughing and screaming, "John Revelation!!! John Revelation!!! Isn't that the funniest thing you ever heard?"

Leslie knew about the pills and the pot, but as far as she knew, this was the first time Todd acted in this manner. She could tell something was very different about his behavior. Usually, he just stared into space, occasionally making strange comments. He had never been this animated before. She wondered if the combination of drugs was finally getting to him. She also hesitated to ask Todd about John Revelation because the guys were always putting her down for not knowing new groups. But his behavior troubled her, so she decided to try and get some answers.

"I don't remember seeing a John Revelation video. Is he somebody new?"

Todd's mood changed from excitement to relative calm, but he still had a vacant look about him. He sat up, reached for a cigarette, and turned down the volume on the television.

"Leslie…There is no John Revelation on TV. There never will be."

"Well, Todd," said Leslie, "If there is no John Revelation on TV, how could he say something funny?"

"He just did, that's all. Forget it. I must be dreaming about something. You wanna go to Jake's?"

"Sure, if you want to. Are you alright?"

"Yeah, I'm fine." said Todd, lighting a cigarette "This reefer must be strong stuff."

"You should cut out the pot and pills, you know."

"Yeah, I'm sticking with beer for the rest of the night. Do you know who I'm not going to be tomorrow?"

"Who?"

"A minister."

"Why?"

"Because Chris says that anybody who calls himself a man of God and owns two suits and there is someone in the world who doesn't have a suit, then that guy is a hustler."

"I think you better lay off the drugs for awhile."

THE END OF INNOCENCE

Chris was lying in bed staring at his John Lennon poster, trying to come up with new ideas for a song. He pulled out a copy of *Premature Coffin* that he thought was pretty good. Billy loved the song and helped with the arrangement. He remembered one night in the old Mineschaft café they put a coffin on stage and Billy crawled out of it and sang the song in a black tuxedo and cape resembling Dracula. The crowd went nuts. They also dropped plastic bats from the ceiling and for a moment some members of the audience thought they were real. It was Billy's idea and Chris thought he was terribly creative until he found out that Screaming Jay Hawkins did the same bit thirty years ago with *I Put a Spell On You*. When Chris asked Billy about stealing someone else's act, he replied, "Who's Screaming Jay Hawkins?"

Chris knew he should be studying for his Western Lit class, but he was not into it tonight. He glanced at the evening's efforts and concluded that Mr. Lennon did not have anything to worry about:

Dark Side of the Blind

When the waves crashed
I held you tight with my eyes closed
On a beach at night; when the sea swells
—and the wind blows

You said we'd last forever
And never know a broken heart
You tossed a shell into the deep
And said we'd never part

Somewhere in the twilight and the dawn
We walked along
Throwing stones into the sea
The fog rolled in, we fought the wind
And you huddled close to me.

Babe, with me you were so compellin'
And I almost lost my mind
Now I know you're willin'
To take a midnight stroll
On the dark side of the blind.

Chris concluded that Billy would hate it, but at the moment he could not find the inspiration to write morbid, grotesque songs like *Bodyburnt, Eyes of a Shark* and *Butt-Ream*. He decided to quit writing and thinking about studying and headed down to Jake's for a couple beers. He took the copy of *Dark Side of the Blind* to show to Billy.

He saw Billy at the usual booth sitting by himself. He was holding a video camera.

"Hey, man, what's up?" asked Chris, sliding into the booth.

"Just call me Hitchcock," said Billy, wielding the camera around to face Chris. "Okay, where were you on the night in question—and don't pretend you weren't there!"

"Get that thing out of my face!"

"Okay, but someday MTV will want early videos of the best band in the USA and you won't be in it."

"I think I can handle that. What's with the camera?"

"Just foolin' around, having a little fun. Maybe I'll make a movie."

"Hey, here's my latest," said Chris.

Billy dropped the camera and began reading Chris's song.

"I don't get it."

"Get what?"

"Dark side of the blind? Is that some kind of metaphor?"

"Christ, Billy, you're hopeless."

"Sounds like a sappy love song—and *Mean Streets* doesn't do crap like that."

"So, my songs are crap. Is that it?"

"No, I didn't say they were all crap. I can't sing a song about taking a moon-light stroll along the ocean. It's too...I don't know...romantic."

"It could fit your range. Why don't you work up an acoustic arrangement? You've sung songs like this before. Put some soul into it. Come on...."

"Soul has to have a hard edge to it. You need tension, or something."

"Like what?"

"Okay, they're walking along the ocean, right?"

"Yeah."

"Well, what are they doing out there? Do they just want to be alone, or is there some other reason?"

"Like?"

"Like maybe they're young and they can't share their feelings in the open, you know...around each other's parents. So, they need a place to get away...to escape. Maybe she wants to escape from him for a while. Do they really think love lasts forever? You can contrast the passion in their lives with some tension. Otherwise, it's too mushy."

"Maybe I'll give it to Marie Osmond."

"Hey! I didn't say it was *that* bad!"

"Thanks."

"By the way, word man, how can you get darker than blind?"

"It's the blues, man. Maybe your lover's leaving in the morning—hard times, blues in the night, funky Broadway...you know...dark...like just before the end of time...all hope is lost...and souls suffer beyond life's torments..."

"Sorry I asked. "Anyway, work on it. I think you've got something there."

"What about my political stuff?"

"You really want to know?"

"Sure."

"Leave the politics to Dylan and Tracy Chapman."

"What's your favorite song?"

"Right now?"

"Yeah."

"I don't know...I guess *Guns and Roses*—the one about paradise."

"Well, my favorite song is *The End of Innocence*. Know why?"

"Why?"

"Because it's about something bigger than the both of us. It's about society, politics—about our generation—important things—not motorcycles, or girls for that matter."

"You saying girls aren't important?"

"Sure they are. But there's other stuff to write about."

"I have no idea what end of innocence means."

"Did you ever listen to the words?"

"No."

"Well, why don't you? There's a line in there about being poisoned by these fairy tales and lawyers dwelling on small details."

"So?"

"So, he's talking about *us* Billy. We've been sold a bill of goods—all this America-the

Beautiful-land-of-opportunity—it's just a bunch of fairy tales—and then they bring in the lawyers to finish off the little guy with all kinds of bureaucratic bullshit."

"Look, I just want to sing rock 'n roll songs. I don't want to change the world. I know it's fucked up, but we're not going to change the world by singing into someone's ear."

"We can try. John Lennon did a hell of a job."

"Yeah, and what did it get him? A bullet in the chest."

"Do you have to be so negative?"

"Okay, I'm sorry I insulted your patron saint of rock 'n roll."

"You don't think rock 'n roll is important as I do."

"That's bullshit and you know it. I dig this stuff as much as you do, but I don't blow it out of proportion. When I'm singing a rock song, I want to change the mood of the people, not the world. If they come into the club depressed I want to make them happy. I want them to feel good."

"I think you can do both. Dylan showed you could change things."

"That was twenty-five years ago. Have you taken a look at people our age? You think they're gonna go marching for anything besides their right to watch TV? They're selfish—just like us."

"Alright, I give up. I can't fight cynicism. I'll work on *Dark Side of the Blind.* Maybe we can try it out at our next rehearsal."

"Which is?"

"Wednesday night—the garage."

"I'll tell Dutch and Todd," said Billy.

"Hey, does Dutch have a new girl friend? I've seen him a couple times with a little girl with blonde hair."

"Yeah, I think he's in love. She's one of those vegans—never eats meat or anything that comes from an animal. She's a real space cadet."

"She might be good for Dutch," said Chris. "He hasn't had a girl friend in a long time."

"Hey! How about me? My next date will be the first one since high school!"

"You mean junior high school, don't you?"

"Very funny. By the way, do you think Todd's alright?" asked Billy.

"What do you mean?"

"I don't know…he's starting to make less sense than you or me."

"Wow, that could be serious."

"I mean, the other day, I suggested that he stick to just beer and pot, you know."

"Yeah?"

"Well, he said something like, 'Obviously, we are talking about the relative value of sensory data. It's simple. I'm trying to dissolve myself in a culmination of reality. Perception is, of course, oblique.'"

"He said that?"

"Something like that."

"You're right. He's making less sense than either of us."

WHAT HORRIBLE LIVES
THEY MUST LEAD

"TO ALL MY FRRR…IENDS!!!! TO ALL MY FRRR…IENDS!!!"

The whole crowd at Jake's suddenly erupted and everyone seemed to be yelling at once. Chris and Todd heard someone scream at the other end of the bar.

"THE GUTS NEED FUEL!!! THE GUTS NEED FUEL!!!"

"Heyyy…no problem," Chris moaned, "You symbolize everything that disgusts meee…obviousness…unoriginal macho energy…ladies man!!!"

"TO HATRED!!!" Todd yelled in response, raising his glass high above his head.

The crowd quickly responded in unison:

"THE ONLY THING THAT LASTS!!!"

Dutch and Ginger were seated at the bar next to Jake. Dutch ordered his usual scotch and water and Ginger asked for a Coke.

"Jake," said Dutch, "Anybody can be a non-drunk. It takes a special talent to be a true drunk."

"Is that from the movie?" Jake asked.

"Jaaake…" Dutch drawled, "…Everything is from the movie."

Ginger sipped her coke in silence and thought about her growing relationship with Dutch. They had been together constantly for two weeks and Dutch had been staying at her apartment near campus. On the surface, she admitted that they were an odd couple. Her friends thought she was being just plain foolish, but it did not bother her. She liked men who were different and traveled to the beat of a different drummer. She liked Dutch's poetic sensibility although she had a feeling he paid for it with a delicate and painful insecurity. Ginger discovered that before she came into the picture, Dutch's life consisted of hanging out at the bar, staying in his room writing poetry, and riding his motorcycle. He told her he was practically agoraphobic, preferring the company of a few close friends and absolute solitude. His choice of vehicle guaranteed him more time alone, and he was prone to taking long excursions high up into the back roads of the Blue Ridge Mountains. Like the rest of the band, he also possessed a fierce, instinctive individuality, and refused to compromise his dedication to being an artist. His poems were loaded with images of sudden cataclysmic collapse, a deep sense of personal loss, a feeling that the cohesion of things had disappeared. One of his favorite sayings was, "The center does not hold." Curiously, she felt he had a yearning for something more spiritual in his life; he was neither ambitious nor materialistic, referring to social practicality as not virtuous enough for his consideration. His poems almost always reflected a world without value, an unbearable abyss to be avoided. Not many things satisfied his interests except extremes, like excessive drinking, fighting, marijuana smoking, and riding his motorcycle. He often said: "Anything worth doing is worth overdoing." At the same time, she felt Dutch had a longing to do or feel something meaningful in a world that was becoming far too mundane and trivial. He seemed like a hippie throwback. His poems were filled with references to people feeling tenderness, joy, humility, ecstasy, and spiritual enlightenment while enduring a world of vacant conformity. There was no doubt in her mind that Dutch thought that where he was right now was the worst of all possible worlds. She looked at him now, hunched over the bar, writing on a piece of scrap paper. His eyebrows furrowed from concentration as he stared into the paper searching for inspiration from his muse.

"How's it going?" she asked.

"It's…I don't know…done I guess."

"Can I see it?"

"Sure, but don't ask me what it means."

Dutch handed her the poem and she read it to herself.

Thief of Death/Requiem

You can't say he wasn't strange
Flinging his arms out, to keep a soul intact
Impossible to know, but what the hell
Blood does bring curiosity.

As if…angry double breasted suits
scrambling for seating space in the capitol
could hear classical music down the river.
As if…flowing to the inner sanction, or in the lotus position
would buy you time in the Gates of Eden.
You, of all people, see the Diamond Sutra
as unholy broken voices hunger over burning tenements.

"It reads really well, but I have no idea what it means," said Ginger.

"That makes two of us," said Dutch. "Hey, let's go for a ride on the bike. Let's cruise up to the parkway—check out the view from the top."

"Sounds good to me."

"HEY JAKE, TAKE A LOOK AT THIS!"

Jake turned around and saw Alicia performing a nasty routine on the dance floor, simulating a sex act. She was dancing alone, whirling and spinning around the tables.

"HEY, ALICIA," Jake shouted, "PUT A LID ON IT, OKAY?"

Alicia, barely standing, looked at Jake cross-eyed, while bracing herself on the edge of a table. She managed to stand upright, then slowly weaved and stumbled up to him.

"Whatsamatta, Jake," she slurred, "Don't you like to see people having a little fun?"

"Alicia, you're disturbing the customers. Knock it off."

"Customers?" she asked loudly, "You mean these barfly fuckin' losers?"

"That's enough," Jake said patiently, "You've had enough to drink. I'll call you a cab."

Alicia slumped on the bar stool, too drunk to argue with Jake, or the arrival of a cab.

"Crazy women," said Jake to one of the customers, shaking his head and motioning to a passed-out Alicia.

"Some people never go crazy, Jake," said the customer. "What horrible lives they must lead."

Meanwhile, two local guys began arguing at the far end of the bar and it looked like another fight was going to take place. Within seconds, the crowd was in full swing, piling out of the bar hollering:

"I'll take Jason for two bucks!"

"Give me three to one!"

"You got it!"

Jake wiped the bar with a rag and wondered where all this was going to end. It seemed to him that all these young kids did was drink and fight and listen to loud rock music. He had no idea what they would do with their time if it were not for these activities. He concluded that maybe that was their problem: too much time on their hands.

ENTROPY

Chris figured he should have seen it coming. Sarah was too formal and business-like when

she called him up and told him she wanted to see him about "something important." He had a feeling this was going to be the kiss of death. She asked him to come to her parents' house. Upon his arrival, she politely opened the door and led him into the den.

"Want a Coke, or something?"

"I'll take a bourbon on the rocks, if you have it."

"Sure."

Returning with his drink, Sarah sat down on the couch next to Chris.

"Chris, I want to talk to you about something."

"Go ahead."

"I have been accepted into the graduate program at the University of Michigan."

"What?"

"I've been accepted to graduate school. I told you I was applying last fall."

Chris took a sip of his drink. His eyes wandered over Sarah's shoulder, resting impassively on a shelf of expensively bound books, lining the walls of the den. "I don't remember that. Are you going?"

"Yes. In September."

"So…"

"I want to know if you think our relationship is worth continuing. I mean…where is it going?"

"Sounds like its going to Michigan."

"Don't be sarcastic, Chris. I can't stay here in Charlottesville. I grew up here. I've been here for twenty-two years. It's just too confining to stay in your home-town the rest of your life. Besides, I've got this chance."

He strained his eyes to catch the titles of one of the books. He wondered what kinds of books really rich people read. He thought he could make out the title, *Fountainhead* on the binding of one of the books near him. He took another sip of his bourbon. "It sounds like you've got everything planned out. What do you need me for?"

Sarah squared her shoulders and turned toward Chris. She looked directly into his eyes. "Why do you have so much trouble discussing the future with me? We've been going out for over three years. I can't wait all my life for you to grow up and accept responsibility."

"That's my parents' favorite word—responsibility."

"Chris, we're not kids anymore. Normal people our age think about marriage, jobs, and kids."

"Well, I guess I'm not normal. Anyway, you're going to Michigan. So, how could we start talking about our future when you'll be a thousand miles away? Besides, I thought I was an emotional cripple, remember?"

"Chris, I was angry with you. I know you have deep feelings for me. I reacted out of frustration."

"Don't apologize. You're right about all that. I'm going to work at being a bit more expressive. I seem to keep a lot inside. I don't think it's good for me."

The sound of lightly falling rain hitting the window of the den caused Sarah and Chris to glance out the window at the same time.

"It's raining," said Sarah.

Chris said nothing. He stared out the window and noticed gray, ominous cumulous clouds rushing across the sky, the countryside darkening behind them.

Sarah continued. "We could still stay in touch and be close. I get all kinds of vacations—and you could come and visit."

"Sure, I'll make lots of trips to Michigan."

"Cut the sarcasm, okay?"

"Look, don't you see that you've already made the decision to break up? If we couldn't get it together when we're in the same town, how do you expect it to work when you're in some other state?"

"We could still stay close."

"Sarah, you must be kidding. Have you ever heard of entropy?"

"Yes."

"Well, then you know what it means. Energy is constantly decreasing. There's no status quo in the universe. Things are always breaking down." Chris inadvertently slammed his drink on the coffee table, causing a loud thud.

Sarah winced at the possible damage to the coffee table. "Is this leading somewhere?"

"A relationship is like that—our relationship is like that. If you don't constantly stay in touch and communicate, it breaks down. In other words, we'll drift apart and you'll find somebody new—probably a nerd who loves John Milton—"

"Goddamn it Chris, I told you to cut out the sarcastic crap. You're getting on my nerves."

Sarah abruptly stood up, folded her arms, and went over to the window. She cast her eyes over the sweeping expanse of the Carter estate. She could see their black and white sheep dog, Cody, romping in the fields below the duck pond, oblivious to the foul weather.

Chris gently lifted the bourbon glass from the coffee table and took a large gulp, finishing off the drink. "I'm sorry, but that's the way I feel."

Sarah turned toward Chris. "So, a commitment is out of the question?"

"Hey! You're the one who's going away. I'm right here, remember? It seems to me like you're the one avoiding the commitment decision, doesn't it?"

"You'll never be ready, will you?"

"I don't know."

"You're a real shit sometimes, you know that?"

"Well, you're the one deserting me. That seems like a crummy thing to do."

"I'm not deserting you."

"Didn't I just tell you about entropy? Out of sight, out of mind."

Sarah paced back and forth between the coffee table and the window. The light rain was increasingly becoming a major storm.

"I guess it's hopeless. I don't know what to do. I think it's selfish of you not to allow me to pursue my career."

"Who said that?"

"The only option you give me is staying in town, working at a job I don't like."

"Do you like English Literature that much?"

"Yes. I want to teach too. I can't do that without a Master's degree."

"Well, how do you plan to go to Michigan and keep our relationship together?"

"I didn't think it would be that hard. If you really loved me…"

Chris stood up and came over to Sarah who was standing rigidly by the window. "I do love you, but let's be realistic. Not many couples survive separation for long periods of time. Personally, I think you could handle it, but not me."

"Why?"

"Do you want the truth?"

"Of course."

"I need attention—no, I mean, I need affection. I need to be with someone on a regular basis."

"What are you saying?"

"I need companionship. I'd be lonely."

"I think I know what you're really saying. You'll want sex and you'll cheat on me. Then it really will be over."

"That's not what I said."

"I think it is."

"Well, maybe you're right…I guess you *are* right. I'm just trying to be realistic."

"Oh, sure. It's unrealistic for you to go through a few lonely nights for the sake of a good relationship."

"I don't think it will be good if you're in Michigan."

"Alright, Chris. You win. I can't believe you're so negative."

"I told you—"

"I know. You're just being realistic…but you're fucking up a good relationship because you're so stubborn and negative."

"Well, I think you're blowing it by going away."

"I told you. I need to go away."

"Okay, Sarah. Time out. Let's make one decision we can agree on."

"What's that?"

"Are we going to keep seeing each other?"

"I don't know…"

"We've got eight months before you leave. Maybe we can work it out by then, okay?"

"Maybe…"

"Well, what do we do now?" asked Chris.

"I don't know…it's raining pretty hard."

"How about a movie?"

"You know we're just avoiding our problems…again."

"I know."

The couple drove in silence to Charlottesville to see *Pretty Woman*. Chris had trouble concentrating all night because he kept thinking about what Sarah had said. He wondered why she did not ask him to come to Michigan with her and if she was telling him all the facts. Chris did not even know what he would have said if she did ask him to come. He felt the only important thing in his life right now, besides her, was *Mean Streets*.

After the movie, Chris took Sarah back to her house. They kissed each other good night and said they would call each other, but they did not say when.

LUNCH

The Ivy Inn was a quaint, rustic, pre-Civil War bed and breakfast located in the historical town of Palmyra, just outside Charlottesville. Sarah pulled in the parking lot next to Leslie's Toyota Corolla. As she entered the restaurant, she spotted Leslie sitting at a table near a large bay window covered with silk curtains.

"Hi Leslie."

"Hi!"

Sarah sat down across from Leslie.

"You look great!" said Sarah. "I love that blouse."

"Thanks," said Leslie. "It was a Christmas gift from my mother."

"She has good taste."

A young, neatly dressed waiter appeared, wearing a ponytail and wire-rimmed glasses. He handed the women two menus.

"Would you like something to drink?" he asked.

"Yes," said Leslie, "I'll have a coke."

"Me too," said Sarah.

The waiter left to get the drinks.

"So, how's it going?" asked Sarah.

"Well…to be honest, not so hot."

"Is it Todd?"

"Yes. He's getting worse."

"In what way?"

"I think he's losing touch with reality. He says things that are totally off the wall."

"Like what?"

"He's always referring to biblical characters, or morbid things that sound like something out of a horror movie."

"Biblical characters?"

"Yes. Like the Antichrist…the Apostle John."

"Is it the drugs?"

"Yes—and no. I mean, I can't be sure. You know he's been doing drugs for years—and he never acted like this. Now, it seems it's not just the drugs. I think he's real sick, you know…mentally."

"Couldn't you get him to go to a doctor, or psychiatrist."

"He says there's nothing wrong with him. He's in denial. I asked Chris if he would find someone at the community college to help him."

"Did he?"

"I haven't heard from him. I hope he can help."

"Chris has a lot of common sense—when he wants to."

"You're right. How are you two getting along?"

"Not so good. We have too many differences…too many…I don't know…ways of looking at the world."

"Nobody looks at the world like those guys."

The waiter arrived with the women's drinks, and he set them down on the table.

"Would you like to order now?" he asked.

"Sure," said Leslie. "I'll have a chef salad with Italian dressing and a BLT on toast with mayonnaise and some French fries."

"Make mine a cheeseburger, well done, with lettuce, tomatoes, and onions, plus French fries too.

"Will that be all?" he asked.

The women nodded and waiter picked up the menus, and left. Sarah took a sip of her coke, looking directly at her friend.

"If Chris would just make up his mind about our relationship, but he's afraid of commitment—to just about everything."

"Including you?"

"Especially me. It's like I'm going to be his ball and chain."

"Maybe they'll never change."

I told Chris that I'm going to the University of Michigan in the fall."

"You are?"

"Yes, I got accepted in the English department."

"What did Chris say?"

"He wasn't pleased. I think he thinks I'm deserting him."

"You would never do that."

"He's more insecure than I ever thought. He doesn't believe in long distance relationships. Are you going to stay with Todd?"

"I don't know. I wish he were the same person as when I met him. He was so sweet."

"Why do you think he's going off the deep end?"

"I don't know for sure, but I think it has something to do with his past—something about his parents."

"Have you met them?"

"Only once. We went to their house for Christmas dinner the first year we were going out. It didn't work out too well."

"Why not?"

"Well, for one thing, they have a lot of money. I know your parents are pretty well off too, but Todd's parents really looked down on me. I think they blamed me for him just wanting to play the drums instead of going to college. He comes from a long line of prominent politicians and lawyers."

"They're snobby?"

"Yes, but, not just snobby…kinda cold and uptight. They gave me the creeps, to be honest with you. They made it clear that they didn't want me to see him again."

"He must be rebelling against his parents and their way of life, just like Chris."

Leslie nodded. "Only Chris doesn't talk to biblical characters."

"Chris has his own problems, although certainly not as severe. I wonder if we're not being a couple of dummies, or…what do they call people like us…enablers…codependents?"

"Maybe just stupid. I'm going to see what happens with Chris getting him some help. If Todd refuses treatment, I'm leaving."

"It's probably for the best, in the long run."

"Our relationship has gone completely down hill. We don't even have sex anymore."

"Why not?"

"Todd has lost interest…at least he has lost interest in me."

"That's hard to believe. Maybe it's the side effects of those drugs."

"Could be. I think he's taking more than just beer and pot. He's been very secretive about his drug use lately. I've seen empty vials of downers and tranquilizers."

"You should get him help as soon as possible."

"What are you going to do about Chris?"

"I don't think there's much hope. I might see him one more time to try and straighten things out."

"Good luck."

"Leslie, I think you're the one who's going to need the luck."

DIE YUPPIE SCUM

Billy Saxon's greatest fear was that he would wind up working in a factory for the rest of his life. With every crummy, dead-end job he held, he stood fast to the notion that he would not be there very long. He would soon be traveling on the road with his band, singing and playing in front of appreciative fans, or recording a great album in a studio. He could not stand the thought of being a local loser—which is what he knew most people thought of him. Most of his thoughts at work were daydreams about rock stardom and escaping the limitations of his small town existence. But his idealistic dreams were becoming harder and harder to maintain, especially on this cold, frosty February day in the Crozet frozen food plant. Billy may have been a daydreamer, but he was still very much in touch with reality, and no amount of faith in the future could erase the harsh reality of factory work and the mind numbing boredom of the everyday routine.

He slid off his forklift and ambled over to the packing area to check the machines. He noticed that one of the packing machines was only loading half the Morton frozen potpies as they glided down the conveyor belt.

"This machine is screwed up," complained a girl at the packing station, wearing a "Die Yuppie Scum" T-shirt.

"Do you know what?" Billy asked her.

"What?"

"It's four o'clock in the morning."

"I know. I'm dead tired."

"Yeah, me too. You know what else?"

"What?"

"Everybody in their right mind is sleeping."

"I know. This job bores me to death."

"It's borgeous, alright."

Billy looked at her more closely and realized that she was an attractive, small-framed brunette with angular features, thin lips, and chestnut brown hair pulled back in a ponytail. Her bright blue eyes dazzled in the glare of the harsh factory lights. For some reason, the girl reminded him of his mother. Perhaps, he reasoned, because his mother was also diminutive, with brown hair and blue eyes.

Billy switched off the machine. He reached into his tool belt and produced a Phillips head screwdriver. He quickly adjusted the angle of the conveyor belt, and then restarted the machine. Soon, the pies were loading to full capacity.

"There you are, good as new."

"Thanks."

Billy walked back into the warehouse and drove a pallet of pies into the rear of the platform, near the loading dock. Sitting on the forklift surrounded by a bunch of truck drivers, he thought about his mother again. He wondered where she was at this moment. The only thing he knew for sure was that she had run off with a computer salesman six years ago. She had left Billy and his brother Sammy to be raised in a series of foster homes. Billy could not help but wonder what terrible sin he committed to have his mother desert him. He thought he was a pretty good kid, at least until he was fifteen. He remembered when he was five years old his mother sat him and his brother down and told them that their father had been killed in Vietnam. It was a powerfully emotional moment and they all cried and hugged each other. Billy's mother told them she loved them very much and she would never leave them. They would be a happy family forever. Well, Billy thought, forever sure isn't as long as it used to be.

"HEY, JERK WEED!!! YOU WITH THE FORKLIFT!!! GET THAT GODDAMN MACHINE OVER HERE!!! YOU'RE ON COMPANY TIME, REMEMBER?!!!"

"Hey!!!" Billy yelled, coming out of his trance, "Chill out. This truck will go out on time."

"Just get it loaded, okay?"

He thought again: Everybody in their right mind is sleeping.

WHEN YOU AIN'T
GOT NUTHIN'

Billy was back in his apartment after the graveyard shift, sitting alone on his battered brown sofa, drinking a beer, and reading an old *Spiderman* comic book. He couldn't help feeling that his life was a total waste of time. He hated the idea of being a loser that no one respected. He felt nauseous all the time and his stomach burned continuously. He was sure he was developing an ulcer. He couldn't remember a good feeling, as if his life was one big, monstrous hangover. He looked down and noticed the skin on his body looked withered and corroded with dirt and cold sores. Yes, he thought, looking over his shabby room, I could easily die here, or maybe I'm already dead.

The room was very dark. He could barely see into the tiny kitchen area where, in the shadows, twisted Domino's pizza boxes piled to the ceiling, forming a small pyramid of red and white abandoned containers. Crushed, empty Budweiser beer cans littered the corner, forming a macabre mountain of aluminum trash. He tried to remember what a home cooked meal tasted like. What a family felt like; the cozy intimacy of having a family member near you. He thought about those early years when his mother cared for him and his brother. He recalled her coming home from work at the drug store, bone-tired with aching feet. "Billy, fetch me my slippers, okay?" she would ask. "Give me a few minutes dears, and I will fix you both a nice hot meal." They would sit together at the dinner table discussing how their day went. Billy would complain about his teachers. Sammy would always get yelled at for not cleaning his plate. His mother would promise that the future would be brighter; that they would have better clothes, a better home to live in. But those memories of good times faded with each passing year until even now he had trouble remembering what she looked like. He knew he probably would not even recognize his brother if he saw him.

He gazed around the room as if in a trance, taking into account his depressing living conditions: An ugly pile of dirty dishes were stacked grotesquely on top on one another, spilling over the counter. A half-eaten, opened box of a chicken pot-pie lay rotting on the stove, a grim reminder of his horrific job. The faded, grease-stained Pep Boys calendar hung crookedly next to the clock was frozen in time on December 1987. He could not detect a speck of sunlight or life in his apartment. Everything about him evoked the smell of death. A cheap, bleached out yellow window shade covered the only window, eliminating the sun, creating a gray, catacomb of vacancy and despair. Particles of dust settled on the window-sill forming a blanket of dull brown snow. Mindlessly, Billy walked over and ran his finger through the layer of dust, creating a miniature dog sled trail down the middle of the cracked, and blistered windowsill.

Smells of abject poverty oozed from every crevice and rat hole, the room engulfed in permanent odors of burnt grease, cat shit left by a mangy stray, stale beer, two day-old Big Macs, the faint stench of Black Flag Ant and Roach killer, the odor of mildew caused by a stack of dank, musty newspapers turning brown by the door. All together the room smelled like a combination of rotting food and kerosene. The walls were bare, crumbling gray cinder blocks covered with obscene drawings left by a former tenant. Pencil penises and crayon vaginas. A lone 40-watt light bulb over the couch mockingly created the cozy intimacy of a jailhouse cell. The water pipes clamored loudly when the toilet flushed. Every-thing was dead here. He had not even seen a cockroach in weeks. The clock on the wall was broken. One of his speakers was busted. There were no curtains, no flowers, no rugs, and no pictures. He felt lucky for the embalmed stiffs next door. He thought he was stripped to the bone, a minimalist joke of a human being, without a hint of hope or optimism for the future. He knew he could not go much lower than this sorry state.

He turned away from the window and ambled lazily over to the other side of the room. He picked up his acoustic guitar and began to strum a few chords of an old Dylan song. Then he sang to himself in a slow, barely audible voice:

"When you ain't got nuthin,' you got nuthin' to lose...
You're invisible now, you got no secrets to conceal..."

Losing interest, he dropped the guitar, then sat back down on the couch. He knew he desperately needed something to break him out of these lonesome doldrums and the vastness of his depression. He thought about an old gangster movie that he saw one time late at night when he was barely conscious. He was halfway paying attention, ready to nod off to sleep, when he saw two guys walk in a motel room to gun down this dude and the guy didn't even flinch. He just stood up and waited for the hit men to blow him away. They shot him dead, and then fled the scene. Billy watched, fascinated by that one brief scene. Why didn't he make a move to defend himself? He just stood there like he wanted to die. Billy was convinced that the man welcomed the bullets. He thought about that one scene more than he cared to admit. He wondered what it would take in life to make you just stand there in front of a spray of bullets, and not care about the outcome. If anybody came into his apartment right now to blow him away, would he try to get way? Maybe that was where he was right now. Just like that guy in the motel room—at the end of his rope with no reason to live.

Basically, he had to make it as a rock star, or perhaps he would end it all. It was the only thing that kept him going—besides his hatred of Alicia. Lately, his obsession with Alicia was getting worse. He was dying to punish her in some way. A litany of wrathful, vengeful thoughts haunted him like the ghosts of his dead ancestors. He was not sure about his motivations; why he despised her so much. Why, he thought, does he waste his precious hate on that scumbag? He watched her all the time now. He was going to catch her doing something worth filming. He was convinced that with the help of his camcorder he could find some way to humiliate or torture her.

He heard a sound outside. At first, he thought it might be a bird singing; perhaps a robin signaling the first sign of spring.

But it turned out to be two guys bringing in another dead body.

SOLITARY EYES OF FIRE

Leslie was in her bedroom reading *Elle* magazine when the phone rang.

"Hello."

"Hello, Leslie?"

"Yes."

"This is Wally Buford from Musicdisc Incorporated. Your uncle Richard asked me to come down and listen to a band called *Mean Streets.*"

"Oh, yes! When can you come?"

"Are they playing somewhere down there?"

"Yes, as a matter of fact they are. I just talked to a manager of a club down here and he agreed to let *Mean Streets* open up for *Megadeth* on the seventh of April. It's a Tuesday night. Can you make it?"

"Sure. I'd be happy to. Can you call me some time next week and give me some more details and directions."

"Sure."

"Great. Do you have a pen?"

"No. Why?"

"My number. I need to give you my number."

"Oh, of course. Just a minute…Okay, what is it?"

"It's 202-544-4663."

"Got it. I'll call you!"

"That would be great. I look forward to hearing from you—and hearing the band."

Leslie was excited to tell Todd the good news. She rushed into the living room, but Todd was not sitting in his usual position in front of the television.

"Todd?"

She did not hear an answer and went into the kitchen to see if he was making himself something to eat. He was not there either, but she did spot a note left on the kitchen table. It read: "Went to Edgar's room."

Leslie could not think of any of their friends named Edgar, but something did occur to her. She went to her closet, put on a parka, and left the apartment.

It was not a long walk to the University of Virginia from Leslie's apartment, but the chilly March wind made the trek slightly uncomfortable as she traversed through the crowd of college students ambling along University Boulevard. Leslie thought she could be wrong about this, but in some perverse way, it made a great deal of sense. The only Edgar Leslie could think of was Edgar Allen Poe. Todd had been reading a lot of the former University of Virginia student's short stories, and she knew that his dormitory room was sealed off somewhere on campus.

"Can you tell me where to find Edgar Allen Poe's dorm room?" she asked a woman coming out of the New York Deli.

"Sure. It's across campus in that direction. Go past two large redbrick buildings, and then turn right. It's easy to spot. It's the only room covered by glass."

"Thanks."

Leslie followed the woman's instructions. As she turned the corner past the second building she saw the dormitory room and Todd standing directly in front of it.

"Todd, what are you doing? It's cold out here."

"It's damn small, isn't it?"

"Yes. It is—but you need to come back to the apartment."

"Okay. Do you suppose he wrote *The Black Cat* at that desk?"

"I don't think he wrote anything here. I think they threw him out for some reason."

Todd leaned forward, placing his hands on the glass, staring into the room.

"He was nuts, wasn't he?"

"I think he was schizophrenic at the end."

"He died lost and drunk in a Baltimore alley, didn't he?"

"I think so—but Todd it's cold out. Let's go home."

"He felt a lingering pity and sorrow for the dead."

"I suppose so…"

"I think he sensed the morbidity of it all…the deep dread of being…a grim legion of suffering souls…solitary eyes of fire…black shadows…dreary abyss…"

"Todd?"

"…Hideous dramas…bloody red death…cerebral congestion—"

"TODD! THAT'S ENOUGH! LET'S GO!!!

Leslie frantically grabbed Todd by the shoulder and pulled him to her.

"YOU'RE NOT MAKING SENSE! DO YOU HEAR ME?"

"Of course I'm not making sense. Any fool can make sense, right?"

"Let's go Todd."

"…Oh…pitiless wave, a final act of delirium tremors…"

Leslie led Todd away from the room and they quietly walked back to her apartment. After Todd had gotten a beer from the refrigerator and settled in his chair, Leslie poured herself a glass of wine, pulled up a chair, and sat down beside him.

"Todd, I want to talk to you."

"About what?"

"You know. You've been acting *very* strange. I think you should get some help."

"Help with what?"

"I think you're losing touch sometimes. It's like you drift off into some strange place—plus you're not coherent all the time."

"It's just too much dope. I'm gonna cut back on the hard stuff."

Todd grabbed the remote control and suddenly the television blared the sounds of a heavy metal rock video. Leslie ripped the remote from his hands and switched off the set. She turned and faced him, her jaw set, lips pursed, her eyes penetrating through him.

"I think it's more than that," she hissed. "You should see a doctor."

"You mean a head shrink."

Leslie sipped her wine, and gazed at the poster of James Dean on the wall. "Call it whatever you want. But it's just not for you. It's for me too. I can't take it much longer."

"You want me to see a doctor for you—"

"Dammit, you know what I mean. Do you think I'm being the selfish one here?"

"No, you're not selfish. Maybe I should get help. I do have some really weird thoughts. But it's just when I take angel dust and mix it with pot. That really sends me off."

"That's really *fuckin'* stupid. Why do you keep doing it?"

"I don't know. It's a weakness I can't control. It's like I want to experience oblivion."

Leslie stood up and paced the room. She went into the kitchen and poured herself another glass of wine. Todd remained in his easy chair, sipping a beer. Leslie returned and continued pacing the floor. Her voice cracked with pain and resentment.

"Is your life with me that bad that you have to shut me and the rest of the world out of it? How do you think that makes me feel?"

"I don' t mean to hurt you Leslie. I love you."

She came toward him, facing him again. "Well, why isn't that good enough?"

"What?"

"If you say you love me, why isn't that feeling good enough? If you love someone you don't want to obliterate your existence. There must be something missing in your life that I can't fulfill. Otherwise, we'd be a happy couple."

"We're not happy together?"

"We were…before you started all this…" She moved away from him and paced the floor once more.

"What? PCP?"

"No, it goes deeper than drugs. You were drifting off into your own world before you ever did PCP."

"Like when?"

"Like when you're with the guys or glued to MTV. I might as well not be in the room."

"I don't do that on purpose," he said.

She marched over to the fireplace, grabbed a black, iron poker and stoked the fire, which was barely surviving. A few fiery sparks shot out from below the stack of logs. She gripped the poker in one hand and drank from the wine glass with the other one. The fire showed signs of rekindling, brightening the room. casting shadows on the walls.

"It doesn't matter. That's how I feel. You used to open up to me more, but lately you just live in your own cave and rarely come out."

"I don't mean to do that. I love you, Leslie."

"How can you love someone and be so non-committal and self-centered at the same time?"

"I'm self-centered?"

"Yes."

"How?"

She leaned the poker against the side of the hearth, turned and faced him.

"That's one reason I want you to go to a doctor. I think people who have mental problems are extremely selfish. They only care about their own thoughts and think they have the corner on the market on suffering. You're not the only one with problems. Try working at the Boar's Head restaurant for a week and see how *you* like it."

"You make good money—"

"Cut the crap! Okay Todd! It's a dead-end, hopeless job that's about as stimulating as watching wallpaper." Leslie took a huge gulp of her wine, finishing off the drink.

"I didn't know you…"

"Now, isn't that my point?" she said, slamming the wine glass on the coffee table. "You're so wrapped up in your own fantasy world that you don't even care enough to look into mine. I'd like to stay home and do nothing sometimes too."

"You want me to get a job?"

"I want my old boy friend back—the one who is great fun to be with and pays a lot of attention to me. I want to do more things together. It's not a matter of you getting a job. I want you to make it as a drummer—if that's what you want."

"I'm going to quit the PCP. It's bad stuff."

"You still need to see a doctor."

"I'm not going to see a shrink."

"Why not?"

"Because they don't know what they're talking about."

"How do you know?"

"I just know, that's all. How can anybody tell what's going on inside my head?"

"For Christ's sake, it's their job, Todd. Just like anything else. It's what they do for a living."

"Well, I think it's all bullshit. They probably think my problems have something to do with my mother."

"Not all psychiatrists are Freudian."

"I'll just cut down on the PCP. I don't need any stupid psychiatrist to tell me something I already know."

"What's that?"

"I'm not crazy."

DR. GILBERT

Chris knocked on the door of professor Robert H. Gilbert's office, the head of the Psychology department at Piedmont Community College.

"Come in."

Chris entered the office and discovered a large, burly, round-faced bald man leaning back in his chair, reading some papers. "Excuse me. Are you busy?"

"No, not really," said Dr. Gilbert. "Come on in."

"My name is Chris Hamilton. I'm a student here. Can I talk to you about something?"

"Sure. Have a seat. What's on your mind?" asked Dr. Gilbert, slumping forward and positing the papers on his desk.

Chris walked toward Dr. Gilbert and sat down in a chair directly facing the professor. "I have a friend who is acting kind of strange. I thought you might be able to help him. He's seems to be losing touch with reality."

Dr. Gilbert stiffened a bit and reached for a tobacco pipe lying in an ashtray on the edge of the desk. "In what way?"

"Well," said Chris, "He says he sees things on television that aren't there—like the Antichrist. And he talks about hallucinating death and dissolving into another reality."

Dr. Gilbert banged the upended pipe on the ashtray, knocking out strands of stale, smoked tobacco. He took his hand and swiped some spilled strands away from the desk onto the floor. Turning away from Chris, he reached down to his left for a pouch of tobacco in one of the drawers.

"How old is he?"

"Twenty-two."

Taking a small pinch of tobacco and stuffing it into the pipe, the professor turned toward Chris, arching his eyebrows that were prominent because of his bald head.

"Is he taking medication?"

"No, not really…but he does drugs."

"What kind?"

"Well…"

"Don't worry, I'm not going to squeal—that's not my department."

"…mostly marijuana, but also some PCP and downers. Alcohol too."

Dr. Gilbert produced a Zippo lighter from his pants pocket. "Do you mind if I smoke?"

"No, not at all."

"I have to tell you one thing before we go any further," said Dr. Gilbert.

"What's that?"

"It's very hard to change behavior."

"Yes," said Chris, "I'm sure it is."

"You don't understand. I mean, it is *very* hard to change behavior. My whole profession is founded on changing peoples' behavior and we are complete failures. You see this pipe?"

"Yes."

"Well, don't you think I should quit smoking?"

"Sure. It's bad for your health."

"Precisely. So why don't I use all my fancy psychological theories to quit?"

"I don't know."

"Because they're useless. Nicotine is the most powerful drug in the world—a lot more powerful than any stupid theory. "Is he a student here?"

"Uh…no, we're in a band together. He's the drummer, but lately he just sits around and watches MTV and smokes dope."

Dr. Gilbert lit his pipe and blew a cloud of blue smoke toward the ceiling. "Do you think you can arrange for him to see me?"

"I don't know. I think he's in denial. I'm not sure he will admit he needs help."

"Well, I need to see him to make an evaluation. Here's my card."

Chris took the card from Dr. Gilbert. "Okay, I'll see what I can do."

"Chris, I want to tell you something. Just like it is very hard for me to quit smoking, it is very hard to cure anybody with any sort of mental illness. I'm not trying to be overly pessimistic, but only fifteen percent of those people diagnosed with schizophrenia ever become normal again."

"I understand," said Chris, "But we need to try, right?"

"Yes, yes we do. We need to always try."

"Okay, thanks for your help. I'll try real hard to get him to come."

"Fine. Nice meeting you."

Chris left Dr. Gilbert's office and drove to Leslie's duplex apartment. He pulled in the parking lot, walked to the front door, and rang the bell. Momentarily, Leslie answered.

"Oh hi Chris! Come on in. Please sit down. Can I get you something to drink?"

"No thanks," said Chris, taking a seat on one of the chairs in the living room. "Is Todd here?"

"No, he went out for some beer, but he'll be back soon."

"I went to a psychiatrist today. He's not actually a psychiatrist, but he teaches psychology and does counseling on the side."

"Did you tell him about Todd?"

"Yes, but he needs to see him in person."

"I'm not sure he'll go. He thinks there's nothing wrong with him."

"How's he been doing?"

"Not so good. In fact, he's getting worse. He just goes off into his own world—it's scary."

"I've noticed. Everybody's worried about him."

Chris and Leslie heard Todd coming in the back door. They heard the refrigerator door open and close and the sound of a bottle cap snapping off. He walked down a narrow corridor, which led from the kitchen to the living room.

"Hey, man, what's going on?"

"Nothing much, said Chris. "Leslie and I were just having a little talk."

"Great. What's the big subject for the day?"

"Actually, we were talking about you."

Todd smiled and took a sip of his beer. "First of all, let me say that I am innocent of all charges."

"That's highly unlikely," said Chris.

"Chris thinks you should get some help Todd," said Leslie.

"Help doing what? Playing the drums better?"

"No," said Chris, "I went to see a psychologist at the school. He does counseling."

"You think I need a shrink?"

"I think it could help," said Chris. "Let's face it, you been drifting off lately."

"Come on! Get serious! So, I get stoned too much. That doesn't mean I'm crazy."

"We're not saying you're crazy, Todd," interjected Leslie. "It's just that you haven't been yourself and we think this guy could help you."

"I don't need any help."

"Look, what's it going to hurt?" asked Chris. "You've been saying some pretty weird things. Maybe this guy can get your head straightened out, so you can better concentrate on your drumming, and other things in your life."

Todd gulped down the rest of the beer in one swallow. "I need a beer." He walked deliberately to the refrigerator, obtained another beer and strode back into the living room. Slumping dismally into his chair, Todd stared into space, his eyes fixed on the fireplace. Chris and Leslie remained silent.

"I guess it is a slow capitulation…"

Leslie leaned in his direction. "To what?"

"I don't know. It's like I'm not always in charge…"

"Well," said Chris, "This guy can help you take charge and get your life back together."

"Maybe you're right. What harm could it do? They're not going to put me in the loony bin, are they?"

"Of course not," said Leslie. "We just want you to meet with him and see what he can do for you. Maybe you just need some medication."

"I'm not into medication. It takes away the buzz."

"What buzz?" asked Chris.

"The buzz I get from beer…dope…going off…"

"So," said Leslie, "That's what we mean. We want you to stay in this world all the time. You've been spacing out too much and it's affecting everything…everything between us."

"I know I haven't been much of a boyfriend…"

"That's not important now," said Leslie. "The important thing is to get someone to talk to you about your problems."

"Leslie's right," said Chris. "Just go to the guy and see what he has to say. He seems real nice."

"Okay, where is he?"

"His name is Dr. Gilbert and he's at Piedmont. He gave me his card. Here you are."

Todd took the card from Chris.

"Don't you think if I just stopped smoking dope and doing pills that I would be okay?"

"Can you do that?" asked Leslie.

Todd thought for a second. "No."

"Well, he might offer you drug treatment," said Chris. "Maybe it's just a matter of quitting dope."

"Maybe…"

"I'm proud of you Todd. I love you." Leslie reached over and gave Todd a big hug and kiss.

"Hey," said Chris, "If you two are gonna get mushy, I'm outta here."

"Leslie's terrific, isn't she?"

"Yeah—and what she sees in you, I'll never know."

"How about a future rock 'n roll star?"

"Well, said Chris, "That remains to be seen."

FOXFIELD

Chris wanted to get the band together after hearing the news about Mr. Buford coming to review the band, so Sarah decided to go to the Foxfield Races with her friend Sally. They arrived at noon... The air was cool and misty. A thin layer of early spring frost blanketed the sloping, grassy meadows. The entire countryside was sculpted with green, gently rolling hills, and at this moment, the diffused sunlight muted the myriad shades of green and yellow bursting from the grasses and flowers. Hundreds of students were beginning to pile into the parking areas reserved for automobiles. Sarah and Sally held orange tickets, enabling them to park close to the track.

Sally eased her black BMW into their spot. The crowd arrived early to tailgate and all the vehicles were loaded up with beer, wine, champagne, fried chicken, potato salad, and other picnic items. The temperature quickly became warmer and some of the guys started taking off their shirts, tossing Frisbees, and playing horseshoes. Sally brought her boom box and shortly the mournful soul-sounds of Bono wailing, *"I still haven't found what I'm looking for,"* filled the air. Sarah absently wondered if the song wasn't written with her in mind.

"Hey Sarah!" Sally yelled, "It's past noon! Time for a beer!"

Sarah reached into the cooler, grabbed a Moosehead, and settled comfortably in a lawn chair. She removed her sweater, leaned back, and gazed skyward. The heat of the sun warmed her face. She could see the horses in the distance, trotting along, loosening up for the races. She did not know much about horse racing, but she knew the race was run on a grassy track. She enjoyed the steeplechases where the horses would gallop at breakneck speeds, gliding smoothly over wooden fences, circling the track a couple times. Already, nearby, she could hear the excited voices of young men starting a betting pool.

One of them, who looked like the lead singer of *R.E.M.*, approached her carrying a cooler and clutching some bills in his hand. He was wearing a pair of black baggy shorts, a long sleeve white shirt with the sleeves rolled up, white deck shoes, and a black Perry Ellis tie with pictures of Marilyn Monroe's face printed on it.

"Hey! Wanna make a bet?"

"How much is it?"

"You can bet as little as two dollars."

"Okay," Sarah said. "How do I do it?"

"Well," He replied, "First, you give me two bucks. Then, you pick a horse. If it wins, you collect money. Simple. What you win depends on the odds of the horse."

"Alright. Give me horse number five. That's my lucky number. Sarah handed the college guy two dollars. "When do the races start?"

"In a few minutes. There are nine races and they run about every thirty minutes. Do you mind if I sit down?"

"No."

The young man sat down, leaned over and grabbed a beer out of his cooler.

"So, where's your boyfriend?"

"Who said I had a boyfriend?"

"I don't know. You look attached for some reason."

"Actually, I do have a boyfriend."

"Where is he?"

"He's in a band...they have practice."

In the distance Sarah could see the horses lining up for the beginning of the race. The resplendent, multi-colored jockeys were leisurely warming up their horses near the starting gate, forming a large circle around the paddock. From the right side of the track several well-muscled thoroughbreds entered an opening in a wooden fence. Cantering smartly down the center of the grassy area, six other horses joined the rest of the field.

"There's number five!" the young man shouted.

Sarah gazed into the arena and spotted a beautiful, deep brown, angular thoroughbred with a waving black mane. Moving easily, the confident looking jockey shifted from a slow loping trot to a medium gallop. The jockey, wearing a blaze of purple and gold, leaned slightly forward as if to aid in the balancing of the horse. The jockey's hands were relaxed and his manner calm and subdued. He drew on the reins in such a way as to cause the bit to slide gently over the horse's tongue and jaw, enabling the horse to bring his head down in conjunction with the use of his legs, creating an image of perfect symmetry between rider and horse.

"What's your name?" asked the young man.

"What?"

"Do you always drift off into space?" He said, smiling.

"Oh, I'm sorry. I guess I was daydreaming. "I'm Sarah Carter…and you?"

"Ben O'Leary. Glad to meet you. So, you've got a serious rock and roll boyfriend. I guess that means you can't come to the Zete mixer with me tonight."

"Thanks, but I have to study for a test."

"Saturday night? Nobody studies on Saturday night. Besides, we're gonna win a bunch of money and we just have to blow it."

"No…no thanks."

"Hey, look," he protested, "You come to the party and I'll get you out of the test."

"Oh, really? How are you going to do that?"

"Easy. My uncle is the Dean of Arts and Sciences."

"You're kidding."

"No, really. Dean Windsor. He's my uncle—dad's brother. "I'll just call him up and say, 'Uncle Dan, I met this beautiful girl at Foxfield and she wouldn't come to the party unless I got her out of this test. He'd say: 'Nephew, I'm glad you called. This is an emergency for sure. I mean, how many times do you meet a beautiful girl at the races?'"

"I have to be home early. I can't stay—and you don't have to call your uncle."

"Terrific."

The horses reached the starting gate and Sarah heard a booming voice from the loud speaker shouting, "They're off!"

GOOEY

Alicia accidentally rolled over in top of the guy. She was tossing and turning in her sleep and she must have smothered him until he could not breathe. He woke up choking and coughing for a few moments. He immediately got on Alicia's nerves and she asked him to leave.

"Sure, let me get dressed. I had a great time."

Alicia figured that he was not only a lousy lay, but a lousy liar as well. She glanced at his ass as he was leaving and realized that he was much too fat for her and wondered how she possibly could have wound up in bed with such an out of shape dude. There were a couple used condoms on the floor and she stepped on one by accident as she was going to the bathroom. It stuck to her foot. She was walking several steps with a sticky, gooey, semen-filled balloon on her toes. She did not quite know how to get it off and certainly did not feel like touching it. She tried to brush it off with her other toe, but tripped on her own two feet, stumbling on the dresser, still mortifyingly condom-stuck. She found an umbrella in the closet and laid on her back with her feet splayed out, like she was having a baby. She reached down and plucked it off with the umbrella and tossed it away. What a way to wake up, she thought. Alicia looked over the side of the bed and there was another used condom lying on the rug. This time she found a pair of tweezers in the dresser drawer and plucked it from the floor. Carefully carrying the condom into the bathroom, she dropped it into the toilet just as her mother's voice called from upstairs.

"Alicia, are you alright? Has your friend left?"

The condom got flushed for good.

Suddenly, Alicia heard a commotion outside her window. She went over and looked at the street below. The guy who just left was chasing someone down the street. Alicia thought that maybe there was a burglar in the neighborhood. Then she thought about what her mother said about a friend being in here with her.

That's really strange because she knows I don't have any friends.

POT...ALCOHOL...
SOME PILLS

It was late in the afternoon when Todd knocked on Dr. Gilbert's office door.

"Excuse me, are you Dr. Gilbert?"

"Yes. Can I help you."

"I hope so. My name is Todd Page."

"Todd Page?"

"I'm a friend of Chris Hamilton's."

"Yes, of course. He said you would be coming to see me."

"He said you might be able to do something for me."

"Well, I'll try."

"Do I have to make an appointment?"

"No, no. I have time now. Please sit down."

Todd entered the office and sat down in a black leather swivel chair. Dr Gilbert took a seat behind his desk in front of Todd.

"Tell me a little about yourself," said Dr. Gilbert.

"There's not much to tell."

"Are you from around here?"

"Yes. I went to Charlottesville high school. I graduated four years ago."

"And you're a drummer in a rock band, right?"

"Yes...but we don't get many gigs."

"Is that what you like to do?"

"I guess so..."

"Tell me about MTV. Chris says you watch it a lot."

"I was on Remote Control. I won $800.00."

"Remote Control?"

"It's a game show on MTV. It's very popular."

"So, you're into rock videos."

"Yeah…"

"Why MTV?"

"You mean, why do I watch it?"

"Yes."

Todd swiveled around 180 degrees in the chair until he was facing the door. He noticed from a schedule on the door that Dr. Gilbert kept office hours every-day from 10:30 a.m. to 11:30 a.m. He wanted to leap out of the chair and fly away from this office, like a bird on the wing. He gripped the arms of the chair tightly, the veins popping in his wrists. He thought if he just took a flying leap, he would suddenly take off from the chair, like a rocket being shot out of a can-non. The murmurs of students talking in the hall disrupted his thinking.

"Todd?"

Todd swirled halfway to his left, facing a wall covered with framed diplomas and assorted pictures. "I guess it's significant."

"In what way?" asked Dr. Gilbert.

"Who's that guy?" said Todd, motioning to one of the pictures on the wall.

"B.F. Skinner. He was a behaviorist, of sorts."

"Looks like a dork."

"He was."

"So, why is MTV significant?"

It's…current…it has all the right…you know…messages…images…"

"What kinds of messages and images?"

Todd swirled in his chair once more, until he faced Dr. Gilbert. "Is this really important? I mean, aren't you supposed to find out what's wrong with me?"

"I don't know. I just met you. Do you think there is something wrong with you?"

"Christ, what do you think I'm here for? To get a haircut?"

"Todd, I'm a psychologist and I do counseling for people who have problems they can't handle. Sometimes it's just a manner of talking it out, and sometimes it's more serious."

"So, where do I fit in?"

"I don't know. Do you hear voices?"

"I'm not sure."

"Do you see things that aren't there? Do you hallucinate?"

"Ah……not sure."

"Are you taking medication of any kind?"

"What do you mean?"

"I don't mean illegal drugs—and don't worry. I'm not going to bust you if you tell me you're on drugs. That's confidential."

"In that case, I'm not on any medication."

"And drugs?"

"Pot…alcohol…some pills."

"What kind of pills?"

"Downers mostly…Darvon…Valium…"

"Do you mix these?"

"Of course."

"You know mixing downers and alcohol can lead to an overdose."

"I'm careful. I'm not going to off myself."

"How are your parents?"

"Fine."

"Do you get along with them?"

"Yeah, I guess."

"Do you see them very often?"

"No."

"Why not?"

"We don't connect that well. They live in a big house with about 50 rooms. You can get lost in there."

Suddenly, the phone rang. Dr. Gilbert picked it up.

"…Yes…okay…I'll be right there."

"There's an emergency down at the hospital. I have to go."

"No problem."

"How about making another appointment?"

"Sure."

"How about Tuesday, same time."

"Okay."

PAROXYSMS OF PLEASURE

Laura Ashton was in the Theta sorority house polishing her nails watching a rerun of *The Brady Bunch*. It was her favorite show. She was thinking about her life right now and how it could be so much better. Sure, she concluded, she was beautiful, popular, smart, and rich, but so what? Sissy McDonald in the next apartment had all those things and she still was anorexic and without a boyfriend. Laura needed to feel better about herself in the worst way. She thought that finding a boyfriend with better social standing would help her feel more secure about herself. Ben O'Leary was okay, but his family did not belong to a country club. She thought about dumping Ben for Everett Morgan, but Everett was only about five feet six inches tall and was already going bald. Laura loved money more than anything in the world and could not understand why anyone would major in anything except business or communications. Laura covered herself on both fronts: she was a business/communications double major. In her freshman year she decided to branch out and take a course in modern poetry, but she hated it. She felt the professor was a complete idiot who constantly made fun of her interpretations of poems. She remembered one poem in which she was sure the poet was talking about the whirring blades of a lawn mower, but the professor ridiculed her by saying it was obviously a hummingbird. Laura was so outraged that she splattered a gallon of red paint all over his car in the parking lot. She felt much better about the course after getting even with that terrible professor.

The Brady Bunch was ending as June Winthrop, Laura's roommate, came sauntering into the apartment, flashing a wide smile.

"Hey, what's up," she asked

"Nothing," said Laura, "I was just watching *The Brady Bunch*."

"Guess what?"

"What?"

"I lost three pounds."

"You're kidding."

"No. I just checked the scale at the health club. Do you believe it?"

"How'd you do it?"

"I just stopped eating. I haven't eaten in two days—except for some crackers."

"That's great."

In reality, Laura did not think it was great that her roommate lost three pounds. In fact, she loathed everything about June Winthrop. She forced herself to be nice to her and pretend she cared about her incredibly small world. Laura had a mean jealous streak that she could barely control. In fact, her three dominant emotions were jealousy, greed, and self-loathing. She looked closely at June and tried to figure out where she lost the three pounds. Laura could not be sure, but she thought her breasts looked a little smaller because her hips still looked about the same. She guessed that June probably weighed about 110 pounds. At five feet seven inches, she was disgustingly perfect. She had long blonde hair, bright blue eyes, and stunning figure made her the envy of all the girls in the sorority. She was hated with a passion, but everybody was real nice to her in person. Laura figured June Winthrop belonged in the highest social group more than any other girl at the school. Laura divided the whole campus into those students who belonged and those who did not belong. She had a habit of immediately putting someone into one category or the other.

"Are you going to the Zete mixer?" asked June.

"Yeah, I guess so. I'm supposed to meet Ben."

"Did you go to Foxfield with him?"

"No, I went shopping. I hate horses."

"Why?"

"I don't know…say, do you think Everett Morgan is too short?"

"He is kinda short. You thinking about dating him?"

"Maybe."

"He's got a nice car."

"His father, like owns Pepsi Cola or something."

"Go for it."

"How tall do you think he is?"

"I don't know. Maybe five feet seven, or so."

"I guess he's too short, huh?"

"I couldn't date anyone shorter than me. It's embarrassing."

"I'd rather die than be embarrassed."

"What about Chip Philbin?"

"You mean to date?"

"Yeah, he's a hotty."

"I heard he's bi."

"Too bad. How about John Fuhrman?"

"No way. He dates townies."

"I heard Dennis Testermann broke up with his girl friend."

"Really? Now, there's a possibility. I heard he got into law school."

"Maybe he'll be at the mixer. What are you wearing?"

"I bought a new outfit at the mall. Nothing fancy, just a pair of black slacks and a brown pullover."

"I am going to take a shower."

"See you later."

June left the living room and went into her bedroom to take a shower. Laura was always bored, but today was more intolerable than most. She could not think of anything to do. She thought about going next door and seeing if Heather Ransome had any marijuana, but then she remembered that Heather was pissed off at her for hitting on her boyfriend at the Pi Kappa Phi mixer last Thursday. She thought about making up a list of all the girls she knew who really did not belong at the school for a variety of reasons, but she quickly lost interest. She considered studying, but she hated to study anything. She went into her bedroom, consumed by a strong combination of restlessness and boredom. Wandering aimlessly about the room, she landed in front of the full-length mirror on the wall. She felt underneath her breasts, pushed them up slightly and squeezed them together to see if she could improve her cleavage. She was not displeased. She looked at her heavily made-up face and made seductive expressions, imitating Marilyn Monroe, pursing her fiery red lips, and pouting like she was in a cheesy porn movie. She tenderly massaged her breasts again and felt an arousing, tingling sensation. She thought about the drunken night that Ben played with them and how he told her she had the most magnificent tits in the world and he loved sucking on them until they were swollen and moist. The thoughts of her sex life with Ben made Laura feel incredibly horny, so she slowly took off her clothes. She positioned the mirror in front of her bed so she could see herself lying naked, spread-eagled. She began to feel herself between her thighs with one hand and gently massaged her left breast with the other one. She glanced in the mirror and tried to see inside of her vagina, but she could not see anything, so she took her two hands and spread the lips of her vagina apart. She strained her eyes to see what there was to see. She could not believe it. There was nothing there. She wondered why guys got so excited over nothing. She placed her left forefinger inside and found her g-spot and rubbed it soothingly. She was becoming excited and rubbed more forcefully, until her whole body was writhing with paroxysms of pleasure. She moaned quietly as she pushed her two fingers further inside of her and made aggressive circular motions. Rising from the bed, she walked over to the dresser drawer and uncovered a battery-operated dildo hidden beneath her panties. She returned to the bed and assumed her former position, clutching the dildo with her left hand. She switched the dildo on and it made a slight whirring noise, so she got up again and went over to the television and turned up the sound. Back in bed, she closed her eyes and thought about Bret, the hot bartender at Trax and how sexy he was in his tight blue jeans. She could feel him slipping his penis in her, moving it gently back and forth, and rubbing the tip of his penis against her throbbing g-spot. *"Ooooh...Bret...that feels soooo... good...* She could feel him kissing her violently on the lips and playing with her tits, squeezing them and licking her nipples with his wild tongue. His penis was now driving faster and faster within her and she moved her ass up and down on the bed, jerking her pelvis into the air, and allowing his penis to penetrate into further regions of her vagina. He took two fingers and found her wet g-spot and massaged her most sensitive area until she thought she was going to burst. She almost screamed with pleasure when she came, but she was careful not to let out any sounds that June might hear. Her whole body collapsed and went limp as she lay on the bed thinking about Bret, the hot bartender at Trax, Everett Morgan, and whether or not he was too short, and if Dennis Testermann was going to be at the mixer tonight. Within a few minutes she was fast asleep.

WHATEVER

Later that night, Laura woke up, got dressed and headed out for the Zete mixer. As she entered the fraternity house, her thoughts focused on meeting Ben and her attitudes about everything else:

I really couldn't care less about Foxfield, but I definitely wanted to catch the Zete mixer. Most of the real Theta girls are here and a couple of wannabes who do not belong at all. Where the fuck was Ben? Someone played Hothouse Flowers and everyone started dancing and bumping into one another like they were a bunch of old punks. In the midst of a lot of confusion, Heather Mason, a third year, who belongs, (who weighs about 115 pounds) stumbled up to me and offered me a sip of her Mountain Dew and vodka. Some guy named Willie (that think I slept with), who was wearing a "Fuck More/Bitch Less" T-shirt and asked me to go upstairs and smoke a joint, and I said, " Okay, but I have to meet Ben, so I can't stay long." On the way up the stairs I ran into Bebe Solen, who almost belongs (who weighs about 110, but was 125 last year) and I asked her if she had seen Ben and she said, "Not yet."

I walked into the room, and of course, it was decorated with The Doors and Deadhead posters. Reggae music was playing. It sounded like AWE or maybe Bob Marley. Ubiquitous Michael Jordan with his legs split wide open, tongue hanging out, soaring towards the rim, loomed larger than life before me. Sports equipment of every variety littered the floor. I stepped on a baseball glove and kicked it rather unceremoniously in the corner. Someone lying on the floor yelled, "Hey! That's my mitt," but I ignored the complaint. I don't know how these guys find their rooms when they're drunk. They all look the same—and they have the nastiest bathrooms this side of Calcutta. I've gotten in the habit of never going to the bathroom at these parties. I go outside. It's a lot more pleasant, although one time at a fraternity party I was wearing a lime green flo-rescent hat. I got so drunk I forgot I had the damn thing on. Anyway, I went to pee in the woods. I squatted next to a tree. As I was doing my thing, I hear catcalls and peo-ple yelling my name, making fun of me. How could they see me? Of course, it wasn't that difficult because I was glowing in the dark. Oh well. Whatever.

Right away, I wished I hadn't come into this cave-world of pasty-faced people. I was hoping it would be mostly Zete guys, but there were dumb, trashed-out Theta wannabes in there who didn't belong. Some totally bleached out cheesy girl in a bright red fuckme mini-skirt and a Florida Gator T-shirt (who weighs 128) and whom I think I saw fucking Chad Overall in his closet last week, said hello to me and I said, "Nice outfit." Her friend, also first year, in a trampy, hideous purple halter-top and painted-on blue jeans (who weighs about 105) was passed out on the couch with her suck-face mouth open in a disgustingly grotesque manner. Another partygirl wannabe, who didn't belong, from Hollins named Lucy Billings (who weighs 112, but I think she had liposuction), barged up to me, totally hammered, blurting out, "HEY!!! DIDN'T WE MEET AT THE PALMS LAST WEEK!!!" And I very politely said, "No, I don't think so." And, of course, she was a nobody, who would never belong because everybody knows it was Van Riper's and not the Palms that was happening last week.

Finally, I spotted Willie hitting on Heather Sampson, a fourth year Theta, who belongs (who weighs about 118) and who just broke up with her boyfriend, so I guess she's gonna fuck Willie tonight. I asked him about the joint and he said, "Sure" and rolled one right away and we smoked it with another guy named Robert in a multi-colored tie-dye T-shirt with the words "Live Free or Dye" painted on the back. He was kinda cute, but too short.

The joint turned out to be pretty good (Colombian I think). Some dude wearing a totally nondescript outfit except for a turned around Chicago Cubs baseball cap changed the tape to The Connells" or maybe "Trash Can Sinatras." I couldn't be sure. They had a lousy stereo system. I leaned back in an ugly blue beanbag chair. I was beginning to feel pretty good. It must be the pot. I absently wondered why I didn't go out with Willie again—especially if he could get pot this good. In the midst of a mar-ijuana haze, as I gazed mindlessly at blue swirls of smoke wafting towards the ceiling, Live Free or Dye Robert intoned mysteriously to no one in particular, "I know God's wife's name."

Oh no, I'm about to be engaged in a reefer deadhead conversation. Oh, please help me. This could be fatal.

"Hey, get a grip," *I advised Live Free or Dye Robert.*

"Mother nature."

"...Huh...?"

"...What...?

"God's wife..."

"Whaaaaaaa...?"

I think the Deadhead said something, but who cares what this geek is talking about? I decided I needed some air.

I strolled out to the terrace. The night air was cool and moist. I saw Daniel Beau-champ, a gorgeous Zete, hitting on Mary Francis, who almost belongs, but she went out with a townie last semester. I walked up to them because I want to know what they are wearing.

Daniel is dressed in very tasteful, contemporary preppy apparel. He is wearing a pair of Ralph Lauren's sturdy, sand-colored oversized, cinch-wasted chino Big Pants; a Zanella abstract print, washed silk, sport shirt; a calf-skinned belt by Allen-Edwards; and leather hand-sewn moccasins by L.L. Bean. On his wrist I noticed a Nobilia Sprint Perpetual World Timer watch. For some reason, he's wearing a Detroit Tigers baseball cap. His cologne is Fahrenheit. I approved of everything, except the baseball cap, of course.

Mary Francis is also tastefully attired in a cute Laura Ashley floral print sundress with large blue buttons down the front; a pair of brown Birkenstock's; an authentic African trade bead necklace with a plain gold bracelet. Her long, black Cher-like hair is festooned upward with a hair scrunchie and hangs down seductively down her face. Her perfume is Eternity. I approved of everything, but I think the Birkenstock's and beads should be left for the hippie wannabes.

I looked out over the balcony and I see a random couple fucking in the bushes. Boy, are they going at it. She is sitting on top of him, smoking a cigarette. A male figure emerged from the side of the building and walked up to the couple and said something to them. She gave the stranger a drag of her cigarette, then he left. I watched them for a few more seconds, got bored, then decided to go downstairs and see if Ben was around.

On the way out I looked at the Michael Jordan picture again and decided I'd sleep with him if I got the chance (and nobody found out).

As I descended the stairs leading to the main party room, I saw Ben across the room with some new girl (who looked like she weighed about 116). He was lying on the couch with his arm draped around her neck. I can't believe this cheatin' son-of-a-bitch. He had not seen me yet, so I circled slowly around the back of the room and came up behind him. I leaned over and whispered in his ear.

"Hi Ben."

He practically jumped out of the couch.

"Laura! When did you get here?"

"Oh, about an hour ago. Aren't you going to introduce me?"

"Sure. Laura, this is Sarah. Sarah, this is Laura."

"Pleased to meet you Laura."

"Hi."

Sarah was cute with medium long, natural blonde hair, and possessed a perfect complexion. I didn't think she was wearing any makeup except for a slight touch of red lipstick. Little brown specks of freckles dotted the bridge of her nose, making her look megacute, like one of those Brady Bunch girls. She was tall, statuesque, and thinly built with a hardbody butt and well-rounded, perky breasts. If I were a judge I'd give her first prize in a beauty contest at the state fair.

She was dressed in a pair of navy Umbro soccer shorts, tan bucks, and an extra-large men's pin-stripped shirt (possibly Arrow). Her only jewelry was a simple black onyx college ring.

Right away I knew she was a threat.

"Ben, can I speak to you for a moment?"

"Sure," he said. "Sarah, I'll be right back."

We went out on the porch and chased away some ugly fat couple who were sucking face under an orange and blue UVA blanket.

"Hey! Get a room!" *I yelled.*

"Ben, who is that girl in there?"

"She's just a girl I picked up after Foxfield—I don't mean picked up—I mean…she was all by herself and looking for a party, so I asked her to come."

"Well, aren't you the fuckin' magnanimous hero. Helping a poor damsel in distress. Gee, were there any dragons to slay in the neighborhood?"

"You don't have to be so cynical. I just met her. She doesn't mean anything to me."

"So, you always put your arm around girls who don't mean anything to you?"

"We were just talking that's all. I had my arm around the couch—not her."

"Sure. Sure you did—And I'm Edie Brickell."

"Come on, Laura. Let's go back in and have a good time."

"You mean with me—or your new girlfriend?"

"With you, of course. I'll just tell her my girlfriend showed up and we're going to spend

the rest of the night together. Right?"

"Yeah, right. Do you know something Ben?"

"What?"

"I think you're a prick."
"Thanks honey. I love you too."

ELIMINATE, ELIMINATE

Billy was sitting on his couch in his underwear, thinking about what happened in the cemetery last night . A few local trash metal freaks were in the back of the cemetery moshing to a tribal war dance, listening to high-level decibels of music about how to kill society, while kicking and smashing everyone around you in the face. Billy could hear them chanting, "Eliminate the rich, eliminate the poor, eliminate, eliminate…" The police finally came and arrested them for performing animal sacrifices and defacing religious statues and tombstones. The newspaper said there was $25,000 worth of marble destroyed. Billy knew one of the boys arrested. His name was Eric and he was 17 years old. He remembered that his mother bought him a 1983 Camaro, and arranged for him to put in a $1700.00 engine. Eric sold the car to buy an electric guitar and some coke. Eric loved songs by Venom, Slayer, and Anthrax. Billy figured the guys had to be pretty bored to wipe out $25,000 worth of marble. He knew that three years ago he would have been out there with them, but he was beginning to mellow out and definitely drew the line at sacrificing animals.

Feeling hungry, Billy went over to the refrigerator and, as usual, there was only one entrée on tonight's menu: frozen chicken potpies. Twelve cartons bunched together in the frozen food section and five Budweisers completed the contents of the refrigerator. Billy appreciated the nice gesture by the company to provide free food, but he was getting really tired of chicken potpies. His thoughts drifted to the time when he first started working for the frozen food company. He was packing hamburger patties in the meat department, wearing gloves for protection. But the gloves did not protect his hands from freezing and turning numb. He hated his breaks. He figured he had the only job in America where you hated to take a break. He would go into the lounge area to smoke a cigarette, but his hands would thaw out and begin to sting. The only way to eliminate the pain was to go back and re-freeze his hands.

Billy was anticipating the beginning of warmer weather. He hated the long winters in the mountains. Growing restless, he switched on the television, surfed a few channels, but nothing caught his attention. He wished he had a girlfriend so they could go to a movie or something. He picked up his guitar and ran through a couple songs, but he couldn't get into it. He figured he would just go down to Jake's.

He reached down to put on his jeans and noticed that they were ripped down the side. He realized that he must have torn them on a fence running away from Alicia's date the other night. He didn't care about ripping the jeans. He was lucky to get away and he consoled himself knowing that he possessed an exclusive video of Alicia having sex with yet another stranger. He slipped the video into the machine and watched the show one more time. Billy became aroused watching Alicia crawl on top of the stranger, sliding down to his erect penis, and giving him oral sex. He got a close up of Alicia's tongue licking the penis and massaging it with her hands as she sucked him off. Billy's emotions were mixed with hatred, lust and envy. At least Alicia could get a partner. Deep down Billy was jealous of Alicia's easy access to sex. Billy occasionally went to whores because he had trouble establishing a relationship with a woman. Women seemed to sense his mistrust of them. They intuitively shied away from him, afraid of his rough persona, his uncaring, sarcastic demeanor. Billy felt that being nice to a woman was a weakness. He was not sure about the difference between kindness and weakness, so he took the safe route and opted for a cynical, boorish personality around women. They did not find any aspect of his behavior appealing. Billy's jealousy of Alicia infuriated him and made him despise her even more. The video, much to his dismay, aroused him and he thought about masturbating to the video, but his repulsion of Alicia overrode his lustful desires. As he was flicking the video off, he heard a knock at the door.

"Come in."

"Hi Billy."

Billy turned and saw his mother at the door. He was shocked to see her, but his face remained expressionless.

"Hi…what…uh…"

"Is it alright to come in?"

"…Yeah…How'd you find me?"

"I talked to a bartender at that bar—Jake's."

Billy's mother was standing in the shadows of the doorway. He strained to see how much she had changed. She seemed thinner, paler, with a deep furrow between her eyes. She was wearing a plain blue cotton dress with matching shoes and handbag. Her hair looked like streaks of gray were blending in with her light brown hair.

"Billy?"

"Yes."

"I'd like to talk to you."

"Sure. Come on in. Grab a chair. You'll have to excuse the place. It's not the Ritz."

Billy's mother came closer to Billy into the glare of the stark light bulb above the room. He was even more shocked as he was able to discern the mature, deep lines on her face and forehead. She lifted a chair from the kitchen table and placed it in front of him.

"I know you're shocked to see me. I'm surprised you even recognized me so easily."

"You haven't changed that much."

"How are you doing?" she asked.

"How am I doing? Are you kidding? Everything's just fine. I gave the maid and the butler off for the evening."

"I'm sorry. I don't know what to say."

"Why are you here?"

"I came because I wanted to tell you why I left you and Sammy. I want to tell you how sorry I am."

Billy stared into her eyes, wondering if she was for real, or if this was some sort of trick. For an instant, he chuckled to himself, thinking that maybe she really wasn't his mother, but an imposter trying to cheat him out of his vast wealth.

"So, why'd you leave?"

"I was scared. I was young and scared."

"You weren't that young."

"No. No, I wasn't. But I was immature for my age...and insecure."

Billy frowned and reached for a cigarette. "I don't understand. What has insecurity got to do with dumping your kids?"

"I thought Fred wouldn't accept me if I had kids. I was afraid kids would scare him off. I felt he didn't want the burden of children...and...if I was without kids, he'd find me more attractive."

"That's not insecurity. It's selfishness."

"You're right. I was very selfish."

"Do you want something to drink? There's beer in the refrigerator."

"No thank you."

Billy looked at his mother, trying to remember what life was like when she was around. He could not remember much of anything, except the time she bought him a baseball glove for his birthday. He wondered how she could have aged so much in so little time. But then again, it was twelve years ago and he thought that could be a long time for a woman under pressure.

"You were never there."

"I know. I was gone a lot."

"All the time. What's the matter? You didn't like Sammy and me?"

"I loved you kids."

"You sure had a funny way of showing it. I love you—good bye."

"I told you I was immature and I felt I was missing out on so much by having to take care of two little children when I was barely twenty-five years old myself. Maybe if your father wasn't killed…"

Billy lumbered over to the refrigerator to get himself another Old Milwaukee beer. This was getting ridiculous, he thought. She must be feeling guilty.

"Don't worry about it. It's no big deal."

"It *is* a big deal. I left you kids with nothing."

"Don't worry. We made out okay. Why worry about something that happened so long ago? You seen Sammy?"

"No. I can't find him. Do you know where he is?"

"No."

"I have some money for you."

"What?"

"Some money. I want to give you some money."

"What for?"

"Because I owe you something. I feel terrible about leaving you and I want to make it up."

"It's a little late."

Billy was feeling uncomfortable. He wished his mother had not come back. She was making him nervous and he did not know what to say to her. It seemed to be getting darker in the room. He could barely see the outline of her blue dress.

"Billy?"

"Yes."

"Do you want me to leave?"

"…I don't know…"

"I want you to take this money."

"I don't want it, really."

"I bet you could use some extra money."

"I'm doing alright."

"Where are you working?"

"Conagra. In Crozet."

"Do they have good benefits? Benefits are important."

"Yeah. I get good benefits. You still with Fred?"

"Yes. We live in Raleigh."

"North Carolina?"

"Yes."

"Would you do me a favor?"

"Sure."

"There's a guy I went to high school with. His name is Bobby Ramsey. He lives in Raleigh and works at a golf course. Could you call him up sometime and tell him I said hello. He's a good friend of mine. He'll remember."

"Sure son. I will do that."

"Look, I gotta split. I told some guys I would meet them…"

"Of course. Do you need anything?"

"No. I'm alright."

"Please take this money. It's yours."

"No. It's not mine. You don't owe me anything. You worry too much."

"I just wanted to make sure you are doing okay."

"I'm fine. Can't you see?"

"Well, you look a little thin. Do you eat right?"

"Sure. I really have to leave. I have to meet some guys."

"I understand. Can I come and see you again?

"Sure. I'm not hard to find."

"Billy."

"Yes."

"I love you."

"I love you too. You worry too much."

"I know."

Billy's mother walked out the door and drove off in a black Honda accord with a personalized license plate reading "BYTE ME."

SAILIN' TO MADRID

Chris arrived early at his uncle's garage and began setting up the equipment. He was tuning his guitar when Billy bounded recklessly into the driveway in his rusty old pickup truck.

"Hey! Give me a hand with this stuff, okay?"

Chris went over to haul equipment and saw the camcorder in the back of the truck.

"Come on, Billy. What are you *really* doing with this camera?"

"Shooting a skunk."

Chris wondered what the remark meant, but decided not to pursue the subject. Todd and Dutch soon pulled in the driveway and Chris was pleased that the band was back in action and rehearsing. Immediately, Dutch began cursing his amplifier, but at least it was finally working. Billy was a bit drunk and cranky. Todd was wearing a new silver cross around his neck, looking dazed and confused as usual. Well, thought Chris, everything appears to be normal. After getting the equipment in order and tuning their instruments, the band started to loosen up, quietly laying down an old Jimmy Reed riff, with Billy singing slow moaning blues...

> *You got me runnin,' you got me hidin'*
> *You got me run, hide, run, hide*
> *Anyway you want me, let roll...roll...roll...*
> *You got me doin' what you want me*
> *Baby, what you want me to do...*

Todd picked up the lazy Mississippi Delta beat with his drums. Chris came in right behind him with a gentle, breezy three note bass line, and Billy sang and played his guitar with Eric Clayton-like intensity. Dutch and Billy traded traditional, deep blues licks. The band was rusty, but the familiar tune gave them renewed confidence very quickly. They jammed on the song for a few minutes until Billy announced that he was "bored with that old shit" and they decided to try out one of Chris' early tunes, *Highway Buster*. The song began with one long blistering scream and today Billy was up to the task. He grabbed the microphone and bellowed:

> *BUSTIN' OUTTA HERE!!!*
> *GOT TWO LANE FEVER, ALL THE WAY!!!*

The band tore the song apart. Todd pounded on the drums, like a caged gorilla wrecking a suitcase, his cross flying wildly around his neck. Dutch was standing on a garbage can pumping windmills with his arm. Billy was playing his own brand of breakneck speed guitar, his hands blazing up and down the neck of the Stratocaster. Billy grabbed the microphone, shouting:

> *YOU SAID YOU LOVED ME*
> *YOU SAID YOU REALLY CARED!*
> *I TOOK TO THE HIGHWAY*
> *SO YOU WON'T FIND ME CRAWLING UP YOUR STAIRS*
> *YOU WON'T FIND ME—ANYWHERE!*

After the song was finished, the band worked on several more songs and a play list for Trax. Chris had reworked *Dark Side of the Blind* and changed the title to *Sailin' to Madrid*. Billy sang the new version, accompanied only by his acoustic guitar:

> *When the waves crashed, I held you tight with my eyes closed*
> *On a lonely coast, when the sea swells—and the wind blows*
>
> *It was late July, the waves were high, as the fog was rollin' in*
> *We gathered shells on a distant beach, and tossed them in the sand*

What did you say on that stormy night, before you ran and hid?
I'm sorry, my love, when the morning comes, I'm sailin' to Madrid.

Yes, I'm sailin' Yes, I'm sailin' Yes, I'm sailin'
...to Madrid...

Sailors rushed back home to shore, the lighthouse looming light
O'er the raging sea, I could hear you sigh
What did you say that night?

I never thought you'd leave me plain, on a beach in late July
The storm raged on; the sails were torn
I began to wonder why

Yes, I'm sailin' Yes, I'm sailin' Yes, I'm sailin'
...to Madrid

Billy sang the song with great passion. He said he would work a little on the phrasing and maybe change a few of the words. Chris' new song about oil spills *The Coast is Not Clear* was rejected by everyone else, especially Billy who found it too political and boring. They included most of the songs Chris had written in the past three years, including some of the heavy metal numbers.

"What are we going to close with?" asked Dutch.

"How about *Vice Grip*?" suggested Billy.

"What about a cover song?" asked Chris.

"What? *Sweet Baby James*?" asked Billy.

"Very funny. What about *Jumping Jack Flash?*

Chris thought the guys would reject the song, but they surprised him be agreeing to end with the Rolling Stones anthem.

RAYS OF
POWERED SODIUM

After rehearsal Dutch went back to his room and found Ginger crawling on the floor, picking up bits of paper.

"Hey! What's up? You attempting *clean* this place?"

"Of course not. You think I'm nuts?"

"Well, what *are* you doing?"

"I'm collecting your poems."

"What for?"

"They should be compiled in some order. I'm going to type them on the same kind of paper, so it will look like a book of poems. Maybe you should send them to a publisher."

"I don't know…"

"Why not?"

"It's really tough to get a book of poems published. Besides, I wouldn't know where to start."

"Don't worry, I'll take care of that. Where are the rest of them?"

"Well…there's some in the bathroom. I think there might be some in my other clothes. I'll look." Dutch searched through the clothes in his closet and found six scraps of paper with poems scribbled on them. He handed them to Ginger. She read one of them:

Black Mission

The ultramarine skies with burning funnels
Racing from Abyssinian plateaus, to the heights of Zanzibar
Days and days with rheumatism in the back, camel trotting

Past the strongholds of Ethiopian monarchs, as Europe crumbles
Caravans plunder from Choa, surrender slaves, exotic women
The Coast of Africa, hotter than Hades in July
Houses the Egyptian army, cavalry, and phantom hoards of gold

"I like this one," she said.

"I was in my Rimbaud period," he said, working his way across the room to the refrigerator. "Want something to drink?"

"Sure. I'll take a coke."

Dutch retrieved a beer and brought Ginger a Coke. He sat down on the couch.

"Hey, I've been thinking." he said. "We've been going out for two months, right?"

"Right."

"Do you think we're boyfriend, girlfriend by now?"

"Yes. I don't want to go out with anyone else, if that's what you mean."

"I guess it's what I mean."

"What *do* you mean?"

"I don't know…maybe something more serious…"

"More serious than living and sleeping together?"

"Yes…"

"What? Getting married?"

"Something like that."

"Something like that? There is no something like that. There's no such thing as being a little bit married. We've only known each other for two months."

"So…?"

"I'm still in school."

"So…?"

"What are we going to live on? The money you make at Jake's?"

"Yes."

"That the most ridiculous idea I've heard in a long time."

"So, what's the answer?"

"Okay."

"Okay?"

"I said okay, didn't I?"

"Of course you did," said Dutch, completely stunned. "I need a beer." Dutch got himself another Old Milwaukee from the refrigerator and collapsed on the couch, sighing deeply.

"I'll be damned. You said yes."

"It'll be tough for a while until I get out of school and get a real job, but we can make it. I'll get a part-time job."

Ginger continued to collect the bits of poetic paper tossed haphazardly about the tiny room. Dutch drank his beer, truly contented for one of the few times in his life. "We'll have to make plans," she said, as she began reading one of the poems found scrawled on the back of a candy wrapper.

> *Giant serpents from gnarled trees*
> *Drool rays of powdered sodium*
> *Smacking terrible irony on the lips*
> *Night farces unabated, into the forest*
> *While exorcists scramble for lost souls*
> *Amid the distant whine of solemn priests*

"I like your stuff," she said, "But it's always so dark and eerie—the language is very mournful and decadent."

"I can't help it. I don't know why, but everything comes out sounding like I'm the angel of death knocking at your door."

"It's not *that* bad. You can knock at my door any time."

"I'm really not that depressed, or anything. I mean, I'm happy. You know what I mean…It's just when I sit down to write something, everything looks a lot blacker."

"Intellectuals deal in despair."

"What?"

"That's what they do. Maybe you're not an intellectual, but look at all the great minds—they were all dealing with dread and despondency—Marx, Nietzsche, Freud…"

"I guess you're right. So, I'm in good company, right?"

"You have a ways to go to top those guys."

Dutch grabbed a piece of paper and began a poem, but lost his concentration. "How are we going to do it...you know...get married."

"I don't think it's that hard. It's quite common."

"What about a wedding? That seems like a big deal."

"I don't want a wedding. I want to go to a justice of the peace, get married, then go away to a nice cabin in the mountains for about a week."

"You got this all figured out already?"

"Well, we certainly can't have a traditional wedding since your parents don't even speak to each other and my parents will simply disown me. They may be ex-hippies, but they're not ready for me to get married right now."

"Okay, so let's do it."

"One thing though."

"What?"

"I want to drive the motorcycle to our honeymoon destination after the ceremony."

"You want to drive a BMW motorcycle?"

"I sure do. And you're going to teach me, right?"

"Hey, no problem. We'll start tomorrow."

DEVIL INSIDE

It was early in the evening when Austin Macon came into Ben O'Leary's dorm room and asked him if he had any dope. Ben told him that he blew his last joint trying to pick up a freshman at the kami kaze party last night.

"Dude, who was she?"

"Who?"

"The freshman, dude. Kamikaza party."

"You mean her name?"

"Yeah."

"Sandy. No, Cynthia…something like that."

"Dude, good sex?"

"No imagination. Hey, I gotta study, ya know?"

To Ben's great relief, Austin left. He had trouble with anyone who used the word "dude" more than once a week. Ben went to the phone to call Laura, but got the answering machine instead. Then he remembered that she might have left for the "fuck-me-red" lipstick party. He was stuck for something to do until he remembered the nice girl he met at Foxfield and took to the *Zete* party. He rummaged through his closest until he found his black shorts. Inside, there was a small crumpled piece of paper with the name Sarah Carter and her phone number. He remembered her as a classy, bright, girl with blonde hair and freckles. He could not, however, remember the line he gave her. Perhaps, it was the one about being raised in a ghetto. Or maybe it was the one about how his father used to beat him all the time. He tried to remember the conversation, but he was very stoned and could not remember any details. He thought perhaps it had something to do with school, or tests. Then it hit him. It was the story about his uncle being the Dean of Arts and Sciences. That one worked every time. Ben reached for the phone and dialed her number.

"Hello."

"Hello, Sarah?"

"This is Ben…from the other night."

"Oh, hi. How are you?"

"Fine. Look, I want to apologize for what happened at the party. It was all my fault."

"Oh, that's alright. I didn't know you had a girlfriend."

"I don't. At least not now. Laura and I broke up."

"Sorry to hear that."

"I was wondering if you want to go to Coup de Ville's tonight. There's a great blues band playing."

"Oh, I don't know. I really need to study."

"I told you! My uncle's got that all fixed!"

"Oh, sure. I don't know…"

"Look, give me one more chance. No foul-ups this time. Honest."

"Well, alright."

Ben hung up the phone and smiled to himself. He reveled in his ability to fool women and charm them with his striking good looks and exaggerated Irish charm. Inside, he really did not like women at all. He held nothing but contempt for such guileless creatures that could be so easily fooled by his dishonesty. He was glad he was young and handsome. Ben reached into his pocket and produced a marijuana joint and lit it. Taking a deep drag, he held the smoke in his lungs a few seconds before blowing a blue plume of smoke toward the ceiling. He opened the window and looked down at a group of guys playing Frisbee on the quad, and somewhere in the distance he heard the thunderous clanging of a church bell. The church bell reminded him that he had missed his two o'clock class, but he couldn't remember what class he was missing. In the distance he could see the outline of Monticello, standing majestically amid the glorious beauty of the Blue Ridge Mountains. He wondered what Thomas Jefferson would think about what had become of his university. Ben could not think of any of his friends that were not on some kind of dope; no one gave a rat's ass about books or ideas, and half the students did not even know that Jefferson wrote the Declaration of Independence. He gazed once again over the breadth of the campus and marveled at the stupidity of it all. No one called the campus a "campus." The grounds were pompously referred to as "the lawns." He tried taking another toke on the joint, but it had gone out. He put the roach in an ashtray on the couch. At this moment the lawns were occupied by students enjoying a moderately warm March day as Ben surveyed the action atop his dorm room. In addition to the Frisbee players, he spotted a tennis foursome playing a heated doubles match, several students who looked like long-haired independents having a conversation under the evergreen trees that lined the quad, numerous random students strolling to class clutching their ubiquitous backpacks, a psychology professor rushing to class, smoking a pipe and saying "hello" to all the students he passed, a few earnest joggers in designer spandex crisscrossing the quad, and two athletic guys playfully tossing a football. He looked back at the Frisbee players and saw that Harry Drew was one of the participants. He tried in vain to remember if he had slept with Harry Drew, but he giggled to himself as he thought about "drawing a blank" about Harry Drew. He went over to the stereo, rummaged through his CD's and found a copy of INXS's latest release. He put the CD in the changer and soon the pulsating, driving beat of "Devil Inside" filled the room. He slumped on his couch, stretched his left hand, and extracted the long roach from the ashtray. He took out a pack of matches and relit the joint. Feeling paranoid, he walked near the window again and turned on a fan beside the half-opened window. He looked around for his spray can of Lysol disinfectant, but he could not find it. Christ, he thought, this place smells like Rashifarian ghangi festival. He heard a knock at the door.

"Uh...who is it?"

"Austin."

"Hey, wait a minute, will ya?"

Ben quickly crushed out the joint and stashed the ashtray under the couch. He opened the door slightly ajar.

"Yeah?"

"What are you doing?"

"Studying—I told you. I'm busy."

"Can I come in for a minute?"

"Look, I'm busy, okay?"

"Just a minute. I want to tell you something."

Ben opened the door and allowed Austin to enter. Austin immediately smelled the marijuana.

"I thought you were out."

"I just had one roach left, okay?"

"Dude, who's that playing?"

"INXS."

"Let me see the CD."

Ben secured the CD from pile of CDs and tapes on his coffee table. He handed the CD to Austin, then sat down on the couch.

"In x's?"

"Huh…?"

"Dude, I don't get it."

"Jesus, Austin, are you that dense? *In excess,* okay?"

Austin frowned and put the CD back on the coffee table. Ben leaned back, listening to the music:

> *Devil inside…devil inside*
> *Every single one of us*
> *A devil inside…*

Ben leaned back on the sofa, closed his eyes, and listened intently to the music, forgetting for the moment that Austin was in the room. Ben was daydreaming about the time he slept with Mary Kennedy and Louise Pentz at the same time last semester. He thought about how delicious they looked performing oral sex on each other while he masturbated in front of them. He opened his eyes half way, feeling drowsy and slightly euphoric. He could barely make out Austin standing before him, staring into space, not saying anything. He wished Austin would go away. Instead, Austin began unbuttoning his blue Izod sport shirt, slowly from top to bottom. He swung the shirt over his left shoulder, letting it drop to the floor. He was bare-chested with no hair on his chest. Ben stared at him, still woozy and unfocussed. Austin did not say anything. Ben was not sure what to do, so he did nothing. Austin methodically unzipped his pants, moving toward Ben, brushing his long thin, blonde hair out of his eyes. Ben stared at Austin as he sat down next to Ben. Austin took off his pants and placed them on the coffee table. Austin was down to his underwear and Ben was feeling aroused. Austin reached over and put his arms around Ben and kissed him on the mouth. Ben turned away, and wiped his lips.

"I don't do that," he said as he took off his shirt and slipped out of his pants, dropping them to the floor.

Austin moved closer to Ben so that the two men were sitting side-by-side in their underwear. Ben pushed Austin away from him and took off his underwear, revealing an erect penis. Ben lay down on his back and motioned Austin to come to him. Austin pealed his underwear away from himself and crawled toward Ben. He placed Ben's penis in his mouth and began sucking and stroking it while Ben moaned, dropping his head further back against the pillow. Austin continued to suck and stroke Ben until Ben was writhing in pleasure, thrusting his buttocks into the air as Austin sucked more violently on his penis. Finally Ben came in Austin's mouth and they both collapsed on the couch, sweating and breathing hard. Within seconds, Ben got up and put his clothes on.

""I've got a class," said Austin.

"Me too," said Ben.

Austin got up from the couch, putting on his shirt and pants.

"See ya," he said.

Ben said nothing. He turned away and looked out the window.

> *Devil inside, devil inside*
> *Every single one of us*
> *A devil inside...*

He could still hear, above the din, the sounds of Frisbee players beneath his window and, once again, the thunderous clanging of the church bell in the distance.

INTO THE
GREAT UNKNOWN

Dutch began teaching Ginger how to ride his bike in preparation for the wedding, but for Ginger it quickly became more than riding one time at the end of the wedding. She wanted to ride all the time. They changed their minds about getting married by a justice of the peace and opted instead to make their vows in a small, cozy historical Methodist church outside of Charlottesville. Ginger picked it out although neither of them were Methodist. She spotted the church one day while visiting a friend and fell in love with the breathtaking, picturesque view of the Shenandoah Valley from the front steps. Ginger was becoming proficient at operating the powerful, yet maneuverable motorcycle. It took her a while to get used to shifting the gears with her feet, and controlling the gas intake with her right hand, while releasing the clutch with her left hand, but Dutch was a very patient teacher. Soon she was tooling down the highways on her own and beginning to get the feel of the motorcycle. It was a 1975 candy apple red R-60 BMW model with a liquid-cooled, 50 degree tandem V-twin engine, multi-reflector headlights, drag-style bars, radial tires, thin aggressive mufflers, mirrors, and a set of cruiseliner bags draped across the back of the bike. Dutch had rebuilt the motorcycle from scratch after buying it at a junkyard for $300.00.

Ginger enjoyed the thrill of motorcycle riding. She loved the way the massive engine responded with power as she twisted the throttle with her right hand, easing the clutch with her left, while shifting the five-speed transmission with her right foot. She began to wear black leather pants, a motorcycle jacket, and a pair of rugged leather biker boots. Dutch bought her a new helmet. She liked to cruise the twisting country roads, leaning sideways as the bike banked the turns with pinpoint precision and delicate balance. She loved the exhilaration of speeding 70 miles an hour with your feet barely five inches above the ground, the wind in her face, blowing her hair away in all directions. She began to go out by herself, sometimes preferring the isolation of riding in a vehicle completely shut off from the rest of the world. With only the sounds of the roaring engine in her ears, she was able to concentrate on the landscape and sights around the valley. She like to travel the back roads free from signs and billboards, where groves, meadows, orchards, and lawns came almost to the shoulder; where little kids on bicycles would wave the arms wildly as she zoomed by; where the old, lonesome-looking people on porches would look at her and think of their younger days; where a whole flock of red-winged black birds would rise up and take flight, sometimes following her in formation along the curvy roads; where dark cirrus clouds signaled a cold front by moving swiftly across the fields and valleys; where the crest of the barren snow-capped mountains dominated your view as she climbed upward toward the top of the mountain. As she sped through the tight, narrow roads, she often achieved a Zen-like state of consciousness, a feeling of being completely free, without worry or regret. Dutch was very excited about Ginger's interest in the bike and encouraged her to ride as often as she wanted. He literally took a back seat to her, letting her ride the bike as he held on tightly behind her.

The wedding day was scheduled for the first of March. They had reserved a cabin on Afton Mountain in the heart of the Blue Ridge Mountains. They planned to stay in the mountains for a week, building a fire every day, cooking romantic candlelit dinners in the early evening, and making love all night. They were determined to live a simple life and felt the cabin was a great symbolic way to begin their married lives together. The wedding was simple and dignified. Dutch asked Chris, Todd, and Billy to be "best men" and the three of them served as witnesses to the ceremony. The reverend of the church read the vows. Dutch slipped a diamond ring on her hand, and they ran out of the church dodging handfuls of rice thrown by the other barfly boys. The townspeople caught quite a sight that day as they looked and heard the roar of a motorcycle on a cold, windy March day, spotting a man dressed in a suit and his bride wearing a black leather jacket over a white, strapless cocktail dress blistering down the a narrow country road.

Ginger was driving the motorcycle and Dutch was clutching to her as they snaked their way around the side roads of the county. Dutch was normally relaxed on the back of the bike and felt very confident about Ginger's ability to control the motorcycle. On this day, he thought that she was driving a bit too fast, knowing she was naturally excited and anxious to get to the cabin. He tried to put his nervous thoughts out of his mind, but as they were careening around a tight corner, he couldn't help but think about the road conditions and the possibility of hitting an icy spot left over from the snowstorm a few nights ago. He almost yelled in her ear for her to slow down and watch out for patches of ice, but he did not want to spoil her mood and the thrill of the ride.

They came upon a loaded dump truck moving slowly in the right lane. Ginger leaned over, looked ahead, and then pulled quickly on the throttle, jettisoning the bike into the passing lane, roaring down a straightaway. She approached a turn in the road, downshifted into third gear and swung the cycle around the blind curve. The side of the mountain cast a shadow on this part of the road throughout the day and the temperature of the surface was well below freezing. There was no way Ginger could have predicted the patch of ice would be waiting for her at the height of the curve, as she adroitly maneuvered the bike around the bend in the road. As it happened, she was traveling much too fast to avoid the frozen section of the road. As she rounded the turn, she made a desperate attempt to veer off and steer clear of the danger, but the tires skidded sideways into the ice patch at breakneck speed. Spinning hopelessly out of control, the bike slid recklessly toward a grove of trees bordering the side of the road. Dutch braced himself for the collision, grabbing onto Ginger, and screaming for her to look out for herself. The last thing Dutch remembered as the motorcycle exploded on impact, was Ginger slipping out of his hands, flying into the air, soaring into the great unknown.

SPRING

Mr. Buford

Driving leisurely down highway 29, Wally Buford could smell the fresh scent of April in the air. He gazed at the sloping rolling hills beginning to glisten from the gradually warming sunshine. In the distance, he could see the eastern slopes of the Blue Ridge Mountains rising majestically above the valley farms and lowlands. Numerous small creeks surrounded by tiny young flowers emerging from winter's retreat honeycombed the land itself, fertile and turning greener. Early buds from may apple, bloodroot, and witch hazel were launching their spring debut. Every few miles he spotted old, wrinkle-faced farmers in blue-jeaned overalls; their sturdy work horses, working together, plowing up the first shards of earth in preparation for spring planting. Bales of hay were already being rolled into tightly wound balls. They dotted the landscape like giant pieces of shredded wheat for a breakfast-hungry giant. The picturesque hillside and former battlegrounds reminded him of the Old South and the Civil War. During intervals on the road, he could easily imagine the boys in blue and gray exchanging gunfire in the open fields, and former battlegrounds. He halfway expected to see a squad of Confederate soldiers come marching out of the woods. But then, abruptly, reality would intrude upon his fantasy and he would encounter a new Toyota dealership with gaudy neon signs proclaiming the latest magnificent no-money-down deals. Occasionally, small herds of horses galloped effortlessly beside the red, wooden fences of the horse farms. Dark green, broad-leafed plants sprung out along the roadside and Virginia pine trees populated the countryside in all directions. He had not felt this good in a long time. At first, he could not understand why Richard did not tell *Mean Streets* to send a demo like everyone else, but he knew Richard loved his niece and so he had promised to send someone in person. Wally was glad his boss sent him to check out this band. He was getting tired of working in the office all day, and felt the road trip would do him some good. As he approached the city limits of Charlottesville, he wondered idly what the real estate prices were like in the area.

After checking into the Sheraton hotel, Mr. Buford called Leslie Richards.

"Hello, Leslie?"

"Yes."

"This is Wally Buford...from Musidisc."

"Oh, yes! How are you?"

"I'm fine. I just arrived in town. Have you made all the arrangements?"

"Yes. I talked to Mr. Greco, the manager, and he said they were on for Tuesday night—around eight o'clock."

"Great. What's the name of the place?"

"Trax. Spelled T-R-A-X. It's on Downing Street, right off Main."

"I'll find it."

"I hope they put on a good show. We've had a rough couple of weeks down here."

"What do you mean?"

"There was a motorcycle accident. Dutch, the guitar player, broke his leg in three places. His wife wasn't so lucky. She's still in a coma."

"I'm sorry to hear that."

"We're all hoping for the best. Anyway, I can't thank you enough, Mr. Buford. This means so much to the band."

"Don't mention it. But don't get your hopes up. I listen to a lot of bands, and to be honest, we don't sign very many of them."

"That's okay—as long as they have a fighting chance."

"They certainly have that."

"Well, thanks, again, Mr. Buford."

"You're welcome. See you Tuesday night."

"Oh, Mr. Buford—"

"Yes."

"We're all going to a local bar tonight. Would you like to come?"

"I might do that."

"It's on Canal Street. It's called Jake's.

"I'll find it. Thanks."

The Only
Thing That Lasts

"TO ALL MY FRRR...IENDS!!! TO ALL MY FRRR...IENDS!!!"

Jake's was louder than usual because the whole bar knew that *Mean Streets* would be playing at Trax on the following Tuesday night. Billy was sitting at the bar talking to Jake.

"How about a beer?" asked Billy. "I can't dig this scene...You know what I mean?"

"I know what you mean," said Jake. "You want a drink."

"Don't be so sarcastic. It doesn't become you."

"Okay, Billy. Have it your way. How are rehearsals going?"

"Terrific. We could play Madison Square Garden tonight."

"Good luck Tuesday night."

"Thanks, Jake. You're okay, you know that?"

"Yeah, sure. Who's that with Leslie?"

"He's a big-time record dude. He's gonna listen to us Tuesday night. If he likes us, we may escape this town."

"Where's Sarah? She's the only one I haven't seen tonight."

"Probably having dinner at the country club."

"Did she and Chris break up?"

"As far as I know. She sure hasn't been around much."

Billy disappeared into the crowd and joined Chris and Todd who were in the process of testing a newcomer to be a certified barfly. The new kid was in his early twenties, dressed in dirty navy work pants and a T-shirt with a chain saw and the word, "Sthil" embossed on the front. He sported a tattoo on his left bicep that read, "Live Free or Die" and his potbelly protruded out from underneath his shirt. He looked like he had not taken a bath in weeks. Billy thought the guy certainly looked the part and thought that maybe he could be the first one in a long time to pass the test. The newcomer was doing very well and he only had two more questions. If he answered them correctly, he would become a regular barfly. A crowd was beginning to gather as the word spread that someone was close to passing.

"Alright," said Chris. "So far, so good. You have two more left. First, What did Tolstoy say?"

The newcomer was relaxed and sure of himself, not sweaty and nervous like most of them. He hesitated a moment, then quoted the famous author:

"Regard the society of women as a necessary unpleasantness of life, and avoid it as much as possible."

Chris looked at Todd and they nodded approvingly to each other.

"CORRECTO-MUNDO!!!" shouted Todd. "One more question for the grand prizes—the trip to Hawaii and the Samsonite luggage!"

The newcomer continually stroked his long, straight greasy hair to the left side of his head. He looked cross-eyed, a bit drunk, yet in control. He tilted his face to the ceiling and raised one eyebrow in a comic motion.

"Okay," said Chris. "This is it. Are you ready?"

"Sure."

"What is more important than truth?"

The newcomer looked at his shoes, tilted his head toward the ceiling one more time, and grabbed a beer. He stared at the beer label, slowly took a drink, and set the bottle on the bar. He uttered one word:

"Stamina."

Several of the regulars groaned. Chris and Todd showed no emotion.

"Sorry," said Chris. "Wrong answer."

The newcomer, unfazed, slugged down his beer, shrugged his shoulders, and said, "Oh, well, time to get wasted."

The crowd dispersed. Chris and Todd went over to shoot some pool. A few people lingered at the bar. Harry, one of the regulars, asked Jake for a couple beers.

"Hey," said Harry. "Give this guy a beer. He came mighty close."

The newcomer started laughing and slugged the beer in one gulp. After he finished, he raised his glass above his head and shouted, "TO HATRED!!!"

To which the whole crowd responded immediately: "THE ONLY THING THAT LASTS!!!"

Someone played a Tom Petty song and people began to yell and dance and shout lines from the movie.

"YOU HIRED A DICK…"

"—TO FIND AN ASSHOLE!!!"

"WANDA LOOKS LIKE…

"—A DISTRESSED GODDESS!!!"

"UNORIGINAL MACHO…"

"—ENERGY!!!"

"HEY, I CAN GET A GIRL…"

"—FOR TEN MINUTES!!!"

"DON'T WORRY, NOBODY'S EVER LOVED ME YET!!!"

The place was so wild that Jake thought the roof might cave in. He was standing near the cash register pouring a draft beer. A customer leaned over and asked him what was more important than truth.

"I don't know," said Jake. "I've never seen the movie."

Another customer named Lionel turned toward the man and said, "endurance."

"Endurance? What kind of an answer is that?" asked the customer.

"Apparently, the right one," said Jake.

FIRE NEXT TIME

...I looked and saw before me the passionless images of the vulgar and the lost.

...began to wander throughout this world immune to the plague before us. Butcher, baker, candlestick maker...auto mechanic, whatever. I'm cat-like in the wickedness of darkness. Watch the police and the taxman miss me, I'm mobile. You can't touch this. I see (what else?) the grimy smudges of life through my MTV and I see that it is good and prophetic. Blessed are those who hear it. For they shall inherit the kingdom, the power and the MTV story...What kind of life is this? I will tell you, listen...It is one riddled throughout with old, cantankerous disquiet, dank rage, and veiled threats. The continuing prophetic exaltations are a true testament to my faith in a supremely happy ending. I am, after all, unscathed upon my dread despair. Put the message in the box or bottle. Janet Jackson is a black cat. I see her with a baseball cap tipped to the side like she's super cool. Super Cool J. Like John Rev. Super Seer, John Rev. Stray Cats, rev it up and go! All of the finest sounds in our land, freeing us from our sins by His blood, as he dresses in His white robe reaching down to his feet, eyes like blazing fire, hands like a sharp double-edged sword, ruling baby, ruling, till the end of time. Till the end of...till the end of...time...time...time...see what's become of me, as I gaze into my possibilities. Time out for the lost requiem for the loveliest dead God conveyed to this world in a sense of the ideal, an eternity of funereal gloom. It's too frightening to behold. My ancestors were slave owners, just like yours. Did you see the scum in my neighborhood? Is it close? Hey, are those Bugle Boy jeans you're wearing? And so, I opened the second seal and changed the channel, and went back to my MTV. Oh, Iggy Pop, you're so skinny. You should wear Levi's 501's and take Totally Pauli off the air. Please, I can't stand him. Take me back, I'm begging please.

Take me back, I'm on my knees. Oh, sweet lips, tremulous with desire. Oh, those really are Bugle Boy jeans you're wearing. Come here, honey. Come on, Gloria. Gonna come to my house. Gonna knock on my door. Come and touch me. Touch the crazy monkey. And say, hey! I feel an earthquake. I hear a thousand peals of thunder. I see a dozen flashes of lightening. A third of the sea turned to blood. It's a revelation! I'm not kidding, this time it's for real. The big ball in the sky will burn you, like a slurn, as soon as He opens the Seventh Seal. But until then it's the same ole situation for us motley crews. And even for you clean-cut types, like Wilson Phillips sitting around a piano. Real clean. It's a clean machine. Do the Bartman. Come on, man. Do the Jane's Addiction. It's a clean machine. Very Strange!

I looked again and saw the filth and vermin at the end of an all night souse. Yahweh's war-bow flashes like lightning, jasper and carnelian emerald, sapphire and diamonds, stoned of paradise. We are swimming in the face of time and everyone is drowning, tomb-like. Rock me, babe. Rock me all night long. Is it close? Can you feel the clinging scum all around us? Ten thousand angels stand before Him and he needs no counselor. These ministers fall down before the cherubim, the majesty of the firmament of the light. Okay, so don't touch me. I'm a monkey. Even for you California girls and gigolos. Hey! I'm just a gigolo. Who could care less? Deal with it. Oh well...another fuckin' planet down the tubes. I'm like...you know...in a lunatic asylum with permission to masturbate. It's great. I don't care if the earth is smeared with putrid bacon grease, or Kevin Bacon. Shock the monkey. Snap! I got the power. You can't touch this. In fact, you can't touch anything. It musta been ice, ice, baby, fire next time...time...see what's become of me. Fight the power. I seem to have contacted a mortal wound, giving breath to the image of the beast. Another mark of redemption flashing before my TV eyes. Who is making that sound like a harp? The Harptones? A loud voice just cried out a condemnation of everyone, except Vanilla Ice. It must be a call for the endurance of the saints. The smoke of their torment goes up forever and ever...Madonna? Hey, whom am I talking to?

...looked once again into the eyes of the beast. He will strike the children dead, you'll see. Just like me...deader than a fuckin' doorknob. Transparent crystal suffused with a warm light by the fireplace. I am dazzled by the vision of the throne...behold the sun chariot. Lumbering memory thrilled at its revealing...what? Chaos? Yellow as sulpher, the brittle earth oozes and moans like an old whore, tired and beaten, with painful sores broken out on every part of her body. Three evil spirits, which looked like frogs, leapt into the blood red sky, as a rider on horseback passed them toward the sun. Riders on the storm. Like an actor out on loan. It's doomsday on Main Street. Close the barbershop, Floyd. Smoke bellows from the heart and liver of a fish, incense in a spoon, smoke rising from the burning coals, dispelling demons. I want my...I want

my MTV. And out of the TV I saw light of the lamb and blood of the new prophets revving up ole John for his last vision. Let's hope he completes his task before the next commercial. But alas, M.C. Hammer comes on drinking a Pepsi and singing "Feelings" which must be an ode to God, or me, or somebody. Feeling profuse perspiration, trembling, delirium tremens, mania a' potu, must be cerebral inflammation. Remember, it had seven horns and seven eyes that are the seven spirits of God set forth into all earth. Hey, mom! You can't touch this! Angels and creation, the earthly disharmony and cosmic catastrophes girded on His armor and waged battles, protecting the host with his sword. Future looks dreary bleak. Another bubble gum teenybopper as—sugarface. But then, look! Idolaters are going to be tortured with fire and brimstone, not the Rolling Stones. I saw on my MTV an angel swinging his sickle on the green earth, gathering the vintage, which he cast into the great wine press of the wrath of God. Ah, the seven angels with the seven plagues see another wonderful portent.

Back to programming as Martha Quinn says, "In one hour, wealth will be brought to ruin." Martha sits down in her director's chair and leans back with a bottle of Blue Nun wine in her hand. "Here's to you whores!" she bellows. "Let's drink to the wine of God's fury.!" Suddenly, from the left side of the studio, a scarlet beast, wearing an Alice Cooper T-shirt, bolts toward Martha and just before she takes another swig of wine, the beast devours her. You can see blood and guts everywhere, as her legs are dangling out of the mouth of the beast. After Martha has been eaten, the beast raises the wine to his lips and proclaims, "Just like sugar and spice and everything nice!"

A voice from nowhere says, "We'll be right back after this announcement."

Hallucinating Death

Billy was sitting in his room watching his latest video production of Alicia having sex in her bedroom. He was fascinated by the images on the screen, the movement of bodies in space and time, the steamy symmetry of sex in heated moments of lust and desperation. In the beginning of the video, he saw Alicia and her lover quietly embracing one another; they kissed softly and displayed a brief moment of tenderness. Billy couldn't believe it. He had never imagined that Alicia could display an ounce of warmth toward any human being. Following a few minutes of cuddling, the sex turned much cruder as her lover pinned her arms behind her back, and stood over her, thrusting his penis into her very violently. Alicia loved it. "Fuck my pussy!" she yelled with reckless abandonment, as her lover jammed harder and harder into her. The sex talk evolved into a litany of graphic exaltations. Billy was amazed at the things people said in bed when they thought no one was around. He heard Alicia scream "Deeper! Deeper!," "Fuck me! Fuck me!!" and "Harder! Harder!." After he came in her, she was still unsatisfied. She wanted oral sex. "Do you want to see it? Do you? Do you want to see it?" "Yes," he said, "I want to see it and suck it and fuck you again and again…" What else do you want to do?" she asked "I want to fuck you up the ass—" Suddenly, Billy heard someone at the door. He quickly pulled the tape out of the VCR and hid it behind the couch.

"Wait a minute!"

He opened the door and found Todd facing him, looking tense and spaced out. Todd did not come around very often. In fact, nobody came to Billy's very often.

"Hey."

"Hey. What's going on?"

"Nothing," said Billy. "I'm not being a bowler tomorrow."

"Why not?"

"Too boring. Unoriginal brain-dead stupidity."

"Yeah. What's the point?"

"Precisely."

"I got a problem," said Todd.

"Yeah? You should try working in a frozen food factory."

"I know your job sucks."

"So, what's the problem? Too much sex?"

"I don't know…things are all messed up."

"Todd, things have been messed up for at least a million years. What's new about that?"

"I'm scared all the time."

"Of what?"

"Death."

"Hey, welcome to the party. I'm the one living next to a funeral home and you're the one who thinks about death all the time? You should be here on Sundays."

"Yeah, I know. But I can't seem to get it off my mind. Like, I'm hallucinating death all the time. Todd looked Billy straight in the face, piercing his eyes with a thousand-yard-stare. There was not an ounce of joke about him.

"What?"

"Hallucinating death."

"What's that?"

Todd paced the room, nervously wringing his hands, casting furtive glances to Billy.

"I'm not here, okay?"

"Say what?"

Todd went over to the window and noticed the layer of brown dust coating the windowsill. He wiped the sill with his finger, retracing the line drawn previously by Billy.

"You need a maid, partner."

"What's this about not being here?"

"I mean, I *am* here. But I'm also hallucinating while I'm talking to you…and I'm hallucinating death."

"Have you been dipping into the L-S-weird?"

"No, nothing like that. I'm straight, except for some pot and pills once in a while. It's just that I see things that are not supposed to be there, but they are. You need a new calendar."

"What things?

"Beasts."

"Todd, you're losing me."

"Sometimes, I drift off into another dimension. And it's nothing but monsters trying to get me—trying to kill me. But not only me. I see destruction everywhere. Aren't you afraid of death?"

"Sure. Do you want a beer?"

"Thanks."

"*Slayer's* new record sucks."

"Yeah, it's bogus."

"Well, from what I can tell, you're one fucked-up dude."

"Thanks, you're a big help."

"Hey chill, man. I think you're taking this life thing a bit too seriously. We're here for a couple of years, then the Grim Reaper comes and snatches us away— and it's all for nothing. It doesn't mean a thing. So, why worry about it?"

"Aren't you religious at all?"

"No. In the immortal words of Jimi Hendrix: 'There ain't no life nowhere.'"

"I've been having religious feelings. I don't know where they came from. I was raised a Methodist. Just a plain simple Methodist. Now, look at me. I'm going nuts."

"Hey, man, you're *not* going nuts. I won't let you. This death stuff will pass. You're stressed because we haven't gotten any steady gigs. We're going to make it and screw every groupie in America. You're not going to go nuts, ya hear? Besides, we need a drummer, asshole."

"It's probably just some left-over angel dust getting to my brain."

"Well, lay off the drugs—see what happens."

"Okay."

"You feel better?"

"Yeah, I'm alright."

"That'll be fifty dollars for shrink fees. Pay the receptionist when you leave."

"I have been to a shrink."

"You have?"

"Yeah, it's a guy Chris fixed me up with."

"Did he do any good?"

"Not yet. We didn't talk long. He had an emergency…"

"Well, keep going. Maybe he can help,"

"I guess it can't hurt. Look, I gotta split. Jake's later?"

"Sure."

After Todd left, Billy called Chris and told him about Todd.

"It's that PCP he's been taking," said Billy. "That stuff will fuck you up."

"He seems to be getting worse," said Chris.

"Yeah, but sometimes he appears to be normal. I don't get it."

"I think that's a symptom of schizophrenia. You slide in and out of reality. One moment you're completely lucid and the next you're talking to Napoleon."

"You going to the bar?"

"Yeah, in a few minutes."

"See you there."

Chris hung up the phone and was about to leave when the phone rang again. It was Sarah.

"Hello, Chris. It's me."

"Hey, what's up? Where have you been? You missed a great night at Jake's."

"I went out with some friends…to Coup de Ville's."

"Did you have a good time? I'm sure you got picked up by some sweater boy."

"To tell you the truth, I did have a date."

"You seeing somebody else?"

"We've been out a couple times."

"What? Some college kid, right?"

"Yes, he goes go UVA."

"Gee, what a surprise. I guess that's it, huh?"

"I just don't think we have a future together."

"If you tell me one more cliché, I'm going to throw up."

"Don't get nasty." Chris could hear her sigh into the phone.

"You're a real fuck, you know that?" said Chris, indignantly.

"That's enough. I thought you might be civil about this, but you're obviously in a foul mood."

"Gimme a break, Sarah. You call me up and dump me and now you're not happy because I used the "F" word? Well, fuck you!—and your college geek."

"I knew you wouldn't understand."

"What did you expect me to do? Wish you good luck?"

"I want to talk to you in person."

"What for?"

"So I can explain all this."

"Shit, Sarah. I've already done the thing at your parents' house, ya know?"

"This will be different."

"It's over, right?"

"I think so...yes."

"And you want me to come over and listen to all the reasons you think I'm not right for you. Gee, Sarah. Sounds great. I think I'd rather take the SAT's over again."

"I want to talk to you."

"No thanks. I'd like to keep my self-respect. Have a nice life—!"

Chris slammed the phone down and went into the kitchen to get a beer. He wandered back into the living room and slumped on the couch. He stared straight ahead.

He tried to hold them back, but the tears flowed anyway.

VIGIL

Dutch and Ginger's mother, Doris, were sitting across from each other in the nursing home beside Ginger's bed. They had not spoken to each other in over an hour. Doris was slumped in her chair, looking worn, drawn, and tired. Dutch looked at Ginger's pale, ashen face and strained to recognize a glimmer of change in her demeanor. She lay curled on the bed in a fetal position, completely comatose, tubes coursing through all parts of her body. Dutch heard the faint sound of a radio playing down the hall. It was playing an old rock and roll song from the fifties. It sounded like the chorus echoed the refrain, *"There's a moon out tonight."* Occasionally, he could hear the sounds of nurses' footsteps coming down the hall, or the intercom in the hallway making an announcement, or paging a doctor or nurse. Sometimes a nurse would peek her head in and ask if everything was okay. But mostly the silence consumed them.

The full-length cast on his leg made it impossible for Dutch to drive a car or a motorcycle, but he managed to get to the hospital every day. Jake volunteered to take him on his lunch hour. Ginger had been in the hospital for five weeks and so far she showed no signs of coming out of her coma. When the motorcycle hit the tree at sixty miles an hour, Ginger was thrown thirty feet into a steep, frozen embankment. She suffered major head injuries and the doctors could not give Dutch or any of her relatives any indication as to when she might out of the coma. After stabilizing her, her doctors moved her from the University of Virginia hospital to the Fairview nursing home outside Charlottesville. The nursing home was efficient, clean and provided custodial care for Ginger. Her life consisted of being confined to a bed, being turned every 3 or 4 hours, occasionally being put in a chair, sometimes for as long as six hours at a stretch. She was fed intravenously. Ginger was void of any visual, auditory, or tactile stimulation, so physical therapy was non-existent.

Although she was housed in a drab undecorated room, she was given adequate care by the staff. She was placed on a life support system and, although she was listed in stable condition, she had already lost 20 pounds and some of her muscles were already beginning to atrophy. The doctor told them that Ginger was probably not responding to any stimuli and was basically in a sleep-like state of consciousness. However, he also told them that it was possible that she could be hearing sounds. Dutch would sit by her bedside every day and pray for her to get better. He would pull his chair up beside her and read her some of his poems, especially the ones she liked. He wrote new poems which were much more uplifting and romantic. He read each of them to her. He felt she could hear him, or at least feel his presence. He looked at her sad, wan face, now pallid and thinly drawn. He often thought about her youthful, radiant glow, and her vibrant energy. The change in her demeanor was indeed striking. Chris, Todd, Billy, Leslie, and Sarah and many of her friends all came by on a regular basis to provide emotional support, but it was Dutch and Doris who came every day to perform their silent vigil.

The nursing home was considered one of the best in the country. Her father decided to stay in California and keep working at his job. Her mother moved to Charlottesville after the accident and got an apartment on Madison Street, near the downtown mall. As the days progressed, Dutch and Doris would sit together every day, keeping Ginger company and hoping for a sign of recovery. In those days since the accident, the older woman and the young man became very close to one another, intimately bound together by the misfortunes of fate, sharing the same grief and loss. In the beginning, Ginger's parents were furious at Dutch, blaming him for the accident. But as time progressed and more information came out about the accident, they realized that Ginger knew the risks she was taking and their daughter was a woman who loved to take new and exciting challenges. Mrs. Grafton was shocked her daughter married Dutch. She could not believe her daughter would get married before she left college and was even more incredulous when she found out she married a local kid who worked and lived in a bar with very little prospects for the future. Neither parent came to the wedding and both of them essentially disowned their daughter. They had not seen her for six months before the accident and Ginger had shut off all communication with them. Now, she was unable to communicate with anyone and Doris felt a deep sense of guilt over her actions before the accident. The terrible tragedy brought two people together who would never have gotten along if the awful disaster had not occurred. They would sit together for hours on end, not saying anything, but sharing the same hope that Ginger would break out of her coma. They prayed and cried together. Now, Doris loved Dutch like a son and she kept hoping that one day she would regain her daughter. Finally, one of them spoke.

"Would you like for me to get you a cup of coffee?" asked Doris.

"No thanks," said Dutch.

"How's the leg feeling today?" she asked.

"Not too bad. I get the cast off in two weeks."

"It will be weak."

"I know. They already prepared me for the rehab."

"I guess you won't be jumping around on stage too much."

"No, you can be sure of that. I just go in the background. I wasn't much of a performer before this happened."

Dutch and Doris lapsed back into more moments of silence. Dutch folded his arms, closed his eyes, and drifting off to sleep. Doris stared out at the window and noticed an old woman with a cane walking into the main entrance. Neither of them noticed a slight movement coming from the patient. It was ever so slight, but the fingers of her left hand opened slightly, then closed again. They could not have noticed the ever so dim awakening of consciousness within her. She awoke to blackness, unable to open her eyes. Minutes passed. She was able to regain her identity. She knew who she was. She summoned some bits of information and memories began to flood her thoughts as she remembered a few details of the last seconds before impact. She remembered entering the curve, losing control of the motorcycle, and being hurled into space. She thought about her parents and her husband. She wondered if they were close by. Within a few minutes, she began to gain strength and tried once more to open her eyes. This time she opened her eyes just slightly, but the room was merely a blur. She tried to focus on an object and get her bearings, but she wasn't sure where she was, or if anyone was in the room. She tried to speak, but she was much too weak to move her lips.

Dutch was drifting off into a comfortable nap and did not notice any activity coming from the patient in room 206. Doris had gone down the hall to get a cup of coffee. Dutch was having a dream about being an Arabian knight, flying in a magic carpet over exotic lands. In the dream he heard someone moan ever so softly into his ear. Perhaps, it was one of his lovers come to visit him in the night. Dutch was suddenly awakened by the sound of the intercom paging a doctor Gerard. He looked over and noticed that Doris was not in the room, then glanced at Ginger. She looked the same. He stared out the window. A flock of black birds flew in formation over the horizon. He thought about leaving. Just before he stood up from his chair, he saw a slight movement in Ginger's eyes, a brief flutter of the eyelid. He moved closer to her. He stared at her eyes, wondering if he had imagined the whole movement. Everything was motionless in the room. Dutch was about to go find a nurse for help, but as he turned to go, he heard a faint voice coming from the bed.

"Hi Dutch."

AUDITION

The Trax club in Charlottesville was an unadorned, black-walled warehouse on Downing Street near the railroad tracks and the Downtown Mall. As Wally Buford entered, he saw Leslie sitting at one of the tables in the back of the club. She noticed him and gave him a big wave to come over to where she was sitting.

"Mr. Buford! It's nice to see you again!"

"Thanks. I liked Jake's. It's quite a place. Good crowd."

"Have you seen any of the guys?"

"No, I haven't."

"I think they come on around 8 o'clock."

"I'm anxious to hear them."

"Leslie..."

"Yes."

"Have you ever modeled?"

"Me? Oh, no. I'd be too self-conscious for that."

"I have some connections in Washington. I could line you up with some very good modeling agencies. I think you'd be great."

"Well, thanks, Mr. Buford. I'll think about it. I'm going to see if I can find the guys. I hope you like them!"

Leslie went back stage and Mr. Buford proceeded to find a good seat in the middle of the club. Gradually, the patrons began drifting into Trax. They were mostly young kids in their twenties looking for a night of loud rock 'n roll music. Mr. Buford did not feel out of place, even though he was the oldest person in the room. He was comfortable in all aspects of youth culture. After half an hour, the lights dimmed slowly, changing the atmosphere into a smoky, late-night club.

Without announcement or fanfare, the band members materialized from the back stage shadows. As they picked up their instruments, and began tuning, Mr. Buford noticed their indifferent attitude and expressionless manner, as if they did not care about anything in the world.

After tuning for a few seconds, Billy calmly stepped to the microphone.

"Good evening, ladies and gentlemen. It's star time. Let's hope we pass the audition."

Mr. Buford took out his note pad. He had no idea what to expect. When he had asked them what kind of music they played, they simply replied, "rock 'n roll."

Mr. Buford had been working in the music business for a long time and loved the job of looking for fresh talent and discovering new rock groups. He may have been the oldest fan in the nightclub, but he loved the sound of a good rock band as much as any young person. He was a firm believer that the right attitude in rock and roll was absolutely essential. He felt one of Elvis' greatest contributions was creating the style, stance, and mannerisms that generations of rockers imitated every time they hit the stage. You have to be young, hungry, and poor and possessed with a desperate, bloodthirsty ambition. You have to be truly desperate because you know that if you don't make it as a performer, that thirteen-dollar-a-day truck driving job will be waiting for you at the end of the day. You also need a dose of cockiness and a curled lip that says: *Eat shit, buddy. You ain't seen nothing like this before.* Mr. Buford did not know at this moment how they sounded, but he felt instantly that they were a rock 'n roll band setting out to prove something.

Mr. Buford thought the band was aptly named. To him, they resembled city thugs transported from the streets of Brooklyn around 1956, looking beat and haggard like they not been out of their garage for seven years. They were all skinny and looked famished. All of them wore black jeans in various forms of chaos, rips and disorder. The common theme was patches of every variety and shape, and plenty of holes with straggly, loose threads hanging from every rip and tear. He stared at the four guys on stage. They were young, longhaired, clean-shaven, and looked like the *Ramones*. They were dressed in T-shirts and black leather jackets with silver studs. The drummer, who had shoulder length hair, was wearing a Jesus Christ Superstar T-shirt with a large cross swinging wildly around his neck. Dutch, the rhythm guitar player, was stationed beside Todd in the background, noticeably limping, yet holding his guitar defiantly,

ready for action. Chris was standing in front of the stage next to Billy wearing a
ripped T-shirt bearing a photo of Frank Zappa. Billy stood motionless on the
stage. Mr. Buford's attention turned to Billy who was gripping the microphone
and checking to see if the band was ready to start. In the smoky light of the club,
he saw a bony-faced kid with beady eyes, and menacing scowl on his face, wearing tight fitting jeans, a Johnny Rotten T-shirt beneath his jacket, and low-cut,
beat-up sneakers. His unkempt hair was greasy and slicked back, hanging loose
around his collar. Billy Saxon was a glorious picture of cocky rock 'n roll bravado.

Instantly, the red, blue, and gold house lights flashed brilliantly onto the stage
signaling the start of the show. But before the first chord came crashing down,
Billy ripped off his jacket and leaped into the air, as if catapulted from a rocket
launcher. Landing lightly on his feet, he bounded into a somersault, then vaulted
into a full split, and bounced up to the microphone bellowing out a blood cur-
dling scream worthy of a gospel possessed Little Richard. From the first note, Mr.
Buford was struck by the sheer intensity and power of the band. The raving, pro-
pulsive guitars chimed together to form a sound similar to *The Black Crows* and
the early *Who*. Billy's vocals were a blistering tidal wave of spit and derision, while
Todd's drumming kept the loose ends of the band from scattering off in a hundred different directions. Sounds, like brilliant sparks, were flying everywhere.
Trax changed into a blazing inferno of raw screaming guitars, rumbling bass
lines, and booming jungle drums. The one hundred watt Marshall amps were
being pushed to the max.

Mr. Buford did not recognize it at first, but the opening song was a cover of
Buddy Holly's "Rave on." Following explosive blasts of guitars, Billy wailed into
the song:

"RAVE ONNNNN!!!! IT'S A CRRRRRRAZY FEELIN'—I KNOW YOU
GOT BE REELIN'—WHEN I SAY I LOVE YOU…RAVE ON TO ME!!!!!!

Every note and movement of the band rang true. In his notes, Mr. Buford
observed that he thought *Mean Streets* was a band rooted in the back street working class culture of drag racing, factory work, beers and bonfires down by the
river, cruising the Dairy Queen for chicks, greasy auto mechanics, and hanging
out down by the boardwalk on warm summer nights.

Following "Rave On" the band broke into an original up-tempo song without
missing an ounce of adrenalin from the first song. It began with a monumental
drum pedal from Todd as Chris fueled the song with a pumping bass riff, while
Dutch and Billy traded nasty guitar licks. As the amplifiers shrieked with pain,

the harsh, electric guitars jammed together in a stereo interplay of feverish rock 'n roll. Billy sang the vocals as if it were his first day in hell—and he was pissed off. His gravely Rod Stewart-like voice belted out a gutsy, soul inflected story about two young men on motorcycles who traveled many miles together. But time and bitter feelings had taken its toll upon the friendship. Approaching a crossroads and knowing they will take separate roads, the two old friends gave a "thumbs up" signal to each other and disappeared down the highways, becoming more detached with every mile of two-lane asphalt. It was a song filled with grimly defiant assertions about faith, loyalty, and the learning hard-earned lessons of life. Mr. Buford was struck by the emotional strength of the song and the graphic imagery in the writing. With the exception of Springsteen, he confessed to himself that he had never heard lower class frustrations expressed so well.

The rest of the songs displayed the same high quality. Most of then were brassy rockers about declarations of the ties that bind, cruising and looking for girls, restless flights from small towns, love gone bad, lost friendships, and promises made, but not delivered. They were simple, but savagely direct. In their sonic, jet-propelled attack on the audience, they combined the irreverence of seventies punk with a sound that rattled at the roots of American black rhythm and blues. Mr. Buford heard Robert Johnson and Muddy Waters in those chords and wrote in his journal that their songs covered the whole hard-life landscape of contemporary youth culture and posited a view of paranoia, resentment, sexual frustration, revenge, and violence.

Occasionally, a beautiful lilting ballad would subdue the audience. At one point, Billy stood absolutely still, a single spotlight gleaming above his head. He looked like a lonely guy leaning on a lamppost lamenting the loss of his lover. As he spoke to the audience, he showed a sense of confidence rarely displayed off stage.

"This is a song written by our word man, Chris. It's called "Mexico." I don't know how the hell he wrote it because he's never been out of Charlottesville in his life."

> *The sun was going down behind a mango tree*
> *And the phosphorescent glow, was there in quantity*
> *…as I dug you diggin' me…in Mexico.*
>
> *We strolled along moonlit Acapulco Bay*
> *While ancient Aztec gods helped us along the way*

And the light fandangoed night surrendered unto the day
…as I dug you diggin' me…in Mexico

We were lovers in the ruins, of tequila's golden beams
And the Mariachi bands sang sweet romantic dreams
In a time remote and lost, a lifetime ago it seems
…as I dug you diggin me…in Mexico

Mr. Buford thought highly of the band because he thought they combined the fulminating power of the fast songs with sturdy acoustic melodies, and showed an emotional range far exceeding their young years. He figured these guys were not used to making compromises with their music, possibly even their lives. He wrote in his notebook that that the band played "with a poetic world-weariness of alienated feelings. Almost every song had a tight concept, a chorus that stuck, and a groove that carried the melody." By the end of the show everyone was shouting: "MEAN STREETS!!!! MEAN STREETS!!!!!

As an encore, the band launched into a rousing rendition of "Jumpin' Jack Flash" leaving the audience breathless, screaming for more. The song abruptly ended with Billy doing a cartwheel across the stage, ripping off his T-shirt, and flinging it into the audience. He was a bundle of raw talent, psychosis, nervous energy, shock, and humor.

"GOOD NIGHT, FOLKS!!!!" Billy yelled, "I HOPE WE PASSED THE AUDITION!!!!!"

As the band left the stage, Leslie came over to Mr. Buford's table.

"Well, what do you think? She asked.

"They're good, Leslie…really good. How long have they been playing together?"

"Since high school."

"They certainly have their own style. They're a very hot band. The crowd loved them."

"Thanks. Will you be coming to Jake's?"

"No. I have to get back to Washington early tomorrow morning. Thanks for the invitation."

"Thanks for listening to them. I really appreciate it. Tell uncle Richard I said hello."

"I will. He should be getting in touch with you about the band. I really can't say too much right now, you understand."

"Sure, I understand."

"Leslie, don't forget what I said about doing some modeling. Think about it, okay?"

"Okay, thanks."

GIRL

Mean Streets must have been practicing somewhere without me knowing it because they never sounded like this before. Billy was actually carrying a tune. And Dutch! He must have been practicing, amp or no amp. Anyway, I'm glad I came, but I don't see anyone I'd like to be with until this chick comes up to me and says, "Hi, Alicia. How ya doin'?" And I say okay, although I have no idea how she knew my name. But she doesn't go away and we just stand there together. The crowd is beginning to thin out, following a hot set by Megadeth. But it's still hot, sweaty, and crowded. We're standing on the dance floor, just drinking beers, when I feel a hand on the inside of my thigh and at first I thought it was one of the guys playing a joke, but then I realize it's this chick who's feeling me up on the dance floor. She's moved so that she is directly behind me. It's smoky and dark. Who would suspect anyway? Her hand moves over my leg and her fingers work her way up toward my private parts. I'm beginning to sweat profusely and I feel her slippery hands, dripping with perspiration, move inside my panties. I spread my legs a little to accommodate her hand that is getting me very excited. A slithering, exploring finger feels along the edge of my panties. I open my legs even more. I'm getting wet. Like some kind of sex expert, she maneuvers a finger around the edge of my panties and slips in me, gently massaging and working her finger in and out of me. I am breathing heavily, rocking back and forth, and I wonder if I will draw attention to myself. But no one seems to notice.

"Who is this girl? Why is she finger-fuckin' me?"

I realize this may not be the best place to get felt up, and besides, it could get embarrassing if the lights came on. I move away and turn around to get a good look at her. She's a little big, but pretty girl with short, close-cropped dirty blonde hair and a pleasant smile. She looks at me like we both got our hands caught in the cookie jar. Hey, she almost got caught with her hand in my cookie jar! Ha ha. She doesn't say anything. So, I guess it's up to me. I think about it and decide, why not? I lean over and whisper in her ear:

"Let's get out of here."

I took the girl to my apartment in the basement of my mother's house. We slipped down the back stairs. I was a little nervous because I have not had much experience with other girls, but considering my luck with men, it could not be much worse. She was very seductive looking and we just stood looking at each other as if we did not know who would make the first move. I asked her if she wanted a coke and she said, "No, thank you." She must have good breeding because she was dressed more like a college girl in a madras baby doll dress. She moved slowly toward me. I did not move or anything. I was standing beside the bed and she came up to me and put her arm around me and whispered, "Lie down." I did what she said and then she positioned herself at the foot of the bed. I watched her remove her clothes. She had a nicer body than I thought. I was not nervous anymore, but I did not know what to do, so I just laid there. She crawled toward me until she was on top of me, and she began to kiss me on the lips. I never tasted lipstick from another woman before. It reminded me of a carnival for some reason. She smelled like Halston. Maybe Dior. I could not tell for sure. I kissed her back, although not really passionate or anything. I was still a little unsure about this, but it was kind of pleasant. She started to feel me in other places. She removed my T-shirt and fondled my breasts. Our breasts are a lot alike. Very round and firm with large pink nipples. She twirled her tongue around my left nipple. I got aroused. She knows this. She has done this before. She moved down to my stomach and belly button. She took off my jeans, then moved to my right breast, then down again. I wondered if I was supposed to do something. As she slithered her tongue down to my pussy, she reached up and gently twirled her fingers around my nipples. They are hard. My hips began to move up and down. I moaned a slow moan. I reached down and found her hands on my breast and held on to them, then I grabbed one hand and began to suck her fingers. I began to feel my left breast while she felt the right one. And then the motions picked up speed and I could feel her finger moving swiftly in and out and I am bouncing up and down on the bed as I reached down and grabbed her down there and felt her in and out, and we flip flopped and she began to suck on me while I sucked on her and her fingers are all over my body. We were making moist, sucking noises with our tongues. And her lips moved up and down and I tasted her. She tasted all right. And I could feel myself cum and cum again right away and the rush was magnificent.

I was about to scream with desire when I suddenly heard a sound…like a thud or something. And the girl jumped up real fast and said, "What's that?" *And I said,* "I don't know, let's go look."

We went over to the window and some dude is at the bottom of our lawn looking like he just fell out of a tree. What the fuck? I looked closer and it is a man, but it is too dark to tell who it is, but he had a metal thing on his shoulder. I did not know what to think. Perhaps it was a gun, or he was stealing our CD player because it is definitely a burglar or worse.

The girl is completely out of her mood, and so am I. "Who is that?" *she asked. And I said,* "I don't know. Looks like a burglar. You better leave. I'll call my mother." *The girl dressed real fast and left. I went into my mother's room and told her I think we had a burglar, and she said,* "I'll call the police."

As my mother was dialing the phone, I wondered what that girl's name was.

Passions Reawakened

Dutch was curious about what Ginger experienced while she was in a coma. He was asking her if she was conscious of her surroundings, or if she could hear or feel anything while they were in the room.

"My brain would move from different shades of color," said Ginger.

"What do you mean?" asked Dutch.

"Most of the time I was in a black place where I could not sense anything. But other times I could sense that my mind was becoming lighter, more alert—even though I couldn't speak, or move. It's like the coma would progress from extremely dark to almost white. That's why sometimes I could feel your presence, and even make out bits of conversation. I even heard you recite some of your poems."

"You sure gave us a scare," said Dutch.

Ginger was resting comfortably at her mother's apartment, still recuperating from the accident while Dutch continued to work at Jake's and play with the band. Ginger had almost fully recovered from the accident. She broke several bones in her arms, but they were mending nicely. She did not suffer any brain damage as a result of the collision with the embankment, but she still felt weak and nauseous. Her memory was a bit sketchier than before the incident. She would suffer short-term memory lapses, and had trouble remembering some people and places she formerly knew by heart. The doctors said she was a victim of a mild case of aphasia and she would improve with time.

"I'm coming to the next gig," said Ginger, authoritatively.

"I'm not sure you're ready."

"I'll be ready. I want to see the band. Leslie tells me you guys are getting really good."

"Actually, we are improving. Maybe we all play better under stress. Todd certainly is stressed out. I'm worried about him. He used to make weird comments once in a while, but now half the time he's out of it completely."

"Has he been getting any help?"

"He's going to a shrink, but it doesn't seem to be doing any good."

"He probably needs medication of some kind."

"I think the only medication he's taking is his own drugs."

"Are you going to write me some more poems, Mr. Poetry Man?"

"Yes, I'm working on one right now."

"Let me see it."

"It's not really finished."

"That's okay."

Dutch reached into his shirt pocket and produced a crumpled piece of notebook paper."

"Read it to me," she asked.

"Okay."

> *I remembered the black room, the windowpanes with yellow paper*
> *Young friends in the parlor, trained in strange, sad errors*
> *Were burning with love, crazed with grief*
> *I prayed, then fell from my chair with a heavy thud*
> *Blacked-out, listening to animated conversations*
> *I was aware of certain deficiencies in my clothes*
> *…alone, red with shame, when my passions reawakened.*

"I never heard you use the first person before."

"Yes, it's a first, alright."

"Are you getting autobiographical all of a sudden?" she asked.

"Maybe I am. Is that okay?"

"I think it's a good sign…You're looking inward, more focused."

"How about me focusing on giving you a back rub?"

"Is that all I get?"

"You crazy women—you're never satisfied."

Welcome Back

It was a relatively quiet Tuesday night at Jake's until the barfly boys and Leslie came storming in around eleven o'clock. It had been a week since their gig at Trax and they were still flying high over their successful performance.

"Hey, Jake!" cried Billy. "Set 'em up. This round's on me."

"Billy's buying?' Chris asked sarcastically. "Let me put this date down on paper. I don't want to forget it."

"Hey word man," declared Billy, "I might even buy you two drinks. One for you and one for your friend, James Taylor!"

"Funny stuff," mumbled Chris. "Jake, give Billy a couple flies from the dumpster out back. He sounded like a frog croaking the other tonight."

"SAVE THE WHALES!!! SAVE THE WHALES!!!" Billy yelled and the whole crowd erupted again, shouting:

"TO ALL MY FRIENDS!!!"

"TO HATRED…"

"—THE ONLY THING THAT LASTS!!!"

"THE GUTS NEED FUEL!!!"

"SOME PEOPLE NEVER GO CRAZY…"

"—WHAT HORRIBLE LIVES THEY MUST LEAD!!!"

"HEY, WHAT DO YOU THINK I AM?…A BUM?"

"DON'T WORRY…"

"…NOBODY EVER LOVED ME YET."

"Hey, Jake," said Billy. "Gimme one for the road."

"Are you leaving already?" asked Chris.

"Yeah. I gotta go to work, remember? We're not rock stars yet."

"You working graveyard now?" asked Dutch.

"Yeah. I need the money."

Billy finished his beer and left. Dutch, Chris, Todd, and Leslie stayed at the bar.

"Billy was great the other night," said Chris. "He deserves better than that crummy factory job."

"Don't worry," said Dutch. "We're gonna make it. They loved us the other night. Even the guys from *Megadeth* were impressed."

"What's mega-death?" asked Todd.

"What do you mean?" asked Dutch.

"I mean, what's it mean? A lot of death?"

"Well…said Chris, "I guess mega means large. So, I guess it means large death."

"I don't think we should warm them up anymore," said Todd. "Their name might spell trouble."

"Yeah, well, we're gonna warm up much bigger acts than that!" exclaimed Chris.

"Hey!" yelled Dutch. "Who the hell is a warm up act? Shit, man. We're gonna be the main headliner across this nation!!!"

"Yeah," said Chris, "Fuckin' *Aerosmith* will be warming *us* up!!!"

"Aerosmith couldn't hold our jocks!!!" screamed Dutch.

"I still think mega-death is trouble," said Todd.

"Don't worry about it," said Leslie. "You guys don't have to warm up anybody. You're going to be major stars."

"Do you think Mr. Buford liked us?" asked Chris.

"Of course he did," said Leslie. "I could tell he was impressed."

There was a brief moment of silence.

"Have you seen Sarah?" asked Leslie.

"No, not recently. We're kinda broken up."

"Kinda…?"

"We just don't connect much anymore. It's like we're on two different planets…so…we're just on hold right now. She's seeing some college guy."

"I hope you two get back together."

"It could happen…"

Suddenly, the bar went quiet. Dutch was sipping his beer waiting for the next pool game. He did not see the girl enter the bar, nor did he see her begin walking toward him. The other patrons remained silent as she put her index finger to her lips, and winked at everyone. She was much closer and Dutch could sense that something was going on. He was about to ask Chris why the hell everyone was so quiet, when he felt a pair of hands cover his eyes from behind.

"Guess who?" she said.

Dutch turned around, tears welling in his eyes, as he hugged and kissed his wife. The crowd responded with thunderous applause as everyone raised their drinks to the sky, welcoming back one of their own.

WE ARE WHO WE
PRETEND TO BE

Once again, Todd knocked on Dr. Gilbert's door.

"Come in."

Todd opened the door slightly and peered into the professor's office."

"Uh…it's me. Todd Page."

"Sure," said Dr. Gilbert, "I've been expecting you."

Todd took his usual seat. The professor was at his desk going over some notes in his hand.

"So, how have things been going?" asked Dr. Gilbert, setting the notes on his desk and turning toward Todd.

"About the same."

"You were telling me about MTV last time. Something about there being images, and meanings coming out of the TV."

"Well, yes, I guess so. I mean, MTV is very important."

"In what way?"

"Well, when I look at MTV I see lots of images and messages about reality."

"Like what?"

Todd stood up and methodically walked around Dr. Gilbert until he was in front of a window in back of the office. He opened the blinds, splashing a yellow flash of light into the room, illuminating the books on Dr. Gilbert's shelves. He played with the cord of the blinds, gently wrapping the end around his forefinger, then unwinding the cord from his finger.

"It's too dark in here. Why do you keep it so dark?"

"Outside is a distraction. It helps me concentrate if I keep the blinds closed."

Todd continued winding and rewinding the cord around his finger. He looked outside and saw a basketball court with a spirited full-court game in progress.

"There's nothing out there but a bunch of jocks."

"Are you being evasive? Tell me about MTV."

Todd continued to play with the cord, working the ends until he formed a miniature noose.

"Hey look!" exclaimed Todd.

Todd simulated being hung by the noose he created, placing it near his neck.

"Very funny," said Dr. Gilbert. "Now tell me about MTV."

Todd dropped the ends of the cord, turning toward Dr. Gilbert. "I'm a strong believer in decadence. I think things are always in a state of dissolution...dissolving into something bad...evil..."

"You mean things in society...people...our culture?"

"The whole ball of wax. I think we're living near the end of time. MTV is just one example of our decadent culture."

Todd went over to one of Dr. Gilbert's bookshelves, glancing at some of the titles.

"Do you think taking drugs has anything to do with your attitudes about society?"

"Of course," said Todd, reaching for a book. "The images coming out of the TV are much stronger on marijuana, PCP, and pills. That's why I take them...so the images will be stronger, more vivid. I need to live a life filled with more flamboyant spectacles...colorful imagery..."

"But you lose touch with reality. Don't you see that as a problem?"

"No, not really. Do you think talking to you is any fun? Where's the buzz in all this?"

"There is no buzz talking to me, as far as I know. I'm just saying that you can't live in a fantasy world. People won't allow it."

"Who's Irving Goffman?" asked Todd, motioning to the book in his hand.

"He's a social psychologist."

"What's his claim to fame?"

Dr. Gilbert stood up and walked over to Todd. He took the book from his hand and placed it back on the shelf. "In a nutshell, he said there's no use asking who the real person is, we are who we pretend to be. In other words, all the world's a stage, and we're just playing different parts."

"He's saying everybody's a phony, just playing games to get over?"

"Yeah, more or less."

"He'd make a great barfly."

"I don't know about that. Now, stop stalling. You're not listening to me. I'm telling you that people are not going to let you continue to lapse into your own fantasy world."

"What do you mean?"

"I'm saying you can't walk around telling everybody you're Jesus Christ. It may be a lot of fun. You may actually believe you are Jesus Christ. But if you don't live in this world, people will not accept it. Sooner or later, you will pay the price for slipping into unreality."

"Like what?"

Dr. Gilbert led Todd back to his chair, and resumed his former position at his desk.

"Todd, listen to me. You'll be ostracized…or worse…they'll put you away."

"I don't lose touch that much."

"Todd, listen up. Most people don't lose touch—ever! Most people occupy the same reality that you and I are experiencing right now. Most people don't smoke marijuana, do PCP, and take a bunch of downers."

"What horrible lives they must lead."

"Is that a quote from someone? It sounds familiar."

"I don't know."

"I would suggest you cut out drugs altogether. I can line you up with some medication. I am not allowed to prescribe drugs, but I can make recommendations to doctors. However, you can't mix them with drugs."

"I don't know about quitting. Maybe I'll cut down."

"I don't think you can afford to do that. The drugs are seriously affecting your ability to deal with reality. They could send you off the deep end."

"What do you mean?"

"Mixing drugs like you do can be catastrophic for the mind. You're playing with fire by altering your consciousness every day."

"I'll think about it."

"You were telling me about your parents. You said you don't connect very well with them."

"That's right."

"Is it because they are wealthy?"

"Money has nothing to do with it."

"Did they mistreat you?"

"Oh, no…nothing like that. It's something about our family history. It's just fucked up."

"What's fucked up?"

"I'm not sure. Did you see that MTV special about the little spider monkey?"

"I don't watch MTV."

"Really? Well, I thought it was the oddest thing. There was this mother spider monkey that was in a cage in a zoo. Anyway, she was pregnant and was having a difficult birth. So, they had to give her all these drugs to ease the pain, and they put her to sleep. She delivered her baby monkey, but there was one problem—"

"What's that?"

"When she woke up she didn't recognize the baby as her own and she didn't want anything to do with it. So, it was raised by a lab assistant."

"Why did you think that was a significant story?"

"I didn't say it was significant. I said it was an odd thing to happen."

"It is—and sad too."

"Yes, I guess so…"

"I have to go to class now. Can you come back and visit again?"

"Sure."

"I want you to think about quitting drugs and letting me get you some medication, okay?"

"Okay."

"How about next Tuesday, same time."

"I'll be here."

Lennon On The Wall

Sarah was in her apartment reading D. H. Lawrence's *Women in Love*, waiting for Ben to pick her up for a date. They were going to Zipper's café to hear a local alternative band named *Everything But the Girl*. Sarah and Ben had been out together several times and Sarah was beginning to like him as a boyfriend. He was bringing out romantic feelings in her that she used to enjoy with Chris. She felt they had many things in common and she loved his sense of humor. She also felt guilty about not attending the Trax party at Jake's, but she knew they did not need her. They were too much into their own unique world to worry about her. Chris had not called her for a week. She was resigned to the fact that it would never be the same with him. Ben already said he would visit her in Michigan and she was getting excited about the prospect of meeting new, interesting people and the challenges of graduate school. It seemed strange to be suddenly hanging out with a completely different social group, but Sarah felt at ease among Ben's friends. They cared much more about social position and middle class careers, but Sarah had to admit to herself that this was her background, the place she found most comfortable. She was enjoying the benefits that went along with living a life of privilege. She also liked Ben's carefree, exuberant attitude about everything; he was always joking and playing the merry prankster. He was not as intuitive, or introspective as Chris, and he certainly was not into writing songs or being a bohemian, but Ben had extroverted confidence that comes from young men born in the upper circles of society; young men who were above the daily grind of the lower class. Sarah was comfortable around people who were groomed for success and who had all the right skills to make it in the world. She concluded that, although fraternity parties may be shallow and superficial, at least they were a welcome escape from the pressures of school, and certainly, they were an escape from the self-conscious seriousness displayed by Chris and the rest of the guys at Jakes. One of the barflys' favorite pastimes was putting down the very people that Sarah associated with in high school and college. For Sarah, the barfly boys had become tiresome and repetitive and she longed to branch out into other areas and meet new people. It was strange to be torn between two very different social groups, and she knew she did not entirely fit in either one. She had no trouble understanding the barfly boys' contempt for her new friends. Sometimes, she grimaced when they would put down someone from the working class, or even poorer students who had to attend community colleges. They could be profoundly cruel toward those who were disadvantaged and not born with a silver spoon in their mouth. It was the one thing that bothered her about Ben. He did not possess the slightest empathy for anyone outside their group, and he could be extremely callous and insensitive to those who were less fortunate. To her way of thinking, it was just not a perfect world. If she had to choose, she would choose her own kind. It was so much easier for her to move smoothly through all the social rituals—the ways of thinking, dressing, talking, making plans, discussing the future, networking, shopping at the mall, buying cars, going home for the holidays, planning a career, applying for graduate school, creating a stock portfolio, going boating, skiing, weekend trips to New York, reading *Cosmopolitan* magazine, buying designer clothes, evaluating law schools, drinking cocktails at five o'clock, working out in the gym with a trainer, buying macro-biotic foods, and going to the beach house in the summer. It was all part of a neat package given to her by her parents; a lifestyle she thought would be the envy of everyone on the planet—everyone except the barfly boys, of course. Occasionally, when she was alone she would wonder about her decision and if she was being just another phony sorority girl with nothing to say, and no sense of social commitment. But these doubts were short-lived. For the most part, she was enjoying her new lifestyle.

From her apartment window she saw Ben drive up in his flashy red Saab convertible. She waved to him from the window, motioning that she would be right down. She put down her book, gathered her keys and makeup, put them in her pocketbook, and hurried out the door. They drove to Zipper's. Ben parked the car in the parking lot and met Sarah at the entrance.

"We're going to meet Geoff and Megan here tonight," said Ben. "They're friends of mine. You'll love them."

The couple entered the small, cozy confines of the café. There was a bar to the immediate left, and a dozen tables set up in front of the stage. It was early in the evening and not many patrons had arrived yet.

"Let's get a table," said Ben.

The young, well-dressed couple walked down the isle separating the room and secured a table in the second row.

"I'll get us a pitcher of beer," offered Ben.

Sarah looked around the nightclub and noticed a gallery of pictures and posters of various rock stars lining the upper perimeter of the room. She spotted some of the enduring sixties icons including Jimi Hendrix, John Lennon, Janis Joplin, and Jim Morrison. The posters reminded her of Chris. Momentarily, Ben came back with the beers.

"Here you are! Sweets for my sweet!"

"Thanks."

"Hey! There's Geoff and Megan!" Ben shouted.

Sarah turned and saw an attractive college-aged couple holding hands, looking around the room. They heard Ben's voice and came over to the table.

"Sarah, this is Geoff and Megan," said Ben

"Pleased to meet you."

Geoff and Megan sat down and Ben poured them each a beer.

"So, what have you guys been up to?" asked Ben.

"Not much, just hanging out, waiting for the end of the semester. We're going to Cancun after graduation."

"Awesome," said Ben. "Sarah got accepted into grad school at the University of Michigan. She's going in the fall."

"That's awesome," said Megan, "What discipline?"

"English literature."

"Gosh, that's great," said Megan. "I was never very good at English. Too much reading."

"I agree," said Geoff. "I don't know how you can read that much."

"It's not so much," said Sarah. "Besides, it's fun to me."

"Do you know when you're reading a book and you get so excited that you can't put it down?" asked Geoff.

"Yes, of course," said Sarah.

"Well, I can always put it down!" exclaimed Geoff.

Everyone laughed except Sarah who stared beyond Geoff and Megan to the picture of Bob Dylan on the wall. She thought to herself that these were probably not Dylan fans.

"What are you going to do after graduation Ben?" asked Megan.

"I'm not going to work right away, that's for sure. I plan on going to Europe for the summer."

"You are?" asked Sarah.

"Yes, I was going to tell you tonight. My parents are giving me a free trip to England, France and Germany. Is that exciting, or what?"

"Awesome," said Megan.

"Wow," said Geoff.

"What time does the band come on?" asked Megan.

"I think about 9:30," said Ben. "I can't wait. This band is awesome."

"What does the name of the band mean?" asked Megan.

"I guess it means that guys always feel that they can get anything, but getting the right girl is pretty hard," said Geoff.

"Or maybe it means nothing," said Ben.

"Say, isn't that Laura?" asked Megan.

Ben and Sarah both turned in the direction of the bar. Laura Ashton was by herself sipping a Corona Light. Laura was looking at the television above the bar.

"Yes, it sure is," said Ben. "I wonder what she's doing here?"

"Has she gained weight?" asked Megan.

"I don't think so," said Ben.

"What time did you say the band comes on?" asked Megan.

"Around 9:30," said Ben, reaching for the pitcher of beer. "Hey, let me fill up that pitcher!" he exclaimed.

Ben scurried over to the bar next to Laura and handed the pitcher to the bartender. He exchanged a few words with her then returned with the pitcher. The subject had switched to the difference between men and women's sex drive. Geoff was explaining his latest theory in the battle of the sexes.

"Men want it more than women, let's face it," said Geoff.

"You got that right!" exclaimed Ben, sitting down next to Sarah.

"I'm not so sure about that," said Megan.

"It's no contest," said Geoff. "Did you ever hear of a woman paying for sex? It's unheard of—in any place on earth. Women never pay for sex. They don't have to! They just point to a man and say, 'Hey! You're the lucky one tonight!'"

"Don't be stupid, Geoff," said Megan.

"I'm not being stupid. Sex for women is like having a nice car in the garage."

"Would you like to explain that Doctor Freud?" asked Ben.

"Okay," said Geoff, "So, you own this real nice expensive car that everyone wants to drive all the time. But even though you like what you have and you appreciate the fact that someone wants to drive your car, you really don't want them to. I mean, what's in it for you? You don't get pleasure from somebody else driving your car. In fact, they could wreck it. Maybe it wouldn't be a bad thing to lend your car, but you don't have an overwhelming urge to free up your car for the evening. You're happy with it in the garage…and that's where women's sex drives are—parked in some garage going to waste.

Megan looked at Geoff, clearly annoyed. "Geoff, have you ever thought about a lobotomy? They can do wonders these days."

"See, that hot looking girl over there?" Geoff asked Megan.

"Yes."

"See, that beautiful smile! That beautiful, engaging, glorious smile! Us guys think that means something. Guys put so much into a woman's smile and it doesn't mean a thing."

"Come on! Geoff, what do you mean it doesn't mean anything?" asked Ben.

"There are three things in life that promise more than they deliver," said Geoff, "The smell of coffee brewing in a pot, the aroma of bacon frying in a pan, and the smile of a woman. None of them lives up to their expectations. It's sad, isn't it?"

"Yes, Geoff, it's really sad. It's also sad that you don't have a clue about women."

Sarah interest in the conversation was waning and she absently surveyed the room to see if she could spot anyone she knew. There were the usual collection of college students and locals, and more men than women were coming through the door. Toward the entrance, she saw Dutch and Billy arriving and getting stamped on the wrist. They walked to the bar and ordered a drink. Sarah wanted to go up to them and say hello, but she decided against it. Dutch and Billy got their beers and walked toward Sarah's table, looking for a place to watch the show. As they idly wandered over to a table nearby, Dutch suddenly recognized Sarah.

"Hey, Sarah!" what's up?"

From the short distance Sarah waved her hand energetically.

"Hi Dutch! Hey, Billy! How's it going?"

"Hey, it's going great! We were a big hit at Trax!" yelled Dutch.

"I heard! That's great!"

"See ya!" screamed Dutch as he and Billy turned toward their table, sat down, and waited for the show to begin.

"Friends of yours?" asked Megan.

"Yes," said Sarah, "They're friends...of a friend. They're in a band called *Mean Streets.*"

"Never heard of them," said Geoff.

"Are they townies?" asked Megan.

"Yes," said Sarah.

"They look a little rough," said Megan.

"They're nice guys," said Sarah.

"I don't know what I would have in common with a townie," said Megan. "I don't know what I'd talk about."

"It's easy," interjected Ben, "Just talk about cars, motorcycles, Nascar, and head-banger music."

"They're not really into Nascar," said Sarah, turning away from the group and looking once more at the picture of John Lennon on the wall.

MOTHER AGAIN

Billy's ankle hurt from falling out of the tree, but he consoled himself by the realization that he got some good shots of Alicia and the girl. Billy was surprised to find Alicia with another woman, but he was glad it happened. This made his movie even more valuable to him. He knew he would have to be careful not to limp around, or Alicia would get suspicious. He was soaking his ankle in Epsom salts when he heard a knock at the door.

"Yes?"

"It's me, Billy—your mother."

"Come in."

Billy's mother entered his apartment and stood in the doorway.

"Oh, did you hurt your ankle?"

"Yes. I tripped down some stairs."

"I'm sorry. Is it broken?"

"No. Just sprained. I'll be all right. Have a seat."

Billy's mother went to the kitchen area and grabbed a chair, placing it in front of Billy,

"Gee, two visits in two weeks. This must be some kind of record."

"Well, it is for me, I guess."

"You want something to drink?"

"No thanks. I came to tell you that I found Sammy."

"Where is he?"

"He's in jail—in Richmond."

"Jail? What for?"

"He's in for drugs. They caught him with several pounds of marijuana."

"How'd you find him?"

"I played a hunch. I figured that because of my negligence, he might have run into trouble with the law. I checked out all the prisons in Virginia. It's my entire fault. I've ruined everything I ever loved."

"Did you see him?"

"Yes. I went to visit him last Thursday. He's doing okay, considering his predicament. He comes up for parole next September."

"Do you have his address? I'd like to write him."

"Yes, I'll write it for you."

Billy's mother reached into her pocketbook and produced a pen and piece of paper. She wrote down the address of the prison.

"Here," she said, handing it to Billy...

Billy shifted his weight in his chair and pulled his ankle out of the soaking pan. He took and towel, washed off the excess water, then limped over to the refrigerator and got himself a beer.

"I can't believe what a mess I've made of my life. I had two wonderful boys, now I have nothing."

"Don't be so hard on yourself. Like you said, you were young and immature. Sammy didn't have to deal drugs. That's not your fault."

"I think it is. If I had been there for you kids, I could have kept him out of jail."

"Maybe, but you'll never know. Why drown yourself in remorse? Sammy will be out soon. He's not doing twenty years, or anything. He can still make a comeback. I'll go and visit him and I'll help him after he gets out. You worry too much."

"I should have worried about you kids more when I was younger. I was so selfish—and now I'm paying the price."

"Hey, cheer up! You're making me depressed! Things will get better. You'll see."

"How have you been doing? How's your job going?"

"It's going fine. I'm working a lot of overtime. The band is doing good too."

"Have you been performing anywhere?"

"Yeah, we played Trax, and we may get some studio time with this record company."

"I hope you make it with your music. You know I used to sing in the church choir?"

"Really? I didn't know that."

"Your father could also sing. He loved country music and he would always walk into the room and start singing a country song. I remember I'd be in the kitchen and he'd come in and start singing, 'Hey, good looking, whatcha got cookin'...?'"

"Hank Williams..."

"I know it was tough for you to grow up without a father. Every boy needs a father for direction and guidance."

"I turned out okay. I'm not a criminal or anything."

"I know. But maybe you could have gone to college...and had more material things..."

"I'm okay. I won't live in this dump forever. Say, mom, my foot is beginning to bother me..."

"Sure, son. I just wanted to come by and tell you about Sammy. Take care of that foot."

"No problem."

Billy's mother got up, put the chair back in the kitchen, and walked out the door.

Again, The Rain
Soaked Drunkenness

Okay, Edgar, give it to me straight. I have been through a period of mournful remem-
brance and I need your advice. You of all people should know my situation. After all,
you have lingering pity and sorrow for the dead, right? Cold lips have sought me too. I
have been drunk in Baltimore. These demons are appearing more often and they are
telling me things…things maybe I shouldn't be listening to…like taking care of the
harlot, brandishing her with fire. Is this correct? Do my ears deceive me? She says her
name is Leslie. See what I mean? Obviously, somebody is playing a big joke. Do you
think it's Gilbert? Bang the drum, slowly…What does he know about the tremulous
desires, the shaky fits and starts that I've been through? You know how the soul sickens
and becomes giddy when you gaze into the abyss. The whole universe seems extinct, as
if anyone would notice. Am I supposed to pay for all these foul-ups? I am not a violent
person. So, why choose me? I loathe the time I spend by the fire, an inner upheaval of
passion in my heart goes out to all the lonesome demons. I can't do the dirty deed.
It's…I don't know…immoral. God sure works in mysterious ways. I just saw a thou-
sand blue devils dancing in the air wishing me luck on my latest cosmic caper… But I
have deep reservations. She says her name is Leslie. America, this is serious. It's dem
Russians…dem Russians. Isn't it kind of odd that they want me to howl in the streets,
writhe on the floor, and drink my own blood. I don't even own a branding iron. But
like I say, I am only a conduit for the Prince, and I guess I must perform my sacred
duty. Quoth the Raven: "Let's kick ass!" It does seem odd. I mean, she should be slain
and punished for being ungodly? How quaint. I see the glory of the Lord coming from

the east. Any day now, I shall be released. The scorching seals must be delivered from the blazing desert fire…burning coals…another day of distress and doom…faces grow pale as they climb into the windows like a thief. My ancestors were slave owners. What were yours? Rich, snooty Richmonders? Tell me about it. Quothe the Raven: "Smells Like Teen Spirit"…The ancients knew the horrors of a smoky den fire, hissing into the bleak night, like a descent into the maelstrom, reeking of all sounds that were not forgiven. The savages are dancing ceaselessly, your cheeks look so hollow and forlorn, and you had to invite the Red Death!!! Don't worry about it. Everything here resembles death anyway. My easy chair looks like a coffin. I just might collapse from grace joined with new violence. Quothe the Raven: "Father, I want to kill you…"…This nightmarish domain, this bewildering melody, what demon hath tempted me here? You should know Poe…poe, pitiful me…I pass through a vacant lot somewhere near Jerusalem where a wild dog feasts on a half burnt corps; terrorists mingle on the corner like ugly refugees. Is this a sign of things to come? The whole universe seems extinct, grave worm twining itself amongst the matted locks, covered with rotten skull…again, the rain-soaked drunkenness…

She says her name is Leslie…

MEETING

Mr. Buford returned to his office the day after he got back from reviewing *Mean Streets*. Richard was in a meeting with a client and the secretary offered him a seat in the waiting room.

"He'll only be a minute," she said.

She was not entirely correct. He waited for forty-five minutes before Richard finally emerged from his office, accompanied by a youth dressed in western jeans, cowboy boots and a rawhide vest. A guitar was slung over his shoulder.

"Hello, Wally. Sorry to keep you waiting. Come on in."

Mr. Buford entered his boss's office and sat in one of his finely upholstered red leather chairs."

"Want some coffee?"

"No thanks."

"How was your trip? How's Leslie?"

"Leslie's fine. She's a great girl. She was very helpful getting things lined up."

"Takes that after her mother. A great organizer. She should quit that waitress job. She can do better than that."

"I'm sure she could. She seems very sharp. I told her she might be able to get some modeling work up here."

"What'd she say?"

"She was pretty non-committal. I think she wants to stay in Charlottesville for the time being."

"Well, what's the verdict? How was the band?"

" I think they're the best local band I have heard in a long time. Most of their material is original and it's good. Mostly fast, hard-driving songs about the usual problems of growing up and distrusting authority. It sounds fresh, but rooted in black delta blues. I thought they sounded a little like the early *Who* or *The Black Crowes.*

"What do you recommend?"

"I don't think they're ready to record right now. I'm sure they've never seen the inside of a studio. They could use some polish."

"Anybody looking at them?"

"No, I don't think so. They're a strange bunch. I don't think they've played many live performances. They seem to have spent years practicing without any exposure. Leslie says it's because all the clubs want them to play cover songs. I really don't know."

"What about their musicianship?"

"The lead singer has the most talent. He has a more than passable voice that we could record without any trouble. He also plays lead guitar most of the time. He's gone beyond a few Chuck Berry licks. Technically, he's very proficient."

"Stage presence?"

"From what I could tell he's got the power to hold an audience. He does flips, somersaults, and splits—a real acrobat on stage."

"The others?"

"Well, the rhythm guitar player is quite good. He plays lead sometimes when Billy—that's the lead singer—takes a break and just sings. They also play well together. We wouldn't have to overdub too much or bring in any of the usual session guys. They would be good enough, as is, for the studio. As far as the rest of the band goes, I'd say they were very respectable for a young, inexperienced group. The bass player is skilled and complements the other guitars. He keeps them moving. The drummer is also very competent and has a good sense of timing. I wouldn't replace any of them in the studio."

"What's your recommendation?"

"Well, like I said, I think they definitely have enough material right now for a CD. We would need to trim down their repertoire and get about ten songs we could work with. We'd have to figure out which songs would be suitable to record. With the proper help and guidance, they'd be ready in a couple months."

"Should we make a demo?"

"I think that's the best way to go. We can invite them up and see how they sound. We don't have to make a commitment. If we like them, we can contact one of our smaller labels. We can keep control without too much risk."

"Alright, let's get them up here in a couple weeks. I'll check the studio schedule. I've never asked a band to come up without hearing a demo first, but I'll take you word for it. Don't mention any contract yet. Tell them to come up. We'll pay all their expenses and give them plenty of time in the studio. We'll see what happens."

I AM THE ANOINTED

Richard called his niece and told her that Mr. Buford loved the band and he was trying to schedule studio time. Leslie thought Todd would be excited when he heard the news, but he did not respond very enthusiastically. He was watching MTV every waking minute, sitting in front of the television, eyes luminous and unblinking, smoking dope, and talking back to the incessant flow of videos. He continued to say things that nobody could understand. She could see him from the kitchen, curled up in his chair, eyes wired to the tube.

"Hey, Leslie."

"Yes."

"Come on out here. I want to show you something."

Leslie came into the living room, but did not see anything particularly different. On the television screen was a typical heavy metal video with guys screaming into the camera, swiftly cutting to images of a Roman-like toga party with men and women lounging around a fountain eating grapes and simulating an orgy of food and sex. The video focused on a young woman in a skimpy outfit drinking red wine while surrounded by admiring men. Leslie had seen the video a couple times.

The temple of the tent of witness in heaven is opened. A sea of glass mingled with fire. Foul and evil sores have appeared on the bodies of those who had the mark of the beast.

"Look at her," said Todd. "She's the great prostitute."

"Who?"

"The great prostitute. The woman on the beast."

The wicked blasphemed the name of God. The judgments are just because those who are being punished shed the blood of the Christian martyrs.

"Todd, I don't know what you are talking about. You should stop watching MTV all the time. It makes me nervous."

Todd laughed hysterically, jumping up and down in his chair.

"It's the scarlet beast! She's dressed in purple and scarlet!"

The woman in the video was dressed in a red and purple Roman gown, but Leslie could not see what was so significant about it.

"She's drunk with the blood of the saints!" he hollered. "And she glitters with precious stones!"

"Todd! Stop talking this nonsense. You're scaring me!"

He is coming suddenly, like a thief in the night. Babylon the great, mother of harlots, and of earth's abominations and the impurities of her fornication.

"You shouldn't be scared," he protested. "You're going to be part of the one hundred and forty four thousand."

"The what…"

"Never mind. Leslie, come here."

We should ascend from the bottomless pit and go to perdition. We will make the harlot desolate and naked. We will show her fire and brimstone. Every foul spirit is now the haunt of demons. All armies of the beast must be slain, angels will gore their flesh.

Leslie wished that Chris, Dutch or Billy could be here. She went over to the phone.

"Todd, let me call Chris, Dutch and Billy. They can come over for dinner, right?"

"Leslie, look. Do you see the seven hills and seven kings?"

Leslie looked at the screen, but all she could see was a bubble gum commercial.

"Todd, there is nothing on except a lousy bubble gum commercial. That Roman video is over."

"That's what you think, he said. "I'm going to bring ruin to the prostitute."

"What?"

"And after this video, I saw another angel coming down from heaven, and the earth was illuminated by His splendor. Shout! Shout! Knock yourself out! Babylon, the Great has fallen! Black Crowes in fluffy shirts. This is a home for demons—and Bon Jovi weekends. Faith No More! All my sins are piling into heaven. Leslie, don't you get it? We will be consumed by fire! And the Lord punishes the ungodly with destruction! You purchased for God your blood?"

"Todd!" Leslie screamed, "I cant' stand it any longer! I am going to get somebody. You wait here!"

Todd reached back, grabbed Leslie, and pulled her close to him. His hands formed a tight vice grip around her neck.

"You must understand," he hissed. "There's not enough love in the world. Not even for monkeys, let alone human beings. We're all descended from slave masters, pariahs on the land. Loveless, bloodless, stiff-eyed hypocrites!"

Leslie broke away from Todd and ran out of her apartment. She was not sure where she was going, but she knew she needed help.

She bolted down the stairs and into the street. As she was leaving, she heard Todd scream from an open window:

"Come back, Leslie! God has judged you for the way you treated me!"

And what may I ask was that all about? Before them peoples are in anguish. Hailstones of mighty power, I am the anointed. Scorching seals will deliver a separate, older fragment of desolation, heat, and cold, followed by the inevitable locust and noxious winds. At the flash of my glittering spear, perhaps an eclipse of the sun might jeopardize this meticulous observance of the four horns at the golden altar of God…in the pit stands in sharp contrast to the worship of demons. Ah yes, another day of distress and gloom. The sea may recede into the abyss and the waters may fail, and MTV may suffer no more, but the great day of wrath will come, like a drunken thief in the long lost city of night…city of night…

TODD SLIPPING

In a panic, Leslie drove to Chris' apartment. As she pulled into the parking lot, she was praying that he would be home and was relieved when she spotted his car. Quickly parking the car, she bounded up the stairs, and banged on the door. Within a few seconds, Chris answered.

"Chris, I've *got* to talk to you! I need help!"

"What happened?"

"It's Todd! He's acting *very* strange."

"I know…I know…calm down…come in and tell me all about it."

Chris led Leslie into his apartment. "Okay, settle down, have a seat. Now tell me what happened."

"He talks nonsense all the time. I have no idea what he is saying. He's in a different world."

"Maybe he is."

"What do you mean?"

"Todd's is slipping into schizophrenia."

"Why do you say that?"

"Because he can't tell the difference between reality and fantasy—tell me what happened."

"He was watching MTV as usual and I was in the kitchen. He called me in and asked me to look at some stupid video. Then he just kept saying weird things."

"Like what?"

"Well…he said there was a woman on some kind of beast and she was dressed in scarlet and purple."

"Scarlet and purple?"

"Yes, I'm sure of it."

"Go on."

"He said something about her being the great prostitute."

"The woman on the beast?"

"Yes—and she must be brought to ruin."

"What else?"

"I don't know! God! It's so hard to remember. Oh! He said something about being part of the hundred and forty four thousand."

"A hundred and forty four thousand what?"

"I don't know. It came out of nowhere."

"Anything else?"

"There was something about seven hills and seven…oh, hell! I can't remember!"

"You're right about one thing. It sure sounds strange."

"I do remember something else. He said Babylon was falling and we'd be consumed by fire."

"Who?"

"I don't know, but he kept talking about the video after it stopped and they went to a commercial."

"Was he still seeing the video?"

"It sure seemed like he was still watching it. What do you think it all means?"

"Well, he's been saying that he's feeling more religious lately, right?"

"Yes, he bought that big cross to hang around his neck…and he's been telling Billy that he's hallucinating death."

"I haven't heard that one."

"Has he been reading the Bible a lot?"

"No more than usual. He's always been interested in the Bible."

"Any particular books?"

"Not that I know of."

"Well, obviously the references are to the Bible. I don't know which books, but it sure sounds like the New Testament."

"Well, I hate to admit it, but I wasn't a good Sunday school pupil."

"Me neither, but I survived a couple years of Bible class."

"What should we do?" asked Leslie.

"Maybe Dr. Gilbert at school has some answers. I know Todd's been to him at least twice."

"Todd says Dr. Gilbert is a quack," said Leslie.

"I wouldn't take Todd's word for anything right now. Let me call Dr. Gilbert."

Chris dialed his office, but got the answering machine.

"Maybe he's at home."

Chris looked up Dr. Gilbert's home number, then dialed. A woman answered. "Hello."

"Hello, is Dr. Gilbert there?"

"No," she answered, "He's not in."

"Do you know when he'll be back—this is an emergency."

"Not for awhile."

"Where is he?"

"Who is this?"

"Chris Hamilton—I'm a student."

"I'm sorry, but he's not here—he's not available."

"But this is an emergency! I have a friend who's freaking out—he needs help!"

"Alright, calm down. I really don't think you should bother him."

"Lady—!"

"Son, this is Mrs. Gilbert—and you're way out of line. This is Dr. Gilbert's day off."

"I'm sorry, but I *have* to see him. Please tell me where he is."

"There must be someone else who can help you."

"There isn't! Dr. Gilbert is the only one who can help! Please!"

"Alright, but this is highly irregular. He's at his son's soccer game—Langsdon field, near the stadium."

"Thanks!"

Chris hung up the phone.

"Let's go see Dr. Gilbert!"

Leslie was pacing back and forth, sweating profusely.

"No, you go ahead. I'll stay here. I need to relax. My nerves are bad. I need to just relax for a little while."

"Alright. I'll be right back. Make yourself at home—and don't go anywhere!"

Chris hurriedly left his apartment, got in his car, and drove directly toward Langsdon field. Along the way, he had a chance to think about his friend Todd and his deteriorating mental condition. It occurred to Chris that he, and the rest of Todd's friends, had been taking Todd's problems far too lightly. No one wanted to admit to themselves that Todd was no longer capable of functioning in this world. It was easier to just pass off his behavior as a temporary drug experience that would go away, like a bad cold. Chris was convinced that Todd's condition was a severe mental breakdown and went far beyond the simple use of a particular drug. He hoped it was not too late to get Todd some real help. He realized that he should not have listened to Todd's casual dismissal of his strange remarks. He should have seen this collapse much earlier, but he was in denial like the rest of the people around him. He admitted to himself that he did not know the first thing about mental illness and he could not tell the difference between just "acting crazy" and lapsing into something more serious. Everyone tossed the phrase "wild and crazy" around like it was some sort of jocular, carefree badge of youth and rebellion. Chris knew enough to know that there was nothing funny about going crazy and losing your mind. If there was anything serious in his life right now, it was the condition of his friend. How often did they dismiss Todd's rambling incoherent monologues to "That's just Todd," or "He's under stress right now," or "It's just a phase," or "Get him to quit drugs and he'll be alright." Everyone just stood around and watched this happen, like paralyzed robots, unwilling to admit that Todd needed to be institutionalized. They should have intervened and physically taken him to the hospital for detox and treatment. They should have had the courage to do the right thing instead of hoping it would go away. Chris thought how easy it would have been if Todd had something physically wrong with him; that would be easy to deal with. If someone breaks their leg, you know how to respond—you buy them a card, or bring them a gift. It's easy. But when someone suffers a mental problem, the rules are not so clear; no one knows quite what to do. Now they were all paying the price for denial. All of his friends were hoping against hope that he would improve, but this latest incident convinced Chris that Todd was no longer capable of dealing with his problems. He needed help—and he needed it quickly.

Langsdon field was a former high school football field that was now used exclusively for little league soccer. As Chris pulled into the parking lot, he noticed, in the distance, a vigorous game in progress. A group of energetic children were running helter skelter up and down the field, and a small section of parents in the stands were screaming their lungs out in support of their team. It all seemed so normal; so unlike the insanity that was dominating his life at the moment. He spotted Dr. Gilbert in the bleachers, sitting next to two middle-aged men who also looked like professors. Chris hated to interrupt him, but felt he had no choice.

"Dr. Gilbert?"

Dr. Gilbert turned and faced Chris. He was surprised to see the student. "Chris?"

"I'm sorry to bother you, professor, but there has been an emergency."

Dr. Gilbert turned toward the men with whom he was sitting.

"Excuse me, guys. I'll be right back."

Dr. Gilbert stood up and motioned Chris to go around the back. They shuffled their way past the other spectators, and went around to back of the stands.

"What kind of emergency? Todd Page?"

"Yes. He's going off the deep end—not making sense."

"What do you mean?"

"He's totally lost it. Leslie—his girlfriend—came to me and told me that he's totally out of touch with reality—he's mumbling verses from the Bible and he can't tell the difference between television and reality."

"You mean MTV."

"Yes—MTV—and the Bible—there's some connection."

"He must have gone off his medication."

"Medication?"

"Yes, I recommended an anti-psychotic drug for him to Dr. Benjamin—he's a psychiatrist at UVA."

"And Todd's been taking it?"

"I thought he was—at least he told me he was taking it."

"It doesn't sound like it's working, if he is taking it."

"You know he's had these episodes before."

"I know, but this time it's different. Leslie was scared."

"Scared?"

"Yes, she's at my apartment right now. I told her to stay there. Do you think Todd could get violent?"

" I don't know."

"What should I do?"

"Go back to your apartment. Tell Leslie to stay there until I can talk to him. I don't think he will get violent. I don't think it's that kind of an emergency."

"You mean the kind where we'd have to call the cops, or something?"

"Yes."

"No, I don't think that's necessary. Todd wouldn't hurt anybody."

"Just stay at your place. I'll call him after the game and check in on him. I'll see if he's gone off his medication. Don't be alarmed. This is quite common. Patients think they're getting better and they don't need to continue their medication—then they have a reoccurrence of the problem."

"Doc, what *is* the problem?"
"Todd is schizophrenic."

Shock The Monkey

Leslie waited a half-hour for Chris to come back, then decided to go back to her apartment. After she calmed down, she realized that Todd would never do anything to hurt her, no matter what his mental state. She figured he just had an over reaction to the drugs he was taking. Perhaps the pressures of getting the band together were stressing him out. On the way to her apartment, all she could think about was Todd's erratic and strange behavior. She wished that she knew more about what makes people do strange things. Living with Todd had become a nightmare. She knew she was ill prepared to deal someone who had major psychological problems. She tried to be as empathetic as possible, but try as she might, she could not fathom why someone would want to wipe out their existence on drugs. She was not a die-hard conservative about drug use; she had done plenty herself in high school. But Todd's drug taking was radically different; he *wanted* to obliterate his whole being. He did not want to feel anything remotely connected with everyday reality. That's what scared Leslie the most; the thought that Todd would go off one day and never come back. She longed for the Todd she knew when they first met and hoped that he would straighten out and return to some semblance of normality. But after this last episode, the odds were looking pretty slim.

She pulled in the driveway. Everything seemed quiet and normal. She had made up her mind not to get excited, no matter what happened. She had invested two years into this relationship and this was no time to desert him. She walked in the door. Todd was nowhere to be seen.

"Todd? Are you here?"

"Who's that?"

"It's me. Where are you?"

"I'm on the hill."

"Todd, don't be silly. Where are you?"

Leslie thought he was speaking to her from the kitchen, but when she went into the room, he was not there. She walked out to the patio, but he was nowhere to be found.

"Todd? Are you hiding from me?"

She was walking through the hallway toward the bedroom when Todd suddenly jumped out from behind a curtain.

"TODD! You frightened me! Why were you hiding from me?"

"I was on the hill watching all your actions."

Todd, please stop this nonsense. You're making me nervous."

"I saw you."

"What Todd? You saw what?"

"I saw you sit on many waters."

"DAMMIT!! YOU'RE NOT MAKING SENSE!!!"

"Are you the blood of the saints?"

"I'm getting out of here. You need help!!!"

"Wait! Don't go. I have something important to tell you."

"I'm leaving."

"No, you're not."

For the first time, Leslie was felt more than just uncomfortable: she was scared. She searched for soothing words to calm him down.

"Todd, listen to me. You need help. Let me go and get Chris."

"I don't want you to leave. The time is near."

"Todd, just relax and sit down. I'll get you a beer, okay?"

"Come with me."

"To the living room?"

"To the seventh seal."

She looked at him and he stared back at her. She did not want to make any quick movements because she knew he could easily catch her. She moved slowly toward the door, tip-toeing as softly as she could. Todd walked along with her, step by step.

When Todd spoke again, she did not recognize his voice. He sounded like he was speaking through a block of ice. It was chilly, icy, and calculating."

"Prostitute."

"Todd, I am *not* a prostitute. You know that. I'm Leslie, you're girlfriend—and you love me. I'm going to get Chris now. You remember Chris? He's your buddy. Surely, you remember Chris?"

Leslie did not know if he heard her. His face did not register any sign of recognition. She did not even think he was seeing *her*. His eyes were bloodshot, bulging, and unblinking, as if he was a terrible monster in a horror movie.

"Todd, I know what we can do," said Leslie. "We can watch TV, okay? How about a little TV before we go to bed?"

"Alright."

They walked down the hall toward the living room, Todd remaining close to Leslie's side. As they entered the living room, Todd automatically headed for his easy chair and the remote control. As he reached down to turn on the remote, she sprinted swiftly for the back door. Running as fast as she could, she tore down the hallway, cutting sharply into the kitchen, the sound of heavy boots thundering behind her. She groped for the kitchen door, managed to open it quickly, but the screen door was locked. She fumbled awkwardly with the latch, then busted through the screen. Flinging the door open, she was about to dash into the open air, but instead of freedom, she was stopped dead in her tracks by a cold, clammy hand gripping her throat.

I was witness to it all. I want you to know that. I was amongst the few who saw the whole thing coming.

Shock the monkey. I was there when the first signs were given for the Great Fall. And I looked into Pergamum and was visited upon by John Revelation. And he told me of things to come. Horrible things. Things only the angels could tell. He said he would come back from the desert. And he was right. Pagan blood returns. The spirit is at hand. Why does Christ not help me? Why doesn't he grant my soul freedom and nobility?

I think I see her now. Did she think she could avoid punishment for her heinous crimes? The beast and his woman are coming out of the abyss and they must go to their destruction.

Babylon must fall.

Shock the monkey.

Shock the monkey tonight.

No need to weep and mourn any more. All things must pass. Even the Beatles. You missed the Beatles, sucker. John, Can you hear me? Imagine this. That bitch. This whore wreaking havoc upon the world. Love, it's a bitch. But where is it? Not from these objects of ruin and disgrace. There are no objects of love in my family. Family of Pillagers. And I heard the voice tell me: The beast and the ten horns you saw will hate the prostitute. They will bring her to ruin, and leave her naked, and they will eat her flesh, and burn her with fire.

I am the beast...Shock the monkey...Eat her flesh...

Burn her with fire...

KNIFE

When Leslie awoke she was bound and gagged. She had no idea how long she was unconscious. It was very dark in the room. She strained to hear something familiar, like the sound of a car passing by, or rain falling on the roof. In the background she could make out the faint sounds of a video being played on the television. She surmised that Todd was probably watching MTV somewhere in the room. She rolled over on her side to get a better look. Gradually, her eyes became accustomed to the darkness. She saw Todd sitting in the chair on the other side of the room, staring into the television. The ropes were excruciatingly tight around her hands, her wrists burning red and raw. She tried to sit up, but her legs were tied together. She stumbled backwards onto the cold wooden floor. She wondered why Todd wasn't saying anything. Finally, she squirmed over to a chair and raised her back against it, so she could face Todd in a sitting position. She felt more comfortable in spite of the fact that she was entirely naked. Todd was about twelve feet away, but he still had not spoken.

She assessed her situation. Todd was no longer her boyfriend, but a total madman. She thought how foolish she had been to leave Chris' apartment and hoped that he would come looking for her. But then again, she had no idea how long she had been left unconscious. Todd continued to stare monotonously at the television. Her only hope seemed to be to talk Todd out of this craziness, or hope that Chris—or somebody—would somehow rescue her.

"Todd," Leslie pleaded, "Please let me go. You're very sick. This is Leslie, your girlfriend."

"Prostitute," said Todd in a flat, diabolical voice.

Leslie fought to keep her senses. She almost asked Todd for a tissue, but it seemed like such a ridiculous request.

"What did you say Todd? Did you call me a prostitute? I'M LESLIE, FOR GOD'S SAKES!!!"

"I will not share your sins. You will not receive any of the plagues."

Leslie tried to get control of herself. She realized that she must remain calm. Screaming hysterically was not going to do her any good. She took a deep breath. Her face felt swollen and irritated from the tears flowing down her cheeks. She wished she knew what Todd was talking about. *What did he have in mind? Was he going to hurt me? He looked really bad. He looked crazy...*

He looked like a killer.

Methodically, Todd stood up from his easy chair and lumbered toward the kitchen. Leslie struggled to free herself, but it was useless. The ropes burned into her flesh like scorching needles. She crawled toward the phone, inching her way gingerly across the floor. But then Todd returned, this time with a knife in his hand.

"You came down from the seven hills, but you will not escape. Eat the flesh, burn the fire, eat the flesh, burn the fire..."

RED PUDDLE

Following his discussion with Dr. Gilbert, Chris hurried back to his apartment, but when he got there, Leslie was nowhere to be found. Sensing danger, he drove straightaway to her apartment. Leslie's car was in the driveway. He jumped out of his car and ran to the door. He was going to barge in, but at the last second, he decided to go around the back of the duplex and sneak in.

The screen door was unlatched and damaged. He crept inside the kitchen. He could not hear anything except the low drone of the television in the distance. His hands were shaking uncontrollably, as he reached into a drawer by the sink and took out a long, thin knife with a serrated edge. Chris could not believe this was happening, but he was carrying a knife to protect himself from one of his best friends. He walked cautiously down the narrow corridor leading from the kitchen to the living room. The floor was carpeted; he barely made a sound. He could see before him the faint outline of the living room, lighted dimly by a flickering fire. He crept along the edge of the hallway and positioned himself so he could see the entire room from his vantage point. He peered into the room. Immediately, an odor of burnt wood forced itself into his nostrils.

It was shadowy, cave-like inside and it took a couple seconds for his eyes to adjust. Finally, he could see the silhouette of Leslie curled up in the corner, her hands and feet apparently bound. She wasn't moving. Chris couldn't tell if she was dead or alive. *Where was Todd? Where was that son-of-a-bitch?*

Chris risked his cover and leaned forward so that his head and chest were visible in the room. He turned to his right and saw Todd in the center of the room, facing the fireplace. He appeared to be relaxing in his easy chair like he was watching a Sunday afternoon football game. Chris looked toward the fireplace and did not notice anything out of the ordinary, but again smelled something burning. Perhaps, he figured, it was just the smell of the coals.

He ducked back behind the door. He felt his heart pounding so much that it seemed to freeze up. Todd got up from his chair and walked like a zombie toward the fireplace. He reached into the flames and emerged with a long, thin piece of metal, glowing at the end. Chris strained to see what he was holding, then it struck him that it was a branding iron.

Todd walked across the room, and stood over Leslie. The tip of the branding iron flickered red and pulsated, like a laser beam, casting a grotesque snake-like shadow on the wall.

Todd stood motionless, muttering to himself. Chris could not make out what he was saying; he seemed to be cursing under his breath. Chris waited for the right moment.

Todd ceased mumbling. He raised the branding iron high above his head. That was enough for Chris.

In a mad rush, he lunged toward Todd, catching him completely off guard. They both hit the wall with a tremendous thud, the branding iron flying out of Todd's hand. Todd was swift and strong, and he recovered quickly. Before he knew it, Todd grabbed Chris by the hand and wrenched the knife out of his hand. But before Todd could grab the knife, Chris kicked it over to the other side of the room. In an instant, they wrestled to the floor, arms flinging in all directions. Chris flailed his arms with all his might, landing his share of blows, but Todd was also pummeling Chris with a furious barrage of punches. They were rolling all over the floor, locked in mortal combat, swinging fists, kicking legs, and ripping flesh. Todd rolled over on top of Chris and slammed his head into the floor, almost knocking him out. Dazed and disoriented, Chris blocked a volley of blows to his head, the kicked Todd in the back of the head, sending him on his side, writhing in pain. Chris stood up and advanced, but stopped in his tracks. From under the chair, Todd pulled out a hunting knife. Chris rushed over to the other side of the room and found his own knife. They circled each other, each looking for an advantage. Todd charged Chris, took a wild stab at him, and stumbled, losing his footing.

YOU FUCKIN' BEAST!" screamed Todd.

Back on his feet, Todd resumed stalking his prey. Again, they slowly circled each other, looking for a chance to strike. Todd lunged toward Chris, swinging the knife at his throat. Chris dodged him to the right, spotted a quick opening, and swung his blade savagely into Todd's stomach, ripping into his guts. Todd bowled over in agonizing pain, clutching his stomach, making animal noises, interrupted by retching sounds. Blood oozed from his stomach; a red puddle quickly forming on the carpet.

Chris was going to drive the knife through him and finish him off, but he couldn't do it. He went over to Leslie. He felt her pulse. Apparently, she was knocked out or fainted. Todd was listless and moaning in the corner. He shook her several times

"Come on! Leslie, wake up! We're getting out of here!"

Leslie regained consciousness, but was still groggy. Nervously, Chris untied her, ripped off his shirt, covered her as best he could, and the two of them raced down the stairs and out the door.

SUMMER

REVELATION

Dr. Gilbert had a busy schedule on Thursday, but wanted to check on the progress of Todd Page. Following a budget meeting in the Dean's office, he arrived at the ward just before lunch. Todd was being held in the special unit designated for the criminally insane. He opened the door to his room that was a simple eight-by-eight cell, with a bed, and a window with bars across it. He had his own bathroom. The attendants had prepared Todd for Dr. Gilbert's visit. He was handcuffed to the bed.

"Good morning, Todd."

"John."

"Excuse me. Good morning, John."

"Good morning. Can I have a cigarette?"

"Sure."

Dr. Gilbert reached for the pack he always brought and held the cigarette to his lips. He had long since developed the ability to smoke a cigarette while handcuffed.

"How are you feeling?"

"Hot."

"I mean your wounds."

"I'm physically healed, but that's not what you're worried about, is it? Now fix my head. Speaking of my head, this medication sucks. You're giving me too much. I can't think right."

"I think it's the right dose. Do you know what you're taking?"

"Of course. Fifty milligrams of Haldol. It could kill a monkey."

"I'm going to keep it at that level until I see some improvement. Do you think you are improving?"

"Improving what?"

"Your state of mind."

"It's as good as yours. How much Haldol are *you* taking?"

"That's not the issue, Todd."

"I told you not to call me that."

"But that's your name. Your parents are Dr. And Mrs. Fulton Page from Charlottesville, Virginia."

"My family never did anything but rise up and pillage. I belong to a race that only moved to conquer or enslave."

"Why do you say that all the time?"

"What?"

"Belonging to an inferior race. I don't understand."

"There's a lot you don't understand."

"Why don't you tell me."

"You're the shrink. You figure it out."

"Your mother and father care about you."

"How do you know?"

"They come to see you all the time."

"Why should I be concerned about the actions of these people? Where did you say they were from?"

"Charlottesville."

"Is that near Ephesus?"

"No. Ephesus is a city in the Bible. It is one of the seven cities where God sent the Apostle John in the book of Revelation."

"I know that. I went there."

"Tell me what you've been thinking lately."

"Lately?"

"Yes."

"Well, I was wrong about MTV."

"Why?"

"He fooled me. Satan fooled me into thinking that it was the word of God."

"MTV?"

"Don't patronize me. The images…the things I saw on MTV were not coming from His vision, but Satan's."

"How do you know this?"

"God told me, of course."

"Why didn't He tell you before?"

"He was testing me…to see if I could carry on His true word."

"And what is that?"

"My revelation. It's all there for everyone to see."

"You mean the Book of Revelation in the Bible?"

"I told you not to patronize me. Of course, you dipshit."

"Did you write the Book of Revelation?"

"Yes, I wrote it twice."

"Twice?"

"Yes. I wrote it two thousand years ago and I wrote it from the scrolls of MTV. It came out of MTV."

"The new Book of Revelation came out of MTV?"

"Yes. It was all there. Prophesy—angels—monsters—destruction—heavy Metal—burning—burning flesh—eating flesh."

"Do you need anything?"

"I could use a set of drums."

"Would you like to begin playing again?"

"No. I think God would use them to send me his new message."

Goes Belly Up

The day was blazing hot and Billy found it ironic that he had to go into a frozen food factory and freeze his butt off. He decided to go into Jake's for a beer before work. It was in the middle of the afternoon and no one was around, except for Jake.

"Gimme a beer, will ya, Jake."

"Aren't you supposed to be at work?"

"Yeah, in a couple minutes."

"How are things going?"

"Great—if you hate your job and live next door to dead people."

"How's the band going?"

"We're auditioning a new drummer in here tonight."

"In here?"

"Well, shit, Jake. He has to pass the barfly test first. Then we'll see if he can play. We're not looking for technical wizardry, you understand. If that were true, they would have kicked me out a long time ago."

"Who's the prospect?"

"Some guy from Atlanta. Friend of Eddie Sealy. I hear he's a hot drummer. Just moved into town a few weeks ago. I also hear he's been watching and studying a lot."

"It's a tough test."

"Damn right. We're a tough band."

"Have you heard from Todd?"

"Not lately. We all go visit him once in a while, but it's useless. He doesn't recognize me half the time. They've got him drugged to the max. The last time I was there he had shaved his head. He also told me not to get too close to him because I might have germs. Really weird."

"That's a shame. I really liked him."

"Me too. Best damn drummer in three states and he goes belly up. How do you figure that shit?"

"I guess you don't. You just accept it."

"Yeah. I shoulda known the record deal was too good to be true. Do you know that record company guy called Leslie the day after Todd flipped? Of course, he was in the hospital tranked up. He wanted to tell her we should come up and make a demo in Washington. We had a chance. A real chance. We've got rotten luck."

"Are you rehearsing?"

"A little. It's tough without a drummer. Besides, nobody has been in the mood, ya know what I mean? I gotta go. See ya later on tonight, Jake. Let's hope he passes."

"Good luck. Give him an easy test."

"Easy is not in our vocabulary."

As he was walking out the door, Billy ran into his mother.

"Hi, Billy."

"Hi."

"Can I talk to you for a minute?"

"I don't have much time…"

"I know. I just wanted you to know that I have moved back into town."

"Really? Why?"

"Fred left me."

"He did?"

"I saw it coming. Believe me, it was no shock. He left me for a woman with three kids. How's that for irony?"

"Where are you living?"

"I have an apartment on Beverly Street—212."

"Look, I gotta go…"

"Son, it has two bedrooms. I wanted to tell you that you could stay anytime you like…for as long as you want."

"You mean that?"

"Yes."

"You know I might take you up on that. I'm having a little trouble with my landlord. We may be getting some good gigs. I wouldn't be around all the time."

"That's okay."

"I've got to warn you. I'm not the neatest person in the world."

"No problem."

"Okay," said Billy, moving toward his pickup truck, "…You said 212 Beverly Street, right?"

"Right."

Billy jumped into his truck and roared off, waving to his mother as she stood on the sidewalk.

BUZZ

Buzz Mahoney was not sure how he felt about replacing a drummer who became mentally ill. He hoped the guys in the band did not have anything to do with it. Everyone he talked to assured him that the guys were okay and didn't have anything to do with Todd's mental problems. He had been hanging out with them for a couple weeks and found it very strange that they had not even heard him play the drums. Buzz never heard of having to pass a test on a movie before auditioning. It seemed like a waste of time to him, but he figured it was this barfly routine that kept the band together. He could also not believe that they took it so seriously. He remembered when Chris told him about learning the *Barfly* movie, Buzz laughed out loud. He thought Chris was joking, for sure. Immediately, Buzz knew he made a mistake. Chris got up and headed for the door.

"Obviously, you're not suited for our band," said Chris.

"Hey! I didn't mean to be disrespectful—you gotta admit it's a little strange."

Chris calmed down, but Buzz was careful not to make that mistake again. He had watched the movie about twenty times and he hoped it was enough. He had taken notes on every frame and every piece of dialogue. He knew the color of every piece of furniture. He knew exactly what everybody was wearing and what drinks each person ordered. He knew that the screenwriter Charles Bukowski made a cameo appearance as a street person. He knew the bar scenes were not filmed in Los Angeles, but in Asbury Park, New Jersey. In spite of all his preparation, Buzz was still nervous. He concluded that this must be what college students feel like before taking a big exam. He went to the refrigerator, took out a

Budweiser, and then suddenly heard the sound of Chris' horn blaring. He ran to the window.

"Be right out!" he yelled, gulping his beer while running down the stairs.

"Hey, man. What's up?" asked Buzz, sliding into the seat.

They drove in silence for a few blocks. Buzz thought Chris was driving surprisingly slow for a hard rocking guitar player.

"How did you get your nickname?" asked Chris. "Isn't there an astronaut named Buzz something."

"Aldren. Buzz Aldren. No, I wasn't named after him. My real name is Scott. The nickname came from a character in a movie."

"Who?"

"James Dean's rival in *Rebel Without a Cause.*"

"His name was Buzz? I don't remember him."

"He drove off a cliff. He's the one who lost the chicken game when his sleeve got caught on the car door handle."

"Oh, yeah. That was a great scene. James Dean jumped out in time and Buzz took a flying leap."

Chris did not say anything for a couple minutes. Finally, he spoke.

"Did your parents give you the nickname?"

"Yeah."

"Don't you think it is a little strange that your parents named you after a character who drove off a cliff and killed himself."

Buzz laughed. "No, not really. They loved the movie and they thought about naming me James, but they felt it would be too much of a burden to find out you were named after a legend. You know, a hard act to follow. So, they decided to give me the nickname Buzz because he was a leader too—only not a *lucky* leader. They said the second Buzz was going to be a winner this time around."

"Sounds like you have interesting parents."

They drove in silence the rest of the way to the bar. As they pulled into Jake's, Buzz was surprised by the large number of cars in the parking lot. He hoped that all these people had not come to see him take this test. As the two men entered the bar, they were greeted with a rousing cheer from the patrons.

"I COULDA BEEN A CONTENDER!!!"

"TO ALL MY FRIENDS!!!"

"MEAN STREETS!!! MEAN STREETS!!!"

"LET'S HEAR IT FOR DRUMMER BOY!!!"

"BAR-RUMP-A-BUMP-BUMP!!!"

"GIVE THAT GUY A DRINK!!! HE'S GONNA NEED IT!!!"

There were about thirty people crowded around the bar talking to Jake, Billy, Dutch and Ginger. Chris walked up to the center of the bar and offered Buzz a stool. A crowd gathered around him. Someone shoved a beer in his hand and a local guy in a scraggly ponytail leaned forward and shook the other hand.

"Good luck, buddy," he said.

Buzz realized that the whole crowd was behind him and really wanted him to pass the test. He hoped he would not disappoint them. Chris stood on top of the bar and commanded everyone's attention.

"Okay, listen up, you dirty bunch of barflies! We're here tonight for the latest international barfly test. Tonight's contestant is none other than Buzz Mahoney, the best damn drummer in the state of Georgia!!!"

"TO ALL MY FRIENDS!!! TO ALL MY FRIENDS!!!" Everyone shouted.

Chris continued:

"…AND IF OLE BUZZ COMES THROUGH TONIGHT, HE'LL BE ELIGIBLE TO BE THE BEST DAMN DRUMMER IN THE BEST DAMN BAND IN THE WORLD…MEAN STREETS!!!"

The crowd gradually settled down and waited for Chris, Billy, and Dutch to begin the test. According to the rules laid down by the band, each band member was allowed three questions of their own choosing and Buzz would be given one minute to answer. It was clear that the answers had to be exactly correct.

"Alright," Billy bellowed, "Time to begin!"

Dutch was the first questioner. He sat on the stool next to Buzz. The bar became quiet and for a second Buzz could almost feel the ghostly presence of Todd Page hanging over his shoulder.

"Okay, Buzz. First question. Name the five bars in the movie."

Buzz did not hesitate. "The Sunset. Oasis. Golden Horn. Silver Platter. Hollyway."

"Correct," said Dutch. "Now, question number two. In the beginning, Henry is walking down the street with a paper bag in his hand. He spots a vicious dog barking out the window of a vehicle. He approaches the dog and leans in his face…"

"Yes?"

"What I want to know is, what kind of store is located in the back of Henry when he talks to the dog?"

"A pawn shop."

"You're right again."

A few murmurs rustled through the crowd. They were impressed.

"Okay, this is the last one from me. Henry goes out for a sandwich for a couple losers in the bar, right?"

"Yeah, he needs guts for the fuel."

"What kind of a sandwich is it and what does it have on it?"

"It's a ham sandwich with mustard and relish."

"He's right. That's it for me."

Chris was the next questioner. Buzz took a gulp of beer and sighed. He thought they were very tough questions and he was not sure he could pass this test. He wondered if it was all worth it. It seemed to him like such a silly thing to do, yet at this moment, it also seemed like the most important event in his life.

"Okay, Buzz," said Chris, "What was the name of the first song played on the jukebox in the Golden Horn and who sang it?"

"Born Under a Bad Sign—Albert King."

"Correct. Number two. When Henry walks into his room for the first time, what color shirt is hanging in the room and is it long-sleeved or short-sleeved?"

"Blue-colored shirt. Short-sleeved."

"Correct again. One more. What brand of peanuts was on the coffee table?"

Buzz immediately thought this was a trick question. It seemed too easy. He knew it was Planters, but even if he did not know, what other brand of peanuts would be on a coffee table? He could not think of any other brands. Maybe, thought Buzz, this was Chris' way of letting him know that he wanted him to be in the band

"Planters."

"That's me," said Chris.

Billy was next. Buzz did not know what to expect from Billy. From what he understood, he was not alone. He knew that on stage Billy had the reputation as a volatile, unpredictable entertainer. Off stage, people told Buzz that he was moody, sarcastic, and sullen. "Don't get on the wrong side of him," was what several people had told him. Others said, "He's nuts and doesn't give a shit about anyone but himself." Buzz realized that Billy was very cynical and a hard person to get to know. The last time Buzz and Billy got drunk together on tequila, Billy told him that he thought everybody on earth was pure scum. "People are real scum." He said, "Not your everyday, run-of-the-mill douchbags, but authentic, one hundred percent slime bags. You look into peoples' lives for ten minutes and it will turn you stomach. Even Todd was scum. He knew it too. That's why he flipped out. He couldn't stand the thought of being scum and it drove him crazy."

In their state of drunkenness, Buzz asked Billy why the barfly boys played this game of not wanting to be somebody. "Because we don't want to be scum," he said, "How can you grow up not to be scum when all the things that are available to do are money grubbing, phony, or meaningless?"

Billy approached the bar, ready to deliver his three questions.

"Okay, first up. Henry is talking to Wanda at the bar before he leaves for his job interview. What does he get from Jim before he leaves?"

"Mints. Jim gives him some mints."

"Okay, second. What is the name of the company he goes to for the job interview?"

"Shifrin."

The Space Cadet game suddenly went quiet. The pool players put down their cue sticks and wandered toward the bar. Someone reached up and turned off MTV on the widescreen. Buzz heard the sound of Jake popping the cap off a Budweiser. Buzz looked up at the picture of Hank Williams for inspiration. No one had gotten this far in a long time and the crowd moved closer to Billy and Buzz.

"Alright, number three. The final question of the evening. Silence, please. Now, Buzz I want you to think about the final scene at the end of the movie. In the exact words, what does the white-haired gentleman say to Eddie?"

The question caught Buzz off guard. He knew what the man said, but there was a catch. It was a very difficult question for one reason: How many times did the old man say "ha?" Was it two or three? Buzz did not know. Billy had asked a question to truly test the professional barfly. How many times did the man say "Ha?" Did he say, "Ha, ha, or Ha, ha, ha?" It was a fifty-fifty shot, so Buzz decided to roll the dice and hoped for the best.

"Well," he declared, "The old man said: 'You gonna fight him again? Ha, ha, ha, that's a laugh.'"

Billy's face remained expressionless. He turned and looked at Dutch and Chris. Buzz was not even sure it *they* knew the correct answer. Moving slowly, Billy leaned over and asked for a Budweiser. Jake handed it to Billy. Billy stared at the bottle of Bud and paused before raising the bottle high over his head in an act of defiance and loudly proclaimed:

"TO ALL MY FRIENDS!!! TO ALL MY FRIENDS!!!"

"WE HAVE A NEW BARFLY AMONG US!!!"

Everyone came up to Buzz and congratulated him like he had just won the heavyweight championship of the world. The crowd went berserk.

"BUZZ IS A BUM!!! HAIL TO THE NEW BUM!!!"

"TO ALL MY FRIENDS!!! TO ALL MY FRIENDS!!!"
"A NEW BARFLY IS BORN!!!"
"THE GUTS NEED FUEL!!!"
In the midst of the hysteria, Dutch came up to Buzz and whispered in his ear, "Gee, now all you have to do is play the drums like Keith Moon on speed."

No Touching

Leslie decided to see Todd one more time. He was making no progress and the last two times he did not even recognize her. The doctor said he would probably be hospitalized and on medication the rest of his life. She drove up the driveway to the hospital, parked her car, and road the elevator to the third floor nurses' section. Mrs. Santini, the nurse who was usually present when she visited, greeted her warmly.

"Why Leslie, Glad to see you!"

"Hi, Mrs., Santini. How are you feeling?"

"Couldn't be better. My vacation's coming up in two weeks and I'm going to the Caribbean."

"Terrific! Take me with you!"

"Oh," she said, slyly, "I'm going with my new boyfriend."

"Well, I guess I'd certainly be in the way!"

"I guess you want to see Todd."

"Is he okay?"

"About the same. Nothing ever changes around here."

Mrs. Santini led Leslie down the hall to Todd's room.

"You wait here. I'll get Fred."

Todd no longer had to be restrained all the time. He had not committed a violent act since he attacked Leslie, but there always had to be an attendant present with any visitors. Momentarily, Fred, the attendant, arrived and they went inside Todd's room.

He was sitting on his bed, smoking a cigarette. His head was completely shaved.

"Hello, Todd."

"Hi. Can I have a cigarette?"

"You're smoking one now."

"I mean for later. I'm almost out."

"I don't have any."

"Then why'd you come?"

"I came to see you. I wanted to know how you're feeling."

"I'm okay."

"Todd?"

"Yes."

"Do you know who I am?"

"Sure. Leslie Richards."

"You didn't know me the last time I came here."

"They changed my medication. I'm okay now."

"What are you taking?"

"Lithium and Klonacin."

"And they are working?"

"The Lithium takes care of my mood swings and hallucinations and the Klonacin calms me down a bit. I was drooling all over the place for awhile."

"Are you...ah...doing anything? Writing or reading?"

"No, I can't read or write. Mostly, I just sit here wondering where my next pack of cigarettes are coming from."

"Have you heard from your parents?"

"I don't remember...maybe last week...I don't know."

"How about Dutch, Billy and Chris?"

"Yeah, they come by. I don't know anything about them. I think they're all floating around somewhere."

"Floating around?"

"Yeah. Floating...like unanchored...they could disappear, if they don't watch out."

"How could they disappear?"

"You know, like...I don't know...they haven't found anyone to talk to, so who are they going to talk to when they are alone?" They could dissolve and no one would ever know. Did you say you had some cigarettes?"

"No, I don't have any."

"They're cool, though, aren't they?"

"Yeah, they're a great bunch of guys."

"Well, I worry about them. They make me nervous when they come here. I worry about them."

"Why do you worry about them?"

I think they're around germs too much. Chris goes out with girls. Too many germs. Too much touching. You don't need to touch. Everyone's better off alone. You don't go out with boys, do you?"

"Sometimes."

"Too bad. Now I have to worry about you too."

"Catching germs?"

"You're better off alone."

"Todd."

"Yes."

"I'm glad you're getting along here."

"Hey, I'm fine...Fred?"

Leslie had completely forgotten Fred was in the room.

"What do you want?" asked Fred.

"I want some yogurt tonight. Blueberry."

"Sure, Todd. Blueberry it is."

"Todd, I have to go," said Leslie. "Take care of yourself."

"Goodbye Leslie. Be careful. Remember, no touching!"

"Alright, no touching. See you later."

Leslie got up to leave, and before she left the room, she turned one more time as she was closing the door behind her. Todd was staring off into space, smoking a cigarette, and blowing smoke rings into the air.

Cogs In The Iron Cages

Sarah was taking a summer course in Romantic poets and spending a lot of time with Ben at his beach house in Nags Head, North Carolina. She had met a whole group of new friends from the Zete fraternity and the Theta sorority. Occasionally, she would miss the old crowd; the conversations about music and books, the wild stories Billy would tell about the crazy people at the frozen food factory. The double dates she and Chris had with Todd and Leslie. She even missed Jake, the bartender. Above all else, she missed their brutal honesty when they were talking about themselves and their own insecurities.

Lately, Sarah had been dividing people into those who were real and those who were unreal. The barfly boys were real, if nothing else. They were not successful by the standards of this world, but they did refuse to compromise their anti-social beliefs and their policy not to devote their lives to ordinary occupations. They barfly boys always had the uncanny ability to spot phoniness in people and strip people to the bare bones of their existence. They all, in their own way, wanted to get to the essentials of the real person behind the social façade most people hide behind. She figured they thought the way down was the way out. To them, the barfly test was more than trivia, but a test of character and sincerity, and the risky business of giving yourself up for greater, more important ideals.

Sarah thought the ideals and sacrifices of the barfly boys were higher than any of her fraternity or sorority friends. It may seem like a childish game of adolescent kids, but in denying all those jobs, they were denying the terror of becoming phony and a superficial cog in the iron cages of computers, or anonymous bureaucracies.

The barfly boys looked closely at the majority of young people who lived inside their social roles and acceptable status given to them by lucky birthright. And they came to the conclusion that there is no need for any of them to be stripped to the nakedness of existence. They simply have too much of everything to be left with their solitary personality and character. Too much money and too much physical attractiveness. Too many convenient defensive mechanisms and social graces that their friends never try to penetrate. Too much time to pursue trivial pastimes, like fraternity parties and sports events.

Sarah felt her friends really were "unreal" by many standards. Sometimes she felt as if they were all cardboard cutouts, all image with no substance. She knew they would be the ones joining the country club, playing bridge once a week, drinking too much, playing around on their spouses, acting like regular, upper-middle class Americans—just like her dad.

The barfly boys were like large unformed masses of paper mache sculpture. Each time they refused to be a niche in society; each rejection of a meaningless job, added little by little, to the final product, or work of art. Each rejection stripped away a part of the unformed mass, like a whittler carving a delicate bird, each slice of the knife bringing one closer to a final creation. She figured all the people she knew started out as potential works of art, but by accepting the limitations and demands of the adult world, they lost the capacity to make themselves into a definable self that is nothing but free-form, uninhibited, honest personality.

Sarah remembered that her father told her that Chris had no "character" because he wasn't connected to any reasonable social influences, but she thought her father was completely wrong—and had it backwards. Her dad thought adjusting to predictable, safe goals like career choices, organized religion, and a middle class lifestyle developed character. How could anybody have character if the were isolated from the "Big Plan?"

The barfly boys did not possess a pattern of adjustment to society, or a plan of life in the usual terms, but they were not without a design for life. They had a design based on absolute individualism and freedom, yet at the same time, it was an organized set of beliefs. The barfly boys were not disorganized in their intellectual attitudes about separating themselves from normal adult goals. In fact, their very separation from society depended on a self-conscious organization of ideas and attitudes. It was not that Chris had no personality or character. Chris had nothing but character and personality.

Ben reminded Sarah of her dad. Ben was very ambitious and responsible and they had many "collegiate" things in common, like fraternity parties, classes, mutual friends, and upward mobility. Sarah realized that Ben was just like her; he wanted to duplicate the lifestyle of their parents. For two years she hung around people who hated her parents' lifestyle, and it made her feel more secure to be around people who wanted the same things that she did.

On the other hand there were things about Ben that mystified Sarah. When they first met, he told her that his uncle was the Dean of Arts and Sciences at the University. When she found out that was not true, he just laughed, and told her he was just trying to impress her. He also told her that he broke up with the girl, Laura, but she felt he still might be seeing her. She spotted him talking to her the other night at Macadoo's and they did not appear to be merely friends. On occasion, Sarah had the uncomfortable feeling that she could not trust Ben.

MAYBE SHE WANTS TO
FUCK BEN, TOO

This is the first time I've been to Jake's and it's, well...different. The crowd is really mixed. I think this is usually a townie hangout, but Judy Perkins (who's gorgeous and weighs about 105 pounds) kept talking about this hot band Mean Streets and how they were going to put on a special show tonight. I would not have come, but Judy is fourth year, and belongs. Apparently, the band can kick ass. Judy said they sounded a lot like the "Georgia Satellites." I asked, "Who?" and she just looked at me real strange and said, "Don't give me no lines and keep your hands to yourself." I thought that was an odd statement. I wonder if Judy thinks I'm queer or something. Maybe she found out that I talk about her behind her back.

There's a widescreen TV playing MTV videos real loud. I watched the screen for a few minutes, but then I got bored because I think it's a heavy metal group called "White Fang" or "White Fug." I can't be sure. They have a lousy stereo system. The heavy metal dudes in the video have identical long blonde hair, earrings, tattoos, and things hanging around their crotch. I guess they want to draw attention to themselves. I thought they were going to sing about hell because a red devil with a pitchfork just poked some cheesy girl in the ass.

I looked around and I spotted an assortment of college guys dressed in two ways: either baggy, cut-off Duck Head shorts and Ralph Lauren polo shirts, or designer blue jeans with an orange and blue UVA T-shirt. The townies, well, they wear whatever is available. They seem dirty for some reason—like they all work as mechanics during the day. I saw Heather Winfield, a Theta, butt-wasted-wannabe (who weighs about

118) slobbering over some skinny, longhaired dude wearing a leather vest and the grimiest pair of jeans in the hemisphere. I'm surprised Heather looks good tonight. Maybe she took a shower. The dude she's talking to looks like he rolls in auto grease for a living. He's even got some kind of tattoo on his knuckles. He's doing a good job of pretending to listen to her, but I can tell he's only interested in staring down her fuckme, low-cut v-neck sweater.

Several wrinkled and fossilized old men, wearing plaid flannel work shirts in the middle of summer, are leering lecherously at me from the bar, checking out my tits, which are magnificent. Cherry Rand, whose name I despise, walked up to me as if she belongs, and said, "How ya doin'?" She's wearing a pair of too-tight floral leggings and a long, oversized blue and white Benetton T-shirt. The T-shirt hides her fat ass pretty good, but her calves are bulging out of her leggings. I said, "Hey!" real cheerfully and lied to her about how she looks. "You look great in that outfit, Cherry."

One of the not-so-bad looking townies, who was playing a "Hotshot" basketball game, approached me, and asked me a strange question.

"Do you hate people?" *he asked.*

"Huh...well, a little bit," *I said.* "Depends on the person."

"Wrong answer. Ask me."

"Ask you what?"

"If I hate people."

"Okay, do you hate people?"

"No, but I seem to feel a lot better when they're not around."

He turned around and went over to the pool table and laughed with some guy with a red bandana on his head. Miriam Cooper, who will not belong in twenty lifetimes, stumbled in my direction wearing a Brew-Thru T-shirt, fuckme tight 501 jeans, a tie-dye headband, and a Baltimore Orioles baseball cap. Before I can escape the intrusion, she came up to me right in my face, smelling like a stale leftover Milwaukee's Best.

"Hi, Laura!" *she squealed,* "Are you going to Coup de Ville's later?"

"Ah...no...I thought I would go to the Virginian."

"Oh," *she said, as if disappointed, but she doesn't even like me. Maybe she wants to fuck Ben, too.*

Ben came in a while ago with his so-called new girlfriend that he cheats on with me. I told him I'm not going to fuck him anymore if he doesn't break up with this prissy new thing. He leaves her place and comes over to my sorority house and bangs on the back door, looking for a piece of ass—which I give him, but not for much longer. I think I'm gonna have a little fun with Ben tonight.

SCHOOL

Sarah saw Chris as soon as she walked in. Ben was hanging out with some of his fraternity friends, leaving Sarah by herself. Sarah spotted Ben's old girlfriend talking to some people at the bar. She was surprised to see her at Jake's. It was not the kind of bar where you found a lot of sorority types. Chris was hanging out by the pool table and waved her over. She approached Chris with caution.

"Hi, Chris."

"How you doin'?"

"Great. We're gonna play later on. It's a benefit concert for Todd's hospital."

"That's a really good idea."

"Well, I'm sure we're not going to raise that much money, but it's the thought that counts, right?"

"Right. What are you going to do next?" asked Sarah.

"We're going on the road to get a tighter sound, then we're going to cut a CD. Mr. Buford's got it all arranged. I'm graduating in two weeks. I was planning on going on to another college, but then, this whole thing happened."

"I didn't know you were that serious about school."

"I don't know…I've been giving it some thought."

"Of course," said Sarah, "You wouldn't turn down a chance with the band for a college degree."

"It's a possibility."

"Really?"

"I don't know. Maybe going to a bigger four-year college wouldn't be so bad."

"I can't believe you'd give up *Mean Streets* at this point in your life. You've worked so hard to get where you are."

"I guess I'm not sure where I am."

"You sound down. Are you alright?"

"Oh, yeah. I'm fine. It's just that so much is happening so fast. I just don't know…"

"Billy is a big hit."

"He's got so much talent, really. You'd never know it by looking at him, or even talking to him. He only expresses himself through music. He's lucky."

"Why do you say that?"

"Because I wish I could be more like him. Everybody thinks he's just some dumb townie with tattoos, but Billy's got a lot going for him. He's more sure of himself than I am."

"Boy, you really are down."

"Yeah, I guess feeling lower than Billy Saxon is *way* down. When do you leave?"

"In three weeks. Classes start September seventh."

"Michigan's a long way off."

"I need the change," said Sarah. "I've been here for twenty two years."

"Are you going to be an English teacher?"

"Probably. If I can make it past graduate school."

"That's great."

"You approve?"

"Sure."

"I thought you hated regular occupations."

"Well…an English teacher. It's not like you're going to sell used cars or anything."

"Do you know what?"

"What?"

"I think you've changed. You may not realize it, but you've changed in the past couple months."

"Like how?"

"Like, you're more serious. More mature. Don't get me wrong, but you don't sound like a barfly boy as much as you used to."

"Are you trying to insult me?"

"No, I'm being honest."

"Maybe you're right. I mean, how long can you stay a barfly boy?"

"That's a question I never thought you'd ask."

"I guess I never thought I would ask it either. Boy, I need a couple beers to cheer me up. I'm getting downright morose."

"Where would you go to school?" asked Sarah.

"I've been accepted at Arizona, Maryland, and Michigan."

"Michigan?"

"Yeah, I applied to Easter Michigan University. I'm on the waiting list. I don't have a ghost of a chance to get in."

"Would you go if you got in?"

"I don't know…everything's happening so fast."

"Chris."

"Yes."

"I miss you."

"We were a good couple, weren't we?"

"Yeah, a good couple."

Suddenly, Billy came over and handed Chris and Sarah a beer and starting talking about the upcoming touring and recording session.

Sarah looked into Chris' eyes and failed to detect any degree of enthusiasm.

Show Time

Sarah left to be with Ben and his friends. Chris and Billy were standing by the pool table, waiting for the next game.

"Hey," said Billy, "I need to go out and get some equipment."

"Band equipment?" asked Chris.

"No, just a VCR and some priceless tapes."

"Are you going to show a movie in here?"

"Yeah," said Billy. "A real Academy Award winner. Should win first prize at Cannes—X-rated."

"Are you going to show a dirty movie?"

Billy grabbed Chris' arm and led him to the rear of Jake's parking lot. Chris followed him until he arrived at Billy's pickup truck. Billy plunged into the front seat and emerged with a plain brown paper bag.

"What's in there?" asked Chris.

"Alicia."

"What the hell are you up to?"

"I secretly filmed Alicia fucking every guy in town.—even some lesbian."

"I don't believe you."

"Oh, yeah? Well, come inside. It's show time! Grab that VCR and help me set it up."

"Billy, listen to me. This is crazy. You can't do it. It would ruin that girl."

"Why do you *think* I am doing it—to make her a star?"

"What do you have against Alicia? She never did anything to you."

"I hate her. That's enough. That whore deserves to be publicly humiliated."

"Why?"

"BECAUSE SHE'S A FUCKIN' WHORE!!! AIN'T THAT ENOUGH? Come on, get the VCR."

"Look," protested Chris, "You're only doing this because you're some kind of weird voyeur and want to show people examples of your work. Don't you get enough attention on stage?"

"Get out of my way."

"Billy, you're not going to do this. It's sick and perverted."

"Perverted! She's going down on some girl and you're calling *me* perverted?"

"There's no law against being bi-sexual. What do you care? She thought she was doing these things in private. You're just as bad as she is. You violated her privacy and it was a cruel thing to do."

"So, I'm cruel. Get out of my way."

Billy pushed Chris savagely into the side of the truck. He rolled to his side, clutching his left shoulder, which had taken the brunt of the blow. Billy calmly reached into the front seat and came out holding the VCR and the paper bag. Chris stepped in front of him.

"Get the fuck out of my way, Chris."

"Alright, asshole. Have it your way. Get your cheap thrills. Have a bunch of laughs at someone else's expense. You'll be a big fucking hit with all the jerks in there, especially the college guys. This looks like a cheap fraternity trick."

"Alicia deserves this."

"Why? Because she sleeps around? You're gonna need a lot more equipment if you're going to start filming all the promiscuous women in America."

"She's a fuckin' whore."

"I don't get it. So what? Why does that bother you so much?"

"I can't stand cheap women. I'm telling you for the last time. Get the hell out of my way."

"You're scared, aren't you?"

"What?"

"You're afraid. Billy Saxon is scared shitless."

"What are you talking about?"

"You're afraid she's too much like you."

"You're nuts."

"No, I'm serious. You want to destroy Alicia only because it will destroy a part of you.—a part that you can't face."

"And what's that?"

"You're both alike."

"You're crazy."

"You want to destroy her because when you look at her you see all those things which you hate within yourself."

"Like what?"

"Like loneliness…like being unloved and uncared for…"

Billy hesitated. "I'm not lonely."

"It's not just loneliness, or being unloved. You know that people put you and Alicia in the same category. You know the college kids think they're better than both of you. You know what they say. White trash—all that shit. You're both outcasts—deviants. And your parents and everything around you have exploited you both. You could both sue life for alienated affections."

Billy stared into space. His arms went limp and the VCR sagged beneath his chest as he lowered and straightened his arms.

"You saying me and Alicia are in the same boat?"

"I'm saying that you both have a lot in common, and I think you realize that—but you don't want to admit it. You want to destroy it. You want to wipe out all those bad feelings within you, but you don't know how. So, you focus your rage on Alicia—instead of yourself."

"You're a regular Sigmund Freud, aren't you?"

"I know it sounds like you're on a couch in some office, but think about it."

Audibly groaning, apparently from the sheer weight of existence, Billy methodically lifted the VCR back into the truck and threw the tapes in the front seat.

"Alright," he said, "No show tonight. I guess it was a dumb idea."

"Not one of your better ones."

"Chris."

"What?"

"Thanks."

"Hey, no problem. What do you think I am—a bum?"

"We're all bums."

PROFESSIONAL DICK

The more I thought about it, the more irritated I became. Ben was a dick. Not just your ordinary run-of-the-mill frat house geek, but also a certified inductee into the Dick Hall of Fame. He'll have his own locker room in the Donald Trump wing of the building and they can retire his number—less than zero. I actually felt sorry for this Sarah Carson girl. She didn't know what the hell was going on. Maybe it was time she found out.

I waited until no one was speaking to her. Finally, I saw her alone, just hanging out watching a "Space Cadet" video game, wearing a delightful J. Crew poka-dotted navy and white sundress. Ben had deserted her. He was probably out back, getting stoned, or fucking some freshman wannabe.

"Hi."

"Hello."

"I'm Laura. Remember me?"

"Yes."

"Yes. The ex-girlfriend. It seems they're always around, doesn't it?"

"I've seen you around, if that's what you mean."

"Are you in love with Ben?"

"I don't see how that is any of your business."

"I just don't want you to get hurt. I don't want you to get the wrong impression."

"Maybe you should just tell me what you're getting at?"

"It's Ben. He's not what you think. He's not…a nice guy…he's not as nice as you think he is."

"I never thought he was a paragon of virtue."

"Sarah…that's your name, isn't it?"

"You know that."

"Sarah, I want you to know that Ben has been sleeping with me. He comes over to the Theta house after he leaves you. If you want proof, I'll tell you what you two did last Thursday night.

"Go ahead."

He came over to your house around eight o'clock. You wore a forest green pair of shorts and a tan sweater. He lied to you and said he was tired from playing golf that afternoon. In fact, he had already drunk several beers and smoked three joints. You asked if he was hungry and he said he would love a pizza. You ordered a large Domino's pizza with extra cheese and pepperoni. You also ordered a coke for Ben. He said he usually likes beer with his pizza, but he was staying sober tonight. The pizza came. Ben paid for it in cash. The bill came to fourteen dollars and twenty-four cents. Ben ate four slices and drank all the coke. You watched a movie that you rented from Blockbuster after dinner. It was "European Vacation." Ben lied to you and said it was funny. He told me it was the dumbest fucking movie he had ever seen. At ten thirty Ben said he was going out for some cigarettes. Actually, he went to the car, grabbed a joint from the glove compartment, smoked it, then drove to the 7/Eleven and called me. He returned at eleven ten, told you he had a headache and needed to study for a test. He left your place at eleven twenty and arrived on my doorstep at eleven thirty five."

"Well," said Sarah, "Thank you for the information. I don't know your motivation, but I'm glad you told me. I can't believe I've been so stupid."

"Ben's a charmer. He got "Most Congenial" in high school. He's also a compulsive liar. He can't help it. He's addicted to lying. He's also very good at it. He's a professional dick. Believe me, I know."

"Well, I'm glad you told me. Are you interested in him?"

"Me? Oh, no. I just use him once in a while."

"I'm not feeling well right now. Excuse me."

BEN'S EXIT

Ben slipped out of Jake's to catch a buzz in his car. He saw Chris and Billy arguing beside the pickup truck, but figured they were two local losers not worth paying any attention to. He got inside his car, lit up a joint of homegrown marijuana, and began wondering how he was going to sleep with Laura tonight. Ben was hoping that he could take Sarah home early, then return to the bar to pick up Laura. He also thought that he might hit on a girl named Rosemary who he felt had great tits, but was too dumb for him. He remembered that he mentioned the word "Rotunda" to one of these local townies and they did not know what he was talking about. One of the guys asked him, "Do you mean that fat girl sitting over there?" He looked over at the two guys arguing and one of them was holding a piece of stereo equipment. He thought they were probably fencing stolen equipment. The one with the equipment pushed the other guy into the truck. Ben decided to go back into the bar. The scene confirmed Ben's attitude about the local guys, namely, they were a bunch of losers who would get into an argument over a lousy couple of hundred bucks. When he reentered the bar, Ben did not see anyone he knew, except Joe Van Fossen, a Lamda Ki geek that he would never speak to in public. Ben was afraid some of his geekiness would rub off on him. Joe Van Fossen had actually entered the "I'm-Going-To-Fuck-The-Most-Freshmen" contest even though he never fucked anybody in his whole life. Ben spotted Laura and went over to the bar to say hello.

"Hey, Laura. What about later on?"

"Have you seen Sarah?"

"No. What about later on?"

"It's over Ben—and not just between us."

"What do you mean by that?"

"Good bye, Ben."

Ben sensed that Laura had told Sarah about their affair, but he had to be sure. He peered out at the motley crew of humanity before him. He saw Sarah talking to one of the townies. He wore a red bandana around his head and an iron cross earring. Ben approached her with caution.

"Hi."

Sarah looked at Ben, but did not say anything.

"I went out to get some cigarettes," said Ben.

"No, you didn't," said Sarah. "You went out to get stoned, or maybe pick up that cheesy freshman in the red sweater…"

"I guess you talked to Laura."

"Yes."

"Well, I guess there's nothing left for me to say."

"Why don't you just leave."

"Sure. This is a dump anyway."

"What are you calling a dump?" asserted Buzz, leaping in front of Sarah and grabbing Ben by the throat.

"Nothing…just a figure of speech."

Sarah stepped between them.

"No, Buzz. It's not worth it."

Buzz let go of Ben. He turned and left hurriedly for the exit.

CALL

Chris decided to just go ahead and call her.

"Sarah?"

"Oh hi, Chris. How are you?"

"Fine. I wanted to talk to you before you left."

"I'm glad you called. I'm leaving on Wednesday."

"Well, I wish you luck. You'll do great."

"I hope so. It's a big move."

"Yeah, I'm making a big move myself."

"With *Mean Streets*?"

"No, I quit."

"You're kidding. Why?"

"I'm not sure. I guess I'm not really cut out for a full-time rock 'n roll career. I don't know…

"Are you getting along with everyone?"

"Oh, yeah. No problem. We're getting along great. It's just that, well…maybe I should really concentrate on something more, I don't know…stable."

"What are you going to do?"

"I got into Eastern Michigan. I'm leaving town too."

"You're kidding."

"No, they actually let me in. I'm leaving next Monday."

"I can't believe it. That's great."

"Thanks."

"That's amazing. You know we won't be that far apart."

"I know. To tell you the truth, that's the reason I called. Maybe we could see each other on a weekend sometime."

Sure…I can't believe you quit. They are really going to miss you."

"Oh, they'll do alright. Buzz has been writing some great material. They're all going out…later on…"

"To Jake's?"

"Yeah, it should be fun…"

"Sarah?"

"Yes."

"How would you like to go to Jake's tonight?"

"I'd love to."

Quiet In Room 421

It was past midnight on the ward. Everything was peaceful and quiet. Fred Williams was walking down the deserted corridor making his last minute rounds. He looked in on Harry Sullivan. He was sleeping contentedly now, but Fred had to restrain him earlier in the day. Fred hated it when they got violent. He knew he was picked for the job primarily because of his strong arms and ability to handle unruly patients. He noticed that Louie, the Great was also subdued in room 402. No one on the ward could remember Louie's real name. He came in as Louie, the Great and that is what everybody called him. Fred moved steadily down the hall. It was a quiet night. Perhaps, too quiet. He passed Dana Kirkland's room and noticed that he was reading "How to Win Friends and Influence People." In three years, that is the only book he had ever read. Fred figured he probably read it a hundred times. He looked in on Bobby Crawford.

"Hey, Fred!" Bobby yelled, "Gimme a cigarette!"

"You know I don't smoke. Why are you always asking me for cigarettes, Bobby?"

"I don't know. Why don't you start smoking like the rest of us?"

Fred proceeded to Todd Page's room. He was usually sitting in bed smoking at this hour. As he passed, Fred was surprised not to see him. Todd was very predicable. He was not sleeping in his bed either. Perhaps, he concluded, he is in the bathroom. Fred unlocked the door and let himself in.

"Hello? Todd? Are you in the bathroom?"

Fred did not hear a sound. It seemed odd. He was always smoking on his bed.

The door to the bathroom was slightly ajar. He hated to disturb someone when they were in the bathroom.

"Todd?"

Fred opened the door a little further. He turned and looked toward the toilet. At first he did not see anything peculiar. But as he glanced away from the toilet, he noticed a dark shadow behind the shower curtain. He thought perhaps it was Todd standing behind the curtain for some reason. He knew he wasn't taking a shower because the water wasn't running. In one sweeping motion, he pulled the shower curtain open and realized why it was so quiet in room 421.

Todd Page was hanging from the ceiling, his body cold, purple, and lifeless.

A Race That
Conquered and
Enslaved

Chris, Sarah, Leslie, Dutch, Ginger, Buzz, and Billy were sitting in Dr. Gilbert's office waiting for him to come back from class. Dr. Gilbert had asked them to come and hear his final diagnosis on the condition of Todd Page. Momentarily, Dr. Gilbert opened the door and greeted his guests.

"Hi, everybody. Glad you could come. Thanks for waiting, but even I have to work sometimes!"

The seven of them were seated on Dr. Gilbert's couch. The professor went to his desk, sat down, and unloaded his books and papers. He swirled in his chair, facing the group. They sat attentively, waiting for Dr. Gilbert to tell them about Todd.

"I've already talked to Todd's parents about this, but I wanted to go over everything with you all personally. I know you all loved Todd and maybe I can shed some light into the cause of his suicide. As you know, he didn't leave a note, so we have to piece together what we have from his comments before he died. I only met with him twice, but I think I can make a few accurate observations. Todd was a complicated case, for sure.

"Was he schizophrenic?" asked Ginger.

"Technically, yes. He had trouble distinguishing between reality and fantasy life. There's no doubt he was experiencing hallucinations. Initially, I thought he had symptoms of functional schizophrenia, but later I concluded that he was suffering from a drug induced disorder. He had apparently been consuming large amounts of drugs for a considerable amount of time. As you all know, he continually took an assortment of drugs—marijuana, LSD, PCP, Lithium, valium, ecstasy, and crack cocaine, to name a few.

"What's functional schizophrenia?" asked Leslie.

"Well, there are basically two types of schizophrenia," said Dr. Gilbert. "Functional and organic. Organic would be something you're born with—a problem with genetics, chemical imbalance, and so forth. Functional schizophrenia happens later on in life, but we don't know the cause. It's still a psychological mystery. Todd was probably on the edge of functional psychosis, then the drugs threw him over the top."

"What about all those hallucinations," asked Billy. "What was all that religious stuff about?"

"Well, Billy, that's a good question. The precise nature of the hallucinations was far from ordinary. In all my years of practice, no one has quite formulated such an elaborate series of bizarre fantasies. Perhaps, this was due, in part, from his well above average I.Q. I found out from his high school records that his I.Q. was 148—that's quite high.

"Todd was no dummy, that's for sure," said Dutch

"I checked with Todd's parents about his religious upbringing. They told me he received a normal amount of religious teachings in the Protestant faith. He was raised a Methodist, and from all accounts, seemed to have experienced the usual church experiences like going to church, praying, and moral counseling. There is no evidence of extreme indoctrination on the part of his parents. However, at some point, Todd began to encounter two simultaneous hallucinations. I think this was brought about by the use of PCP, or angel dust as it's known on the streets.

"We all tried to keep him away from hard drugs," said Chris. "We should have tried harder."

"It's nobody's fault. Todd was too determined to fall headlong into his fantasy world. The PCP was the great rush he needed to fulfill his fantasy life."

"Which was?" asked Sarah.

Well," continued Dr. Gilbert, " First of all, he became so absorbed in the Book of Revelation in the Bible that he thought he was the Apostle John, and then began to think that he had actually written it. Secondly, he became obsessed with MTV. Of course, that was no big secret. As he steadily lost track of reality, Todd was increasingly unable to distinguish the visuals shown on MTV and his own personal visions as the Apostle John. Many of the images coming out of the TV screen were interpreted as signs of the end of time. This is not a particularly ridiculous hallucination. As you know, MTV is filled with grotesque creatures, violence, turmoil, and signs of general decadence in our culture. I am not making a judgment on this point. I am simply saying that Todd's fantasies were not without a rational, logical basis.

Dr. Gilbert stopped talking and swiveled his chair back to his desk.

"Coffee anyone?"

"I'll take a cup," said Sarah.

"Me too," said Buzz.

Dr. Gilbert took a coffee filter and bag of Colombian coffee from a drawer. He took the coffee carafe and went outside to a water fountain and filled the carafe with water and placed it underneath the coffee pot. He shook the coffee into the filter and turned on the coffee maker.

"Just be a couple minutes. Now, where was I?"

"You were talking about his fantasies—the Apostle John," said Sarah.

"Yes, of course. Well, as his condition worsened, he became the Apostle John, and for all intents and purposes, Todd Page no longer existed. The end came when he thought Leslie was the "Great Prostitute" from the Book of Revelation. You all know what happened to Leslie, so I'll not go into that."

"But why did he become violent?" asked Leslie.

"To tell you the truth," said Dr. Gilbert, "I don't know. Certainly the Book of Revelation has lots of violent images, but we don't know why some schizophrenics become violent and some don't. I wish I could be more helpful on this, but we have a long way to go in predicting violent behavior. Anyway, when we first got him into the hospital after the attack on Leslie, and after he recovered from his wounds, Todd settled into the routine of hospital life."

"Did you give him medication?" asked Buzz.

"Yes. He was on 50 milligrams of the anti-psychosis drug Haldol and 25 milligrams of Klonicin, another powerful anti-psychotic drug. He was really a model patient after that. He did renounce MTV as one of "Satan's tools" and became terrified of germs, but Todd's condition did not deteriorate as rapidly as it could have. Remember Leslie, you told me that he was quite lucid when you last saw him and he seemed to be genuinely improving. I reduced the amount of Haldol to 30 milligrams on July first."

"But why did he take his life?" asked Leslie.

"Good question. There is nothing inherently suicidal about having these particular hallucinations. A lot of people have hallucinations, take PCP, and don't commit suicide. Drug use alone doesn't begin to tell the story. I think it is best to see his suicide as a chain of events. I don't think there is one particular reason why he killed himself. I think the first chain, or cause, can be linked to his relationship with his parents. I am not a Freudian, by the way, in spite of the fact that I have a couch in my office.

"What do you mean?" asked Dutch.

"Freud thought that all neurosis and psychosis could be traced to early childhood relationships with the mother and father. He basically believed that the human personality was formed by the age of four or five. Anyway, as you all know, Todd came from a wealthy, powerful and status conscious family. His great, great, great grandfather was John Page, one of Thomas Jefferson's oldest friends. He was also a descendent of "King" Carter, a prominent Albemarle county landowner. John Page served as lieutenant governor from 1801-1805. Todd was a descendent of one of the richest and most distinguished families in Virginia. They are even rumored to be among the "Z" Society, a secret society of wealthy Virginians who donate large contributions to the University. Don't get me wrong. Todd's parents were not mean-spirited people who drove their son to suicide. From what I could tell by talking to them, they are a reasonable and caring couple that loved their son and tried to bring him up as best they could. However, although caring and considerate, neither parent demonstrated a great deal of overt affection toward their son, especially in terms of holding, nurturing, fondling, and general emotive output. Generally, a parent's lack of affection typically produces a cold, alienated offspring. To understand how Todd got where he did, however, you have to look further. The source of the adjustment problems, which eventually lead to his death, may have been a combination of factors which are common enough, but which in Todd produced an effect unique in my experience. So, we have a combination of factors. First of all, his family was considered extremely superior by most social standards. Secondly, we have the parent's absence of expressive emotions, or conversely the parent's emotional cautiousness. However, although practically everyone in his immediate surroundings believed Todd's family "superior," Todd did not hold this view. In my conversations with him he made several references to his family as slave owners. This is an historically accurate statement, although you probably know this was a common practice to employ slaves in Virginia in the nineteenth century. Todd was an extremely idealistic and perceptive person. At some point, he could not accept the fact that his family made their fortune on the backs of slaves. His statements bear this out. He said something like, 'My family never moved a muscle except to rise up and pillage the countryside.' He made statements similar to this all the time.

Todd could not accept the fact that his family was considered superior, and yet, owned slaves. How could a family who owned people be superior? As I said, Todd received a normal religious upbringing, but it would not have taken much religious training to see that slavery was not an acceptable part of the Judean-Christian ethic. So, Todd believed himself "inferior" rather than "superior," and obviously this affected his self-image. One time he told me he I belonged to a race that conquered and enslaved.

"Todd took this conclusion one step further. Since all the objects around him were derived from the hardships of slaves—the house, furniture, farmhouse, animals, crops, and so forth, there was obviously no love behind the development of this material existence. Painful people made it in abject poverty and bondage. Todd reasoned, and not entirely incorrectly, that he could receive no love from his parents because they were inextricably linked to the absence of love all around him. Again, this is not a totally ridiculous idea. If everything around you is devoid of love from its origin, how can one achieve a loving existence?"

Dr. Gilbert paused. The group remained silent.

"I think that coffee might be ready by now," said Dr. Gilbert. He got up from his chair and retrieved three cups from a bookshelf, then poured three cups of coffee. He kept one for himself and handed the other two to Sarah and Buzz. Dr. Gilbert continued his analysis.

"I believe the second explanation for the suicide lies in Todd's relationship with his mother. As we know from earlier studies of orphans, babies need to be fondled, or they literally die. As Todd's mother admitted to me in conversation, she was not a very attentive mother. It is my opinion that Todd did not receive enough physical contact. He became increasingly convinced that he was not properly cared for and he needed a surrogate mother to provide touching and feeling for him. Now, of course, he knew better than to walk around saying, 'I need a surrogate mother'—at least in the beginning. Probably as a result of a PCP hallucination, Todd became to increasing identify himself with a spider monkey he heard about in Georgia."

"Say what?" asked Billy.

"Bear with me on this. It may sound strange, but in the last days, Todd told me about a spider monkey who was abandoned by its mother. A lab assistant raised the baby monkey. He heard the story on MTV, of all places. I asked him why the mother abandoned her offspring. He said because it was a difficult birth. They had to keep her anesthetized, and when she woke up, she didn't recognize the baby as her own. Two weeks later, I asked his mother if Todd had been a difficult delivery. She said it was. I asked her if she was drugged, or anesthetized during labor. She told me she was very drugged and out of it completely. I think this is significant because I think Todd knew he was a difficult baby and he sympathized with the spider monkey. I also think he felt his mother and father were also figuratively anesthetized because feelings were dulled from lack of emotion.

"I picked this up quite by accident because I heard you, Leslie, mentioned that he used the phrase 'shock the monkey' and I began to think about that statement and how it tied in with his later references to the abandoned spider monkey. In effect, Todd *was* the spider monkey. It was he who wanted to be "shocked," or get feeling, or put another way, to get love.

"In summary, let me say that I think Todd wanted very simple things in life— a family, home, love, and a sense of belonging. Unfortunately, he felt that his family life only brought him emptiness and exile. I think in his last days, he increasingly wanted to find a secure place, however small, for him to exist without turmoil and pain. I believe he took his life to give him a moment of mercy and calm which he had never been able to experience in his life. He certainly was not happy in this world…"

Dr. Gilbert's voice trailed off until the room was engulfed in silence. Leslie broke the quiet in the room.

"Dr. Gilbert," she said, somberly

…"Maybe he'll be happier in the next one."

THE UNIVERSITY OF
MICHIGAN
ANN ARBOR,
MICHIGAN
WINTER, 1991

SEXY SAXON

Sarah entered the apartment, clutching several bags of groceries.

"Chris?"

"Yes?"

"Give me a hand, will ya?"

"Sure."

"You'll never guess what happened."

"What?"

"I was in the supermarket waiting in line and I ran into one of the girls in my British Lit class. She asked me what we were doing tonight. I told her we were throwing a party for the band playing at the forum tonight. You won't believe it."

"Had she heard of *Mean Streets?*"

"*Heard* of them? She's practically the president of their fan club. She actually screamed at me when I mentioned their name."

"Wow."

"That not the best part. She was very interested in how I knew them. I told her you and I were old friends with three of the members. Then she yelled, 'don't tell me you know Sexy Saxon!!!'"

"Sexy Saxon?" Chris asked, incredulously. "Billy? Our Billy Saxon? Are you sure she wasn't an escapee?"

"No, she's normally a sane person. Hard to believe isn't it?"

"No kidding. She sure has strange ideas about sex appeal."

"Well, they are getting more popular. I asked her to come to the party."

"Sounds good to me. Maybe Billy will finally get lucky."

"I think he's gotten lucky by now."

Chris helped Sarah unload the groceries and as Sarah watched Chris prepare dinner, she couldn't help but feel pleased about the success of *Mean Streets* and the way Chris and her had gotten along since they moved to Michigan in September.

Mean Streets began touring along the east coast and quickly formed a cult following. Managed and promoted by Mr. Buford, the band began to sell out medium-sized auditoriums. Their big break came when they warmed up *Nelson* at the Capital Center in Washington DC. The reviewer for the Washington Post gave Mean Streets a better review than *Nelson*. Sarah remembered one of the lines from the review. "I have traveled into the future of rock 'n roll and it's on a street called mean." After that, tickets were hard to get. It was Mr. Buford who insisted on including Ann Arbor on their itinerary, just so they could get together.

The campus was buzzing for weeks about their arrival. Chris and Sarah stayed in touch with them. The band members phoned them all the time from their hotel rooms. The new bass player was named Steve and Billy called the night he passed the barfly test. Chris entered Eastern State University in Ypsilanti as a junior and decided to major in journalism. He told Sarah that the world needed more muckrakers and radicals. Eastern State is twelve miles from Ann Arbor and the couple has seen each other every weekend since school began. Chris admitted to himself that he was a different person now. He told Sarah that he was not as cynical and hostile about growing up and accepting responsibility. Sarah had changed too. She dropped out of the sorority and party scene. She told Chris that after awhile those parties seemed to blur in an alcoholic haze. She also said she had the feeling that there were more guys like Ben at fraternity parties than she ever thought possible.

The phone rang.

"Hello."

"Sarah? This is Wally Buford."

"Oh, Mr. Buford! How are you?"

"Fine. How's it going?"

"Terrific."

"Listen, we finally made it to the Hilton. The boys are beat. Our plane was late and we didn't get here until six o'clock. Cleveland was a mad house! Anyway, you can pick up your tickets at the door—and your backstage passes. Chris is coming, right?"

"Oh, yes! He's here right now."

"Great. We won't have time to come over before the show, but we'll see you backstage. Party still on?"

"Yes, I've got all the stuff. Chris bought a keg today."

"I can't wait to see you all again. Well, I have to run. See you after the show!"

"Bye."

"Goodbye."

Sarah hung up the phone. Chris was sitting beside her on the couch."

"Mr. Buford?" he asked.

"Yes. They just got in. Our tickets and backstage passes will be at the door. How's the keg?"

"Iced down and ready to go. You want a beer?"

"Sure."

Chris went out on the terrace to get Sarah a beer. He came back with two plastic cups in his hand.

"Here's to the reunion of *Mean Streets*," he said, raising his beer into the air.

To All My Friends

The new version of Mean Streets played the forum for three and a half hours, tore the house down, and received three encores, before leaving the fans thirsting for more. Billy, as usual, put on a stunning performance, rivaling his energetic shows in Charlottesville. You could tell the band was more polished, more professional, adding a light show, and more sophisticated equipment. Chris kidded Dutch about his amp. Dutch said his old amp was in the trashcan with the rest of the junk. Chris joked with Buzz about getting his sleeve caught on a car door and tumbling off a cliff. They both laughed, knowing the inside joke.

"Hey, Chris!" Billy screamed from the other end of the room, raising his beer to the ceiling, "TO ALL MY FRIENDS!!!"

Instantly, Chris hailed the conquering heroes, "TO ALL MY FRIENDS!!!"

Everyone picked up the old barfly cries.

"TO HATRED!!!"

"THE ONLY THING THAT LASTS!!!

WHAT DO YOU THINK I AM...?"

"...A BUM?"

"I CAN FIND A GIRL..."

"...FOR TEN MINUTES!!!"

"DO YOU HATE PEOPLE?"

"NO, BUT I SEE TO FEEL A LOT BETTER WHEN THEY'RE NOT AROUND!!!"

Dutch and Ginger were sitting on the couch, taking in all the excitement. Ginger reached over and pulled a package out of her pocketbook.

"What's that?" asked Dutch.

"It's a present—a present for you."

"Can I open it up?"

"Of course! I said it was a present."

Dutch tore away the gift-wrapping and uncovered a bound manuscript. "A book for me?"

"Yep."

Dutch turned the book over to reveal the title. The Words, *Diamonds of Affection: A Book of Poems by Dutch Leer* were embossed on the cover.

"Oh my God…"

"There're all there. One hundred and eighty of them."

"I can't believe it. This is great! I never could have done this."

"It wasn't so hard. Now we just have to get them published, Mr. Poetry Man.

"Honey, I love you."

The phone rang. Sarah picked it up and talked to someone for a few minutes, then motioned Chris to come over to her.

"It's Leslie. She wants to talk to you."

"Leslie, how are you doing?"

"Great. I've got an assignment in Rome. Can you believe it?"

"Wow! Maybe we'll be seeing you on the cover of *Cosmopolitan*. Model of the year! Leslie Richards! Next step, Hollywood and the Tonight show!"

"It's Mr. Buford who should be getting the credit."

"He's a great guy."

"I know. I never thought I could model, but he really gave me confidence."

"He's here right now. Want to speak to him?"

"Sure."

Chris handed the phone to Mr. Buford and wandered out to the terrace. Billy was by himself, staring out at the panoramic view of Ann Arbor.

"Hey, superstar. What's happening?"

"What's up?"

"Never better. School's great and Sarah…well, we're getting married."

"You two make a great couple—always did."

"How's rock and roll stardom?"

"It's as good as you can imagine. We're doing everything we always wanted to do, writing our own material, playing our own kind of music—you should know. Half the songs are yours."

"Yeah, the world couldn't live without "Butt-Ream.""

"Well, even Lennon and McCartney had their low points."

"Did you hear what happened to Alicia Powers?" asked Billy.

"No, what happened to her?"

"She got religion and married a minister! Do you believe it? They moved to Myrtle Beach and she's happy as a clam."

"Wow, you never know," said Chris. The two guys remained silent for a few seconds.

"Do you ever play the game anymore?" asked Chris.

"No, we don't. It's funny, but we were backstage after a gig in New York and Buzz asked me in the usual manner who I was not going to be tomorrow and I was going to say something like computer programmer, but it occurred to me that we really didn't have to play the game anymore. We had arrived at a place where it was just not necessary. I really don't understand it."

"It is weird."

"Buzz knew it too. We all did—even Steve who was only playing for a couple months. That was the last time anyone in the band brought the subject up."

"Hey, let's toast," said Chris, raising his glass in Billy's direction.

The two old friends came together, raising their glasses toward the darkening sky. Below them a line of automobile taillights formed a red neon ribbon around the perimeter of the city's downtown area, as early stars made their first twinkling presence in the expansive northern sky.

"To all my friends," said Billy, hoisting his glass further in the air.

"To all my friends," said Chris, clicking his glass against Billy's as the last flicker of light from the glittering sun disappeared below the horizon, surrendering to the darkness of the night.

0-595-27492-7